of
SCARS
and
DUTY

NATALIE DEBRABANDERE

ISBN: 1546446001
ISBN-13: 978-154644600

ACKNOWLEDGMENTS

Once again, thank you so much to Peter at 'bespokebookcovers' for the great work you do for me, and all my marketing goodies!

Thanks as well to all my readers, not only for buying and reading my books, but also for being so kind and leaving me awesome reviews on Amazon. I appreciate it more than you know! X

CHAPTER ONE

Cyrus Constellation 9
Mission HR-10-09J
June 15, 2252

"DON'T LET ME FALL!"

The commando soldier was screaming, holding on for dear life. And still, the heavy military transport vehicle continued to lift, with him just barely hanging off the side. Williams threw herself across the floor, fighting the heavy stretches of darkness that floated in front of her eyes. Her entire world was spinning. She could taste blood in her mouth, and everything had started to feel like it was happening in slow motion. She could recognise the signs... But she could not afford to pass out, not yet. With some difficulty, she reached for the vial of C12 attached to her armour. It was the drug the marines had laughingly nicknamed Zombie Magic. This on account of how the cocktail of mostly pure adrenaline it contained was probably good enough to resuscitate the dead. Either that, or the shock to your system when it was injected into the bloodstream would probably just kill you on the spot. Without a second's hesitation, Williams stabbed it into the side of her own neck, straight into the jugular. Immediately, everything zoomed back into sharp focus, and at incredible speed. When her soldier shouted again, it felt like his voice was coming from the inside of her own head. Everything felt heightened. Colours, sounds, the sight of laser fire hitting the cockpit... And the pain, too. Blinding, searing pain spreading rapidly throughout her entire body.

"I'm gonna fall!" he gasped. "Help me. Help me!"

She reached out for him with her good arm, trusting in the harness that kept her attached to the craft to do its job, and keep them both in. Only he was not on board yet, not by far. And as the vehicle started to gain altitude, she saw his grip on the slippery rubber start to weaken. With intense clarity, and blessed detachment, she realised that the floor was wet... Wet with her own blood.

Shit. How did this happen?

"Hold on to me," she ordered.

At the same time, she glanced in the general direction of the control panel, and shouted to make herself heard over the sound of laser fire. She could smell something burning. But why the hell were they still going up, when she had already ordered the damn thing to wait?

"Abort!" she shouted, as her 2IC struggled in vain to grab hold of her hand. "Control, I repeat: abort take-off NOW! Get us back on the fucking ground!"

The craft got slammed extremely hard by something she did not see coming. *Rocket?* she wondered. *Laser strike?* It was hard to tell. A screeching sound like metal being ripped apart echoed at the back. Williams could see flames to her right, the air in front of her face suddenly shimmering due to the intense heat blasting along the side. She wondered how much damage of this sort they could sustain before the whole thing simply blew up.

And they were still lifting up. But despite the critical position that they found themselves in, she still did not want to leave just yet.

"Control, bring us DOWN!" she screamed, her voice almost breaking in fury.

The drone ship had initiated its ascent, and the AI brain in command, programmed to relinquish control to her whenever she ordered it to, was not responding to her requests. Williams felt the soldier's hand that was wrapped around her arm slide down to her wrist. She tried in vain to tighten her fingers around him. Her right arm was useless. She could not even manage to let it dangle over the side so that he could reach. She felt a sudden flash of despair hit her deep in the pit of her stomach. She had nothing left to give, and it looked like what she had delivered so far was nowhere near good enough.

"Williams, don't let me go," he pleaded. "Please! Please, don't let me go!"

Bubbles of blood blew out of his mouth with every heaving breath he took, and she finally realised what was going wrong with him. He had been hit. He had to be badly wounded. Normally, Sanchez was the kind of ultra-fit guy who could have easily crawled up and over her body, using her as a ladder to get himself back inside the craft, and to safety. But now, all she saw in his eyes was panic.

"Hold on to me!" she urged. "Harder! Don't give up, you hear me? Use your other hand, Sanchez, come on! You can do it!"

He tried once more, and she gritted her teeth against the rush of pain the sudden movement sparked across her chest. It was so sharp that she almost fainted again. But she had to get him in, she just had to. She made another supreme effort to move her right arm.

"Come on!" she screamed.

Her vision blurred as he attempted one last time to pull himself in. She felt something in her shoulder give, followed by more throbbing. But then it was all over, and she saw it in his eyes. The sudden realisation that he was never going to make it hit him hard, and the howling sound that came out of his mouth at that moment was so loaded with terror it did not even sound human anymore.

"Don't," she hissed. "No, Sanchez, don't you dare…"

But he was done, could not hold on any longer. As the craft suddenly accelerated, gaining momentum, his fingers slipped from her wrist, and he disappeared from view. She lunged after him, dangling half in and half out of the vehicle, only held in by the thin safety wire.

"Sanchez!" she yelled. "SANCHEZ!"

In shock, unable to believe that she had lost him, she stared into the void for several long seconds. It was only the door closing shut that forced her to crawl back inside the craft. All of a sudden, there was only silence. Something sticky was dripping into her eyes. It made it a little hard to see clearly. She tried to stand up, and found that she could not. She stared at the hole in her Kevlar armour, and frowned at the sight of bright-red arterial blood pulsing out of her leg in a steady stream. *What the hell…* She was out of breath, and it was only getting worse with every passing second. Williams struggled to lift her head, and she threw a weary glance toward the back of the vehicle. The three hostages that she and her team had managed to rescue were huddled together. She should go check on them.

"Is everyone… Is everyone okay?" she asked.

Her voice sounded far away, even to her own ears. As more blood poured from her thigh, and her entire body became heavier, sluggish, she vaguely saw one of the three scientists rush over to her. She wanted to reassure the woman, to tell her that she was okay, but the words simply would not come this time. She slumped forward. She felt hands on her body, pressing hard against her leg and her shoulder. Faces floating above her. She caught vague words, broken sentences. The disembodied voice of the AI over the speaker system reeled out a bunch of data about something, but it all sounded like a string of meaningless noise at this point. More human voices then came through the fog... *losing too much blood... she's dying...*

Christ, Williams thought, appalled. Who was dying? Had she missed something?

She went through a checklist in her head, although it was almost impossible to hold a coherent thought by this point. She remembered that the hostages were safe. At least, the hostages were safe... But something had gone wrong, too. Had it not? Bad intel. Yeah, that was it. And an AI failure. They had walked straight into an ambush.

As she started to drift deeper into unconsciousness, the smiling faces of her fellow marines floated slowly across Williams' mind. Sanchez, Maxx, Edwards, Collinson. But her team were gone, now. She had failed to bring them back. The hostages were safe, but she had failed, period. *I'm sorry. I'm sorry...* The Special Forces officer lay still on the bloody floor, closed her eyes, and willed for the darkness to hurry up and take her.

∞ .

"Major Williams? Wake up, please, this is your alarm system speaking. Major Williams? Wake up, please, this is your alarm system..."

The polite, soothing female voice gradually penetrated Williams' consciousness. Eventually, it registered. Her eyes flew open in panic, and she flinched. Shifted onto her back, and she stared at the ceiling for a moment, breathing hard all the while. She tried to disentangle herself from the nightmare that still felt so vivid.

"I'm awake," she murmured.

She had been on medical leave ever since waking up from three long weeks in a deep coma, following the mission that had almost killed her. And it certainly felt to her like she should be way past feeling this bad every day now. But, as always when she first opened her eyes after spending any time at all asleep, she felt dizzy, disoriented. Nauseous, even. She struggled for several long seconds before she could remember clearly who she was, where she was, and who the gentle voice belonged to. When she did, she turned over, and buried her face into her pillow.

"System," she muttered. "Reboot."

"Yes, Major."

Most people called their personal AI system something nice; like Jerry, Sam, or Kid. They said *'please'* and *'thank you'* to it, and all that stupid shit. Treated their AI like a member of the family. In Williams' opinion, that was a dangerous thing to do. She much preferred to use a denomination that made it harder to forget that she was essentially just speaking to a computer. Heartless, and uncaring. One of those damn machines she hated so much, because when they failed, people died.

"Time," she asked.

The AI was programmed to wake her up whenever she had a bad dream. When vital signs like her heart rate, breathing pattern and body temperature reached a certain unacceptable threshold. It was efficient, but not good enough to stop her having the dreams in the first place. Of course, she could have used her neural lace, like her doctor kept suggesting… But that was simply not an option the stubborn officer would allow herself to consider.

"It is now 2:38 a.m.," the system informed her.

She ran her fingers through her hair, and rubbed her face with both hands. She was feeling pretty awful, and beyond tired. But this was also her usual time to freak out, so no surprise there. She took a deep breath to clear her head before anger and helplessness had a chance to kick in.

"Window," she murmured.

Major Evan K. Williams of the universally renowned Interstellar Commando Unit threw the covers off her scarred legs, sat on the side of the bed, and rested her elbows over her knees. She stared for a while. Truth be told, it was hard not to. The opposite side of her cabin had become transparent the instant she had asked for it, and sure enough, there it was; the unbelievably beautiful planet Mars, so close it felt like she could almost touch it. Mars had not always looked so magnificent, of course. It had taken about a thousand years to terraform a good chunk of its inhabitable surface, and turn it into a place where human beings could begin to thrive. But after the initial work was done, and once they added an atmosphere to it, Mars started to flourish. From space now, if you happened to catch it at a good angle, it almost looked as beautiful as Earth was.

Williams took another deep breath in, and released it carefully. So, they had made it into orbit, then. *Going to be a lot of happy and distracted soldiers onboard the ship today,* she reflected. For a while now, Mars had been the ICU's planet of choice for R&R. Some of the troops were natives of the place as well, and so, the next few weeks onsite would be an ideal opportunity for them to catch up with family and friends. But Williams herself had been born on a military ship. She had been raised on one, and she had no family on Mars. No desire to spend any time at all on the ground either, if truth be told.

She only glanced at the planet once more, without any emotion, before getting up and grabbing a bottle of juice. She went to the bathroom to brush her teeth, splashed cold water on her face, and threw on her running clothes. Then, she stepped outside into the spacious curved corridor that ran all the way around the officers' accommodations floor, and started jogging. She headed straight for the gym. She knew it would be quiet at this crazy hour, and that she would have the running track all to herself, just the way that she liked it.

It had become a well-practiced routine for her. Nightmare, get up, go running, shower, and coffee. Lots of coffee. Busy days, late nights, everything to stop thinking, and block the memories. Even though it helped, it still did not stop the members of her doomed team all taking turns visiting her in her dreams, each and every night. It was as it should be. Deep down inside, Williams was firmly convinced that this was her punishment for being the only survivor. She accepted it, did not question it for a second. She should not have lived through this horror, and given the choice, she would not have wanted to.

This last night had been Collinson's turn. In her dream, she had watched him burn, again and again. The nightmares always felt so real to her... She could even taste it in her mouth. She could hear the man scream, and call her name. Feel his fear. She watched it all unfold, all the while knowing full well that there was nothing she could do to help. She invariably woke up drenched in sweat, shaking, breathing hard, and that was when she remembered that it had been no dream. Her marines were all dead. And okay, maybe it was not her fault... But her failure? Yeah, definitely.

Don't do this, Williams reminded herself, as she hit the empty track at a fast pace, and started on her first lap of many that day. *Don't dwell on all this stuff. Keep your focus. You know what to do.*

She worked extra-long hours, spent the rest in the gym, and did not discuss her private life with anyone. She lied to the shrinks, her superior officer, and all the doctors they forced her to see on a regular basis. She knew that all she had to do to be okay was stay in control, and she did not need anybody's help for that. Never had, and never would. Just concentrate on the work, on the mission… And hopefully, it would be good enough to keep her from losing her mind.

CHAPTER TWO

Williams had decided that she would handle R&R on her own, onboard the ship, with a few bottles of something strong and nasty for company. No one had asked her what her plans were, apart from the med team, and she had bluntly lied to them about it, as always. Then she had made herself scarce around the few other people who she thought might be able to see through the bullshit.

As she sat alone in the mess hall later on that evening, toying with a plate of synthetic meat drowned in non-descript sauce, she observed the few soldiers who were still waiting around for a shuttle. She was the only one wearing fatigues. Everyone else were in their civvies, displaying a dubious assortment of the latest fashion in trendy flip flops and Hawaiian shirts. Everyone in good spirits, looking happy and excited. *And why the hell not, after all?* she thought. Everybody worked hard onboard this ship, and they more than deserved a little rest. Williams turned to face away from them. She quickly finished her food, and then made for her cabin. She locked the door behind her, and threw her jacket across the room.

"Messages," she ordered.

Immediately, her wall turned into a screen, and an email flashed onto it. She barely glanced at it at first, only to do a quick double-take, and freeze.

"What now, are you kidding me?" she muttered, feeling irritated.

The email was a request from Colonel Ar'yelk Baasim'ha Colrd to join her on the observation deck for a personal chat. Williams stood there, frowning, biting nervously on her lower lip for a while, as she read and re-read the cryptic message. It was extremely rare for the ship's commanding officer to request her company in this way. In fact, it had only ever happened once before, and that had been to inform Williams of the death of her only sibling. *Damn it. What does she want this time?* Feeling highly suspicious, and more than a little worried as well, she immediately made her way to the location of the little rendezvous.

"Oi, beach body!"

"Got your bikini ready, Major?"

A bunch of marines were up there, milling about, chatting, and drinking coffee. The ones who said hello to her and addressed her in this way were men she trained with in the gym sometimes, but no one close. No one who really knew her. It made it easier to lie to them as often and as relentlessly as she needed to.

"Can't wait," she replied, pretending to grin but in fact gritting her teeth. "I can't wait, guys."

She did not join in with their conversations, and simply stood in front of the main window for a while, alone, staring pensively at the gorgeous planet in the background. She could see a shuttle out there on its way to the ground airport terminal. Her thoughts rapidly drifted back to the strategic response report she was working on, and the modifications she needed to apply to her new armour. She did not hear Ary behind her until the woman spoke.

"Major Williams. Good evening. I thank you for coming."

The pointed, lingering look that the colonel gave her when she turned around was not lost on Williams. Unlike as with her, there was not a single scar to disturb the Cretian's beautiful features. Her posture was perfect. The uniform she wore was perfect. Every inch of her, in fact, was perfect. Williams knew that this was not something specifically related to their kind. Perfection was something very personal to the colonel, and she excelled at it.

The Cretian people, originally from a group of planets located in a different star system, tended to look strangely like the ancient Masai people of Earth. The difference being that their entire bodies, including their heads, were delicately sculpted with intricate coloured patterns, mimicking the stripes that could be seen on some species of tropical fish. In fact, their planet Cretios was mostly liquid, and as such, they had adapted to be able to breathe underwater for long periods of time. They operated at a slightly higher level of vibration consciousness than most humans could achieve, and yet, strangely enough, rarely experienced the same range of emotions. This tended to balance out the two species quite well in terms of leadership abilities.

Cretians made for tough, resilient soldiers, and they were well-suited to the Marines. They were generally quite lithe, beautiful creatures, with smooth skin and large, velvet brown pools for eyes. Colonel Ary for short, as she was referred to amongst her human colleagues, also ranked several levels of amazing beauty above everybody else in her universe. Williams stood at attention in front of her, although the lack of enthusiasm in her posture was quite obvious.

"Colonel," she nodded.

Ary noticed her stance, and waved a dismissive hand in her direction.

"Relax, Major. This is just a chat, as I've said. It has been a while since we spoke like this, hasn't it? I think you were still in the infirmary the last time we did. If I didn't know any better, I would think that you are probably trying to avoid me."

Since it was not a direct question, Williams did not offer any comment. It saved her lying about it. Ary flashed a small, hard smile in her direction. She knew.

"Please, have a seat," she invited. "Coffee?"

She studied the human woman as the marine sat opposite her, dumped half a ton of sugar into her cup, and sat stirring it for a while in sullen, reluctant silence. The heavy scar on her face was striking, running as it did from low in the middle of her forehead, over the top of her nose, and across her right cheek. Ary knew there were even worse ones on her right arm, and on her legs. She was the one who had authorised a lot of the medical stuff that had saved Williams' life to be done to her. She knew the score, and how the major felt about it all.

"So, how are you?" she asked.

"Fine. Looking forward to being back on duty," Williams replied, immediately chastising herself for sounding so defensive.

Ary nodded, unsmiling.

"Yes, I'm sure you are."

It had been twelve weeks already since the fateful mission that had resulted in turning the Special Forces officer into a global war hero. While she was in a coma in the hospital, fighting for her life, they had promoted her to the rank of Major. Awarded a bravery medal to her. And pretty much squeezed as much out of her as they possibly could before Williams finally regained consciousness, and flat-out refused to cooperate with any more of what she called *'a PR circus of such fucked-up proportions it makes me sick'.*

Ary had found it hard to disagree with her on that point, although she also knew that an enemy race known as the Scythians were rapidly gaining ground in several areas of the solar system. The forces were in desperate need of more soldiers. And so, if they could use her exploits on the battlefield to generate a few blood-pumping, adrenaline-inducing stories, and inspire more young people to join up with the Marines, she was all for it.

"Major Williams," she addressed her now, "I get the impression that you are not into idle chit-chat, and neither am I. So, let me get straight to the point. It has come to my attention that you have successfully avoided R&R on planet for the last four years. Is that correct?"

She saw the immediate flash of annoyance that crossed the woman's face, and the sombre way she pushed a strand of thick blond hair behind her ear. Patience had never been her virtue, and Ary knew that about her. She tolerated it because Williams was also gifted with above-average intelligence, and a knack for thinking out of the box. She made decisions quickly, accurately, and it saved lives in the field. She was also notoriously short-tempered with the people who she saw as either *limited*, in her own words, or unwilling to take risks, break a few rules, and live on the edge a little. Both unforgiveable failures of character in her opinion, and certainly two things which Colonel Ary could never be accused of.

"Major?" she prompted.

Williams shifted in her chair. She kept her bright, crystal-clear blue eyes fixed firmly onto her coffee.

"Might be," she replied.

"Might be?"

Ary stared at her intently until Williams felt it, looked up, and met her gaze.

"Yeah, I haven't been counting." She shrugged. "Been kind of busy, you know?"

She could not quite keep resentment from creeping into her voice, and Ary nodded. Her gaze fell on the dog tags that she was wearing around her neck. They were a different shape, and made out of a different alloy than all others. They were engraved with her name, rank, unit designation, and blood type. *Williams, E.K. Major ICU/L5 AB-.*

Not many officers were rated L5 within the Interstellar Commando Unit. Only those who achieved expert ratings in such diverse fields as zero-G combat, underwater demolitions, sniper skills, and CQB; along with space diplomacy, alien biology, and linguistics could ever dream of reaching the coveted Level 5 status. It was the equivalent of the Navy Seal rating of old, combined with a few more obscure and harder to grasp specialties. The prestigious designation was awarded by a collective interplanetary military and diplomatic group simply known as 'The Council'. You did not apply to train for the programme, you were invited. Not many officers received the honour, and even less graduated. L5 marines were special, everyone knew that, although Ary, when she was still new to her command, had always prided herself in never treating them any differently. Only with Williams had she come to realise that she was expected to. And definitely not in a good way. She braced herself for what was to come.

"I know you've been busy, Major," she agreed, watching her.

"Yeah," the officer muttered, nodding.

"I know you do not enjoy being on medical leave either."

Another nod, slightly more emphatic this time. *You are a true genius, Colonel,* Williams reflected quietly inside her head. *Awesome. And where the hell is this conversation headed, anyway?*

She glanced toward the window again, obviously eager to get moving, and leave. She wanted to be left alone. But Ary kept her eyes on her, and eventually delivered her punch line.

"I know you have decided to blame yourself for what happened to your team. And behave accordingly. That is a stupid idea in my view, Major. And not acceptable for a marine of your calibre."

Williams looked startled. She suddenly went very still, although her heart was pounding hard inside her chest. The colonel's blunt and aggressive statement made her stomach tighten and churn in response. She paled, and when she did, the scar on her face suddenly stood out in sharp contrast. It was inflamed, just like she was. Ary was pleased to have finally provoked a reaction.

"Trust me, you are the only one adopting that unhelpful point of view," she continued, without much emotion. "Not only did you save the lives of the three high-ranking hostage scientists, but you were also successful in destroying the Scythians' main infrastructure, which allowed us to regain control of the area. If not for your courageous actions on that day, we would have lost the entire planet. There is a reason everyone thinks you're a hero, you know? Why don't you stop being such an idiot about it?"

Williams was visibly upset.

"It's not about that, Colonel," she gasped. "It's not about who did what, or being a hero. It's… I lost my crew…"

"I know. Not your fault."

"That's what people keep saying, but I should have…"

"Oh, save it, Williams, I know the song," the Cretian cut in again. "Shoulda, woulda, coulda are the last words of a fool. And you are no fool, Major."

The marine stared at her in silence.

"By the time we identified the enemy virus that caused the AI glitch in our system," Ary carried on, "and all the disinformation, it was already too late. You and your crew were already on the ground by then, taking fire. You did the best you could with the resources you had available. You knew the risks, and so did they."

She leaned forward a little, her gaze piercing and hot as it roamed all over the officer's face.

"You came back. Now it's time to move on."

"Don't you think I have?" Williams replied angrily.

Ary raised a sardonic, disbelieving eyebrow.

"No, I don't," she replied. "Not for a second."

Williams had to break eye contact with her before she could say something really nasty that would land her in jail for a few days of quiet reflexion. She looked away. A slow tremble started in her body as she remembered the event. They had come under attack almost as soon as they had set foot on the planet. Enemy numbers at the site had been three times higher than their disastrous intel had estimated. Still, they had pushed on, stormed the building, and managed to get the hostages out. On the way back, things had taken a definite turn for the worst. One by one, her team had gone down. Sanchez and Collinson's deaths had not been the worst ones to witness. *Maxx...* Williams closed her eyes at the thought of her, and immediately broke into a cold sweat.

"All right, that's enough. Snap out of it, now!" Ary barked.

Blinking slowly, as if coming out of a daze, Williams turned her attention back to her. She took a shaky breath, and struggled to bring her emotions under control. Not for the first time, she found herself on the verge of a panic attack. She clenched her fists on the table, cursing her own weakness, and tried really hard not to let it get any worse.

The Cretian officer was watching her intently.

"There was nothing at all you could have done," she repeated, with a light shrug thrown in for effect. "My guess is that's the real issue here. Am I right, Williams? Is that what is causing all the nightmares, and the PTSD? Forcing you to drink yourself into a stupor every night? It isn't nice being left powerless on the battlefield in this way, is it? I'll bet that was quite a new, unwanted and disturbing experience for a soldier like you."

Williams swallowed hard. She had no idea how the woman could have found out about her drinking, but it did not matter, not really. Because now, she was getting pissed off, and she was not going to take this lying down.

"Why don't you get to the point, Colonel?" she hissed.

Ary shook her head, displeasure at the L5's reaction obvious in her expression.

"As you wish, Major," she conceded. "And I will. You failed your re-entry test for active duty."

"Yeah, well. I have a few nightmares sometimes," Williams exclaimed, her voice tight with anger. "Who doesn't, right? You spend your life fighting space aliens all over the goddamn galaxy, you're bound to get a few. I'll bet you do, too. Doesn't mean it's PTSD. Doesn't mean I can't do my job, or that I shouldn't be re-instated. And I don't understand why a stupid test…"

"For your information, I do not have nightmares," Ary interrupted bluntly. "And I am not talking about your psy evaluation. Although that is also an issue, and I will deal with it in due time. But you failed your physical as well."

Williams froze.

"What?"

"You heard me, Major."

This was obviously shocking and devastating news for the commando officer. She stared at Ary, stunned into silence. She had never, ever failed anything in her military career. Especially not physical tests. She was by far the best combat marine they had. Fierce on the battlefield, she was driven and tough, and a brilliant strategist to boot. She worked hard, physically and mentally, and she routinely pushed herself far beyond what she ever asked of others. She was considered by many to have a great future ahead of her, possibly even only a few years away from being offered her own ship to command. She deserved it. But now, this?

"Well, I... I'm not sure what to say about that," she admitted.

It was not often that the woman who had come top of her class at the Academy, finishing first out of an intake of 150 hopefuls, betrayed a single hint of vulnerability. But she was doing so now, allowing Ary more and more insight into her true state of mind. The Cretian watched her in silence, as the blood once more drained from Williams' face.

"How could I fail?" she asked. "I passed every gym test..."

"It is your general physiological fitness that isn't up to standards, Major," Ary explained impatiently, as if this were a personal insult to her. "Your recovery times are down. Your HRV stats are all over the place. You are showing signs of autonomic imbalance, along with elevated levels of adrenaline and cortisol in your system. Which I probably don't need to tell you could lead to heart disease if they remain present for too long, right?"

Williams shook her head. She appeared irritated now, and ever so tired as well. Her shoulders slumped.

"It's just overtraining," she murmured. "I'm sure it's nothing more."

"Yes," Ary agreed. "It is not unheard of with people returning from a significant injury like yourself, who push themselves a little too hard, a little too soon. Which is why you will be going planet-side for a while, and make sure you use the R&R you have been so studiously avoiding for the past few years to get yourself back into shape."

Williams drew in a sharp breath, as if to argue. But she suspected it would not do much good at this point. She stayed quiet, and just nodded.

"Anyway, there is another thing I need to discuss with you," Ary said to her. "I know you have been moving heaven and earth to try to find out who authorised your neural lace injection. Why is that?"

Williams looked at her, eyes flashing, her fists clenched in anger.

"You want to know why?" she repeated. "Isn't it obvious?"

Ary glared at her.

"I asked you a question, Major."

"I was rated negative TX, that's why," Williams exclaimed in exasperation. "None of that stuff should have been done to me! I want to know who that person is, who decided to go against my will. I want to tell them that what they did was wrong. Who the hell do they think they are?"

"And then what?" Ary smirked. "Rough 'em up a little too, maybe?"

Williams slammed her hand down onto the table.

"Damn right!" she spat.

Ary looked at her. Her smile suddenly vanished, and her eyes grew hard.

"Well. I'm afraid it was never your decision to make, Major," she stated. "It was mine. And I did."

CHAPTER THREE

When Ary broke the news to her, Williams almost punched her fist through the side of the ship in a striking combination of rage, disappointment, and total astonishment. It was not often that she lost her temper, her training and her general strength of character saw to that. But this was something else entirely, and this time she went completely wild at her commanding officer. For the first time in her entire career, she could not hold herself back.

"You fucking WHAT?" she exploded.

Several off-duty soldiers turned around to glance at them, throwing amused looks in their direction, thinking that they were probably only joking. But as soon as they spotted the savage expression on Williams' face, and the equally angry one on the colonel's, they quickly and wisely returned their attention elsewhere.

"Be quiet," Ary ordered. "Follow me."

She grabbed hold of her arm, rose from her chair, and dragged the furious marine outside with her. The human's face had turned an alarming shade of red, and something in the way that she held herself alerted Ary that it would probably not be wise to push her that much further. This time though, she was only partly correct in her assessment. Because as soon as they were alone inside the colonel's quarters, Williams freed herself from the Cretian's powerful grasp, and she swung a hard, loaded punch in her direction.

Ary's shield activated before she could even consciously realise what was happening. In the next millisecond, Williams found herself flung halfway across the large room. She scrambled to her feet immediately.

"Don't do it," Ary warned her.

She kept her shield up, making sure the protective energy field was clearly visible. Surely, the woman would not be stupid enough to carry on with... *BAM!* Even from behind the shield, Ary felt the rippling shockwave of her next strike. It made her feel a little angry.

"Don't force me to defend myself, Major," she snapped.

But Williams was obviously lost in a world of grief, deaf to her warnings. She slammed her leg against the Cretian's armour, over and over, and when it did not work to break through, she started pounding on it with her fists. One thing she had not lost, Ary had to admit, was her physical strength. It seemed that Williams was just as powerful as she had been before... And now, she was also fuelled by incredible resentment, bitterness, and fury.

"It was you?" she shouted. "It was you who authorised those things?"

"Major, listen to..."

"You were my CO, Ary! You knew I was rated negative TX!"

"Don't be ridiculous," Ary shot back from behind her safe bubble. "You think a Level 5 officer like you would be allowed to die? You are much too valuable an asset. We would have made you 99% AI before we let such a thing happen!"

Williams looked dangerous now, a few orders of magnitude above simply pissed off.

"Get that shield out of the way," she yelled.

"Not until you calm down, Major."

"Stop hiding behind that fucking thing, Ary! I am going to demolish your…"

But before she could finish her sentence, the Cretian woman decided to put an end to the madness. She made a simple, tiny gesture with her fingers, and the shield suddenly expelled a powerful blast of energy. This time, Williams was slammed against the wall with enough force to knock her unconscious. For a second, she struggled to get back on her feet, and then she simply slid to the ground and lay on her stomach, stunned. Knowing that it was probably safe now, Ary went to stand next to her. She looked down at her top marine with a mixture of disapproval and dismay.

"Told you that you wouldn't like it," she remarked. "Now, are you done trying to kill me?"

Williams grunted in response, and pushed herself up into a sitting position. She rubbed her hand against the back of her neck, wincing.

"Wasn't trying, Colonel," she said. "If I had, you would be dead."

Ary burst out laughing. Now, this was a little more like it. She went to sit down next to her, and leaned her back against the wall.

"Good answer, Major."

"I am not joking."

"I know. But those AI works saved your life. You should be grateful instead of angry. I don't understand why this is such an issue…"

Williams stared at her as if the other woman had gone crazy. She was well aware that Cretians struggled to grasp human emotions sometimes, but this should have been such a simple thing for the colonel to get her head around. And Ary was more intelligent than most, whether human or not. Why was she pretending that she could not understand this?

"I had signed a negative TX agreement."

In spite of herself, Williams' voice kept getting louder, and more aggressive with every word that came out of her mouth.

"Major Williams…"

"You knew it! You knew what it meant to me. And yet, you gave me neural lace! I can't believe you would do such a thing…"

"Calm yourself down, Major," Ary warned.

Williams threw her a furious look. She was not ready yet to abandon her argument.

"I don't want to calm down," she raged. "I trusted you, goddamn it!"

She looked away from Ary because she did not want the Cretian officer to see her cry. *I trusted you,* she reflected, feeling something inside herself flutter wildly in panic. *I need to be able to trust you still, because if I can't… If I can't…*

Something would be broken if she could not even trust her own CO, Williams knew. Something important, something vital she could not do without. She had never been particularly friendly with Ary, but she had served under her command for three years. She respected her, and she understood her decisions. Up until today, it had never occurred to her to question her judgment, or wonder if the woman really had her best interests at heart. In Williams' book, officers had their soldiers' back. Always. They fought for them, with them. Sometimes they even died alongside them, too, the way that she should have been allowed to do.

She glanced toward Ary.

"Colonel," she murmured. "Why did you do it?"

She had woken up all on her own in the hospital three weeks after the mission, and discovered the large scar across her face. It was a shock all right. The doctors told her that she had been lucky to keep her eye. They said she was lucky to be alive, period. And then she found out that she had lost her right arm, and that most of her shoulder had gone with it as well. Of course, they had given her synthetic replacements. It was standard procedure to do this, and Williams was not really worried about those. After all, as a front-line marine, she knew that the odds of never ending up with some kind of a prosthetic limb at some point in her career were pretty slim. She was okay with that... Well, past the initial nerve-wracking experience of being told about it, clearly.

But they had touched her brain, too. Enhanced her with a layer of artificial neural lace. And that, she could not forgive. Obviously, it had saved her life. But her negative TX form stated that if she were ever in that type of situation, if an AI transfer was the last thing that could save her life, then she did not want it. She would rather die, simple as that. Thanks to Ary's violation of her deepest wishes, she was now 50% robotic, just like the AI she so despised.

"Why?" she repeated, looking at her.

"Why do you think, Williams?" the colonel replied with an aggravated sigh. "I was ordered to do it. And also, you were too precious to lose, and I agree with that. Do you know how much money and effort has gone into your training as an L5? We could not just let you go. Nothing personal, I assure you."

The marine gave a bitter chuckle.

"Is that supposed to make me feel better?"

"For what it's worth, Major, I am sorry."

A little flicker of hope flashed across Williams' face.

"Really?" she asked.

Ary rolled her eyes.

"No. Now please, do me a favour. Stop acting like such a child, and suck it up."

And on those words, she stood up, and held out her hand.

"Are we good?" she enquired.

Williams did not move. She did not reply, and did not even blink. She looked lost, confused, a far cry from the normally self-assured and sometimes impossibly focused officer that Ary was accustomed to dealing with. So confident that she often came across as arrogant. And yet, so kind-hearted and charismatic with it as well that her soldiers would have followed her to the ends of the world without question. This was the problem here, Ary suspected strongly. Williams cared too much. It would be her downfall one of these days.

The colonel did not share with her that she had laughed when she had found out about the results of her return to duty test. She had not believed it at first. Major Williams, failing a test? Outrageous! That was why she had pushed her so hard this evening, revealed everything that she had, and triggered all of her emotions and insecurities; because she wanted to see for herself exactly how big the problem was with her. It was big, Ary realised now. For all of her brilliance, and talent, if this L5 did not manage to get her mind and her emotions under better control, it would only go downhill from there. And pretty quickly, too.

"Look at me," she said.

Again, Williams did not move. She did not respond. Ary rested an impatient finger against her chin, and turned her head back toward her.

"I said, look at me," she repeated, a little louder this time.

But her voice did not even register with Williams. She remained just as still, and Ary noticed the slight glaze over her eyes, which had not been there only a few seconds earlier. She appeared to be freezing cold, too, and her lips were slowly turning blue. She was going into shock, right there in front of her it seemed.

"Damn it, Major," the Cretian officer exclaimed under her breath. "Don't do this."

She ran to collect a warm blanket from the bedroom, and came back to wrap it around her shoulders. It was almost a full minute before Williams regained her composure. More than enough for Ary to know that she was making the right decision in sending her away.

"Go spend a couple of weeks on Mars," she told her.

Her tone was softer this time, although clearly forced. Ary was not good at pretending to have emotions she did not actually feel, and she did not often even care to try.

"Ace the active duty test when you return, and go back to fighting. That is all I want from you, Williams. Not too much to ask, and as I'm sure you now realise, this is the only choice you've got. Okay?"

Williams nodded, just once.

"Okay," she said.

She had never spent much time before questioning who she was, and what she did for a living. Both of her parents had served in the Marines, and her older sister too, before she was killed in combat. Williams had enlisted at age sixteen, and made her way through the ranks like it was a game to her, easily and effortlessly. She had never had any issues with any of her superior officers before, and certainly never tried to punch one in the face the way she had just done with Ary. But it had never occurred to her previously that she was property. The military meant something good to her, something reassuring, and worthwhile. She was proud to serve, and she loved being a part of something bigger than herself. She used to think that she belonged.

However, all this, the way they had used her so shamelessly to appeal to new recruits, the AI in her brain, and Ary's disturbing revelations, this only served to highlight one thing to her. She was nothing. She was no one. She did not belong, she was owned. She was just a toy in this game of war they played. Just like Ary was in a way, except that the woman knew it, and had made her peace with it. Or perhaps she had never even cared in the first place. Williams was not at peace, far from it. Worst of all was the fact that she had ever been naïve enough to believe that she mattered.

"Major Williams, I asked you a simple question," Ary reminded her.

She passed an arm underneath her shoulders, and helped her to her feet. She steadied her with a strong hand when Williams stumbled forward, as if she would fall, and she looked deeply into her eyes, trying to ascertain her condition. Funny how that gaze was completely devoid of any warmth. Williams shivered.

"Can you... repeat the question, Colonel?" she murmured.

"I asked if you and I are good now, Major."

"Yes, ma'am." Williams nodded quietly. "We're good."

"And you will get that PTSD nonsense under control."

It was an order, not a question.

"I will."

Ary squeezed her shoulder, and Williams tried not to wince. Emptiness was all she felt conveyed in the Cretian's every touch, her every look, and even her apartment seemed to be so cold now, she reflected.

"Return to your quarters, and get some rest," the colonel advised.

Williams trudged back to her own cabin, and by the time she got in, there was already a message from her medical doctor with a schedule for when she would be on Mars. She was not really surprised to see mentioned on it that she was expected to attend daily counselling sessions with a military-rated therapist. She sighed, and suddenly noticed the bruises on her knuckles where she had hit her fists against the Cretian's protective energy field. With a shake of the head, Williams reached for her bottle of whiskey. She grabbed her sidearm as well, and she sat on top of her bed with the bottle in one hand, and the gun in the other. She forced herself to drink for a while.

What would you do, Colonel, if your precious little L5 blew her brains out in the privacy of her own cabin? The thought that came back was immediate, and she knew that it was true; *get another one.*

Williams chuckled darkly. She laid her head back against the wall, and closed her eyes. She lifted the gun to her forehead, and pushed it against the side of her temple until it was nice and snug. Her index finger caressed the trigger. She relaxed, put a little more pressure over it. Ary's words floated unbidden through her mind... *'You think an L5 would be allowed to die? You are much too valuable an asset to us. We would have made you 99% AI before we let such a thing happen!'* Williams' eyes snapped open, and she let go of the gun.

"Shit," she murmured under her breath. *And you think it's bad now?*

What if it was true? What if they really would not allow her to die? It was not a risk she felt that she could take. She put the gun away, slugged another few mouthful of whiskey, and then collapsed on top of her bunk. *Please, no dreams,* was her last conscious thought before she passed out.

CHAPTER FOUR

The next morning, she boarded the shuttle at zero-five-hundred hours sharp. She had slept 3 and ½ hours, dreamt of death and destruction for most of it, and woken up feeling sick, and with a splitting headache to boot. There was a message from Ary waiting on her terminal when she woke up that simply said, *"Good luck."* Two days ago, this might have made her feel a little better, knowing that her CO gave a shit. Now, it was anybody's guess what the woman really meant by it. It was almost like a veiled threat, in fact. A warning, even. *Don't worry about it,* Williams thought to herself. *Just keep going.*

She threw on a pair of jeans, running shoes, and a t-shirt. It had been a while since she had dressed in anything other than armour or fatigues, and it did not feel quite right to her. She did not own any pair of shorts other than her standard issue training ones, and she was reluctant to take them with her because they revealed way too much of the scars on her legs. She was far from self-conscious, but she did not enjoy being stared at. Her face was bad enough as it was. Still, it would be scorching hot where she was going.

The place had been nicknamed the *'Martian Key West'* amongst the many soldiers who had spent vacation time over there before. Although Williams had never been to Key West, and never shown much interest in holiday resorts anyway, she got the gist of it. She was being sent off to a tropical paradise, more or less, and yet it felt to her like the worst possible form of punishment. With a sigh, she shoved the shorts and a change of clothes into a rucksack, grabbed her data pad off her desk, and walked off to the cargo bay.

She sat on her own at the back of the transfer shuttle, hiding behind a pair of black sunglasses. She kept her headphones stuck in her ears, even though no music was coming through, and an extremely pissed-off expression arranged all over her face on purpose. She was hoping that it would discourage anyone from trying to strike up a conversation with her, but she was wrong. Only two minutes into the hour-long flight, she felt someone coming to stand by the side of her.

"Is this seat taken?" the female voice enquired.

"Yes," Williams muttered without looking up.

There was a light chuckle, and the woman plonked herself down next to her.

"Hey, Major," she said happily. "How's it going?"

Sergeant Nicole Holson, one of the control room operators and tacticians, always looked happy to see her whenever she did; whether it was in the gym, in the mess hall, or anywhere else she somehow managed to bump into her, supposedly 'by chance'.

Truth be told, Holson always looked happy to see a woman, Williams knew. Any woman. Anywhere, anytime seemed to be her motto. She looked as good as a Cretian supermodel, she had the brains to go with the looks, and an attitude to match. Discovering that one of the only women she had still not managed to charm into bed was on her way to Mars on the same shuttle as her seemed to spark a little madness in Sergeant Holson. She reached out for the major's sunglasses, and gently pulled them down over her nose.

"What the hell are you doing?" Williams snapped.

"Hmm... One shade away from furious, and a trained killer as well," Holson replied with a teasing grin. "Very attractive, Major. I like a little temper in a woman. And I really don't think that such beautiful eyes should be kept hidden."

Williams pushed her off, and she yanked her sunglasses back on. She knew her eyes were red from too little sleep, and too much drinking the night before. She was not particularly keen to put her condition on display.

"Save it," she muttered. "I'm not interested, okay?"

Holson chuckled again, and settled a little more heavily against her shoulder.

"That is only because you have never bothered to find out what I have got to offer, Major," she breathed against the side of Williams' neck. "But you're off duty... I'm off duty... So, why not? You want to play?"

Her left hand came to rest on the officer's thigh, waited there for just a second, and then rubbed languidly against the inside of her leg. She felt the woman's hard muscles tense nicely under her touch, only a millisecond before Williams grabbed her wrist, pulled her hand back roughly, and dumped it on the armrest in between their two seats.

"Leave it alone, Holson," she growled.

She jerked her head back in annoyance when the sergeant reached up to caress her cheek with a long-nailed finger. Holson could feel the heat under her skin which even such brief contact had managed to spark. She laughed knowingly.

"Are you sure?" she whispered.

The intentional, tantalising, yet ever so light brushing of her lips against her skin made it a little harder for Williams to respond in the affirmative this time. But she managed. Just. Holson smiled before she allowed her hand to drop. She caught the relieved look on the marine's face, only there for a second before that rigid mask of detachment fell all over her features again. Well. This one might have been saying one thing, Holson knew, but her body definitely signalled something else. She always liked a challenge.

"So, where are you staying?" she enquired.

"Same resort we all are. At the beach."

"Good. Wanna bunk together?

The woman was relentless. Williams got rid of her shades and headphones, and she turned her head to look at her. She spotted the teasing glint in her eyes, making it obvious that she was enjoying herself. Still, there was a serious undertone to her proposition. Holson was definitely not joking about it. Williams looked away before she could lose her countenance.

"No can do, Sergeant. Sorry. I'm sure you won't have any trouble finding someone else."

"Well, I thank you for the compliment," Holson replied with a delighted wink. "And you're right, I will not be sleeping alone tonight. Or every night for that matter. But it is with you, Major Williams, that I would rather be playing naked on the beach. Not someone else."

She was funny, to be fair, and even her persistence came across as kind of sweet in a way. Despite her best intentions, Williams found it quite impossible not to chuckle.

"Why?" she smirked. "Ran out of options?"

"Yeah," Holson replied in the same tone, grinning. "Fallen on some hard times. You know how it is."

"Looks like it, yeah," Williams agreed. *And you really have no idea…*

She ignored the seatbelt warning sign that suddenly came on, signalling their imminent entry into the Martian atmosphere. She knew full well that if something went wrong with the craft now, it would explode, pure and simple. Wearing a seatbelt would not change the outcome of that. *Health and safety bullshit,* she reflected darkly. The military kind was always the worst. She noticed that Holson did buckle up though, and then the woman pretended to want to look out of the window, and proceeded to lean all over her in order to do so.

"Beautiful," she whispered.

Her hand was resting flat on Williams' stomach, and she could feel the strong muscles under her t-shirt twitch with every bit of pressure that she applied. *Not interested?* she thought. *Yeah, right!*

Williams decided to ignore her. She willed her body to be still, and she turned her head toward the window instead. The view was beautiful, mesmerising, breath-taking... None of those words were an exaggeration. A blue sea, lagoons and white beaches extended down below as far as the eye could see. It was one of the most amazing things she had seen in a long time. The thought flashed in her mind: *I don't deserve any of this.*

"You like that?" Holson enquired, clearly not talking about the view.

Williams spared her a single sideways glance.

"You've been down there before?" she asked.

"Oh yes. Many times. You mean you haven't?"

She sounded incredulous. Williams shrugged.

"Nope. Never been."

"But you have been to the beach before, right?"

As if talking to a child. Williams peeled her fingers off of her t-shirt, as a memory flashed in her mind of the last time that she had been to the beach. It was during her L5 training, on exercise. In the middle of winter, on a planet in the vicinity of Pluto the Council had acquired as their training ground. For almost a week, it had been a steady regime of punishing runs, always timed, getting longer and harder with every passing day; challenging, dangerous swims in the freezing ocean with no wetsuits allowed; sleep deprivation, low food intake, and constant beastings. Williams was not really sure what it meant about her personality that she had actually enjoyed every minute of it.

A thin, dreamy smile appeared over her lips.

"Yeah, I've been to the beach," she murmured.

As they hit some turbulence, bringing her back to the here and now, Holson suddenly tightened her seatbelt, and gripped the armrests.

"Shit," she groaned. "I hate this stuff."

Williams glanced over at her, surprised at her reaction, and she raised an amused eyebrow.

"You okay, Holson?" she enquired lightly. "I would have thought you of all people would enjoy a bit of rough stuff going on?"

"Yeah. It's fine."

"Not feeling seasick or anything, are you?"

Holson visibly swallowed.

"Don't..." she hissed in between clenched teeth.

"Damn, Sergeant, you look a little pale. Feeling a bit woozy all of a sudden? Are you going to throw up? Do you need a sick bag to..."

But Holson shot out of her seat and ran for the heads before she could say anymore. Williams sat back, grinning, feeling pleased with herself. *Saved by the turbulence,* she reflected. *Good.* Contrary to what Holson seemed to believe, she had noticed her long before the woman had even shown an interest in her. It would have been hard not to, really, and there also something about Holson that piqued her curiosity. It was often with her in mind that the L5 did what she had to do, late at night in the privacy of her own cabin. She found it a little shameful. Making it a reality with the beautiful operator was absolutely not a part of her R&R plan.

Still, just before landing, and because Williams was wired that way, she went after her to make sure that Holson was okay. And then she exited the shuttle quickly, ahead of everybody else, not giving the woman a chance to tag along or even suggest sharing a ride to the resort. She made her way across the busy terminal, not thinking much of it at all. It looked like any other cargo bay, any other passenger airport on any other planet she might have been. It was only when she stepped outside that she noticed the difference. Taken by surprise, she immediately froze into place.

"Wow," she murmured.

The first breath of fresh air felt like she had just stepped inside of a wonderful green house. Humid, hot, and with the most delicious fragrance floating on the air. It brought an instant, unconscious, delighted smile to her lips. One thing you did not get on ships were nice smells like that... And there it was as well, the scent of fresh earth, wet grass, and something else that Williams did not recognise but smelt absolutely divine. She had forgotten how good all this stuff could feel, and she stood on the tarmac for a while, breathing it in, with her eyes closed and her face tilted up to the sun.

Four years, she reflected to herself. It had been four years since the last time she had been out on any kind of planet for anything other than a combat mission. It startled her a little to realise it. *No wonder I feel so destroyed.*

"Major Williams, hi!"

Williams opened her eyes to find a young woman standing at attention in front of her. 5'3, slender, with ultra-short blond hair, and a goofy smile plastered all over her face.

"Uh, hi... Do I know you?" she replied.

The woman's smile widened even more.

"Oh, no, but I do. I work for Doctor West, and I'll be your driver and personal assistant for the duration of your stay. It is such an honour to meet you, ma'am," she added, blushing hard. "I hope to join up very soon, and my dream is to serve under your command one day. I mean, well; I know it wouldn't be like, straight away, but maybe in a couple of years. I've just aced all my pre-entry tests, I think, and, well..."

More blushing and excited grinning followed, as Williams simply stared at the youngster in complete silence, her face expressionless. Inside was a different story altogether. This woman's eagerness and heartfelt enthusiasm reminded her of Maxx all of a sudden. *Maxx...* Williams allowed her picture to form inside her head, and the next thing she knew something heavy at the back of her mind started spiralling down, and draining all the light from her brain.

"Aw, shit," she muttered.

"Major, are you okay?"

The woman's voice sounded so far away... Williams' surroundings suddenly grew dim. Her vision was reduced to the size of a thimble. She struggled for air. Took a couple of steps to the side, and felt like she was going to fall down. *Focus. Find something to focus on, and don't think about her, damn it!* she instructed herself.

"Major?"

"Yeah..." Williams stammered. "Yeah. Just a minute..."

She focused on the lovely smell. She took some deep breaths, concentrated briefly on the sun's warmth she could feel, and how wonderful that was. Back to the gorgeous scent. Anchoring her mind on simple things, not allowing the stress reaction to get any worse. It worked. After a few more seconds, her vision went back to normal. Thankfully, the young woman by her side appeared calm, patient. Ready to catch her should she need it, it seemed, which would not be necessary. Absolutely not. But Williams was grateful for her cool and measured reaction, because she was not really in a position to reassure anyone at this stage.

"Are you okay, Major?"

The struggling officer nodded eventually, and even managed to flash a weak smile.

"Yeah. Sorry about that. I, uh... It's been a while since I breathed some real air," she lied. "What's your name?"

Another bright, delighted grin that tugged at her heart. *So much like Maxx...*

"My name's Christina. Christina Spiller, Major."

Williams used her t-shirt to wipe the sweat off her face. She briefly caught sight of Sergeant Holson, standing in line with a group of other soldiers, waiting to board the military transport craft that would take them to the resort. Clearly dying of curiosity, obviously wondering whether to walk over or not. And leaning toward doing it.

Williams snapped into action.

"Christina, did I hear you say you've got a vehicle with you?" she asked.

"Yes, right over here, Major."

The L5 quickly shouldered her rucksack, and she started walking in that direction before Holson had a chance to make up her mind.

"Let's get out of here," she declared.

"Yes, ma'am!"

"Christina?"

"Yes, Major."

"My name's Evan, by the way."

"Yes, ma'am. I know."

Williams let out an amused chuckle.

"As in, feel free to use it anytime you like."

"Oh..." Christina looked surprised, then pleased. "Sure thing, Major! Will do."

Williams rolled her eyes.

"Never mind," she sighed.

CHAPTER FIVE

After this, she quickly discovered that her wannabe-commando recruit was polite, thoughtful, and subtle in her interactions. She did not ask any probing or unwelcome questions. She did not try to fuss over her the way the medical crew usually did, and she got her excitement under control, too, which was a huge relief to Williams. The last thing she needed on her hands was a kid with a crush.

She started to relax a little more as Christina drove them along the beach toward the resort that was situated at the end of town. The views were magnificent, the weather outstanding, and after such a long time up in space, the weary marine had a little trouble not being distracted by all the sights. It took her a while to remember Christina's initial introduction. When she did, she recalled the name that she had first mentioned.

"So, who's this Dr West, by the way?" she enquired.

Her young guide shot her a surprised look.

"That's your therapist, Major."

"Right," Williams grunted. "Thought that might be."

"You, uh, you haven't read your paperwork yet?"

Williams gave her a pointed look. She raised a bored eyebrow.

"There was some paperwork?"

Christina started laughing.

"Yes, and quite detailed too."

"I'll bet. Can you fill me in?"

"Sure! So, you have a private apartment on the other side of the resort, only a 5-minute stroll away from the beach, and separate from all the rest of the troops. Colonel Ary was quite specific about that. She said she did not want anyone bothering you there, or intruding on your private time."

"Kind of her," the L5 murmured ironically.

She was well aware that every second she spent off duty ended up costing the Council extra money. Personally, she had never thought about it in these terms before. It was not why she fought. But no wonder they did not want anything interfering with her recovery.

"Everything you need will be free for you at the resort," Christina continued.

"Great."

"Apart from alcohol."

That figures, Williams reflected with a smirk. Good thing her new rank had also earned her a significant pay rise. She would spend good money on quality stuff if she wanted to, and fuck Ary and her stupid rules.

"You can request any food you want, and we can put a specific menu together for you if that's something you would like."

"Okay, thanks. Don't think I'll bother with that."

"No problem. We also have several gyms on site, a couple of swimming pools, a spa, massage specialists, a doctor, dive instructors..." Christina recited off the top of her head.

"Can I swim off the beach here?" Williams interrupted.

"Oh, yes," the woman replied with a quick glance in her direction. "There are no sharks or anything you need to worry about. The waters are safe, except when the red flag is up."

"What then?"

"Then, don't go in."

Williams laughed easily.

"What? Why not?" she challenged. "What will happen if I do?"

"The rip tide will swallow you up, and we will never see you again, Major."

"Evan."

"Sorry. But yeah, be careful with the red flag, okay? I know... Well, I don't know for sure, really, but I've seen videos of L5 swim training, so... I'd love to learn more, by the way. I mean, not that it's your job to tell me, of course. I just..."

Christina must have caught herself babbling suddenly, because she appeared to give herself a mental warning.

"Yeah, whatever," she concluded. "All this to say I'm sure you can handle yourself out there in the water, but that rip tide means business. So, now you know."

She flashed another excited grin, and the commando officer smiled again in response. She liked this Christina after all, she decided. Even though she reminded her of Maxx, it was refreshing to be around someone like her for a change. Enthusiastic, bright, and full of energy. Obviously bursting to ask questions about all the L5 and military stuff, but too polite to do it. She was sweet, Williams concluded.

"So, what else?" she asked.

"Well, the beach is twelve miles long, and it's great for running."

"Excellent."

"Anything you need, anywhere you want to go, just let me know. Also, I am supposed to remind you that you are scheduled to see Dr West at 5 o'clock every afternoon. That's important."

Williams' smile faded. Now that she was on the ground, and had been made aware of the facilities available at the site, she was in no doubt whatsoever that this was the ideal environment to help speed up her recovery. But the thought of having to talk with a shrink every single day still did not sit right with her at all.

"5 o'clock, noted," she muttered.

Her mood darkened even more when she spotted the billboard by the side of the road, and recognised herself on it. Dressed in full armour, aiming her laser rifle at something in the distance. She looked fierce and formidable, and like some movie war hero or something. Was it even her, or had they simply pasted her face onto someone else's body? *I can't believe I am seeing this,* she thought, astonished. The eye-catching, clever caption across the huge picture simply read, *'INTERSTELLAR COMMANDO UNIT – BE THE BEST'.* Williams groaned as they drove past it, and Christina followed her gaze. She gave a little shrug.

"Oh, yeah, sorry. I guess I should have warned you. They have a lot of these things over here. You're quite famous on Mars, Major. And... People really appreciate what you've done, you know?"

The so-called famous soldier shot her a piercing look.

"But people are being fed stories and lies. It's got nothing to do with the truth, or what really happened. You realise that, don't you?"

"Yes, but..."

"Is this why you decided to join up? Because of all that fake motivational shit?"

"No, it's not."

Williams shook her head, and she sighed in barely hidden frustration. She did not believe Spiller entirely. Of course, it may

43

not be the full reason, but she knew that this stuff always played a part, no matter what people said. It was also clear from the woman's behaviour, and her initial comments upon first meeting her that she had this huge hero thing going on about her.

"Why then?" she pushed.

Christina was calm and collected when she replied. And she gave a good answer, genuine, and honest. It was pretty much exactly the same one that Williams herself had stated on her recruitment paperwork all those years ago.

"I want to join because I'd like to make a difference," she said softly. "I want to save lives. And help make the world a safer place for the people I love." Then, in a much quieter voice, she added: "My older brother was in the Marines too, you know."

Williams exhaled sharply. *Was.*

"What happened?" she murmured.

The bright, energetic woman behind the wheel suddenly looked much older than her years. Williams knew pretty well what the answer to her question would be, and she had not wanted to ask it. Still, it felt to her as if Christina wanted to tell her.

"He was a pilot. He was killed defending a Pleiadian colony against a Scythian raid. It happened just over a year ago. I was still in school back then."

"I'm sorry, Christina."

Those were words that she had said hundreds of times, to lots of different people all over the galaxy. And still, there was emotion in Williams' voice when she said them, each and every time. She knew how much it hurt. She was genuine about it. It was something that Colonel Ary would probably never understand, and clearly considered a weakness. But Christina threw her a timid smile. She appeared grateful for the sentiment.

"Thank you, Major."

"Evan," Williams repeated absently.

Christina laughed.

"Sorry. Okay, I got it now."

It felt a little strange to have company, Williams reflected. And even weirder to realise that she was enjoying it. For the first time, it occurred to her how lonely she had actually felt since the loss of her team. She was always surrounded by doctors these days, of course, with a bunch of specialists/scientists to monitor her new AI. And even though she was technically off-duty, she still had some involvement with the strategists onboard the ship, and she had spent some time in the war room discussing objectives and tactical decisions. She had been with and around a lot of people, yes, and also completely shut down, unwilling and unable to connect. But it was hard to resist Christina's refreshing candour, and not respond in kind. Especially when the woman turned to her suddenly, and pointed to a wooden shack a little way ahead on the beach.

"Hey, are you hungry?" she asked.

She was already licking her lips at the thought of food, and Williams burst out laughing.

"Are you?"

"Yeah, but I'm supposed to be at your service. So..."

"So, in this case," Williams cut in, "I think I am starving. This place do burgers?"

"The best," Christina replied, eyes glinting in anticipation.

Ten minutes later, they sat side by side under a canvas awning, at a small table near a tiny food shack with killer views of the beach. The food consisted of two ridiculously juicy burgers, the thickest chips Williams had ever seen, and the best mayonnaise in the entire world. A cold beer for the off-duty major, and a tall iced tea for her driver.

"Cheers," Christina said, raising her glass.

"Cheers," the L5 replied in kind.

Christina looked at ease in a pair of short shorts, a tank top, and no shoes. She had left her sandals in the vehicle. Williams was sweating in her jeans and heavy t-shirt, and after a while, it simply got too much.

"Sod it," she muttered.

She kicked her shoes off, grabbed a steak knife, and cut the legs off her jeans. They became short shorts as well, revealing pale skin, hard muscles, and a bunch of scars that still looked red and painful even after so many weeks. To her credit, Christina only looked at them once before she shrugged, and returned her attention to her burger.

"Feeling better?" she asked.

Williams felt the warm breeze on her legs, the sand in her toes, and decided that she could not remember the last time she had felt quite this good.

"Much," she replied.

She took a huge bite off her burger, and reached for the beer. In front of them, it was nothing but mesmerising white sand and glittering blue sea.

"What an amazing place," she reflected. "Were you born here?"

"Yes. Lived here all my life too."

"How old are you?"

"Seventeen."

"And you want to enlist. As an officer?"

"Yes."

"Just waiting for the results of your tests now?"

"Yes, ma'am."

Williams nodded. There was something about this young woman that told her she had probably scored top marks on every single one of her assessments. This kid appeared nothing but extremely clever, and massively determined. Williams gestured toward the sea, and the food on Christina's plate.

"You will miss this," she remarked.

It was not a question. She knew for sure that Christina would. Badly. They all did eventually, the soldiers who were born in nice places, the ones who grew up on a planet instead of on a ship. And not a single one of them ever believed that they would never return. The bad stuff would happen to someone else. Of course, it would.

"You're right," Christina said. "I know I will."

She gave a light shrug.

"But I have thought long and hard about it, trust me. And I want to do it. Join the Marines, and maybe one day, serve under your command."

Williams was trying to get her eyes accustomed to the bright light and sunshine. She took her sunglasses off at that moment, and gave the woman a long, lingering look. She resisted the urge to ask her what she thought it would be like. Resisted the temptation to at least try to talk her out of it. Her brother had died in combat. She doubted that Christina's motivation stemmed from seeing a few photos of her looking good on some billboards around town, but still...

"Ice," she said instead.

Christina appeared confused.

"Ice? Uh, you want some?"

"No, I just decided that 'Ice' is going to be your nickname, Spiller. You can't serve in the Special Forces unless you've got one. So, yours is going to be Ice. Do you like it?"

Christina clearly did.

"But wait, why Ice?" she enquired. "How did you come up with that?"

Williams grinned.

"Guess," she prompted.

Christina was quick to frown.

"Oh, I get it," she said. "That's because I drink iced tea."

She sounded disappointed.

"Nope. Try again."

"Hmm…"

The marine finished her burger, and she polished off her chips whilst the younger woman tried to come up with the right answer.

"Hey, do you know why I'm really here, Spiller?" she asked her then, her eyes fixed onto the sea in the distance. "On this so-called R&R thing?"

There was a serious, focused look back on her face now.

"You mean why you're seeing West?" Christina replied immediately.

She was quick, this one, for sure. Williams nodded.

"Yeah."

"I don't know. I'm just your driver."

"But you must have an idea."

"Some."

"And yet, you would still want to serve under me? Despite knowing for a fact that there must be something really wrong with me?"

Christina looked confused.

"Why do you say that?" she asked.

Williams rolled her eyes.

"Because otherwise," she pointed out, "I would be on the front line doing some good right now, instead of down here talking to a shrink. Right?"

In that instant, Christina proved to her that she deserved her new nickname.

"I don't care," she replied with a simple shrug. "What, you really think I am stupid enough to believe the stuff on the posters? And all the bullshit the recruiters tell you?"

Williams gave a faint smile.

"I wondered," she admitted, truthfully. "You seem to think I am something special. But I am just a regular marine, you know? I do my job the best I can, and sometimes that's not enough. I'm not a hero. Don't put me on a pedestal."

"I'm not."

"Are you sure?"

Christina blushed, but she stuck to her argument.

"I look up to you, Major, that's all. You're an officer, and L5-rated as well. To me, you're a model of excellence, and that's what I aspire to be. The other stuff is not important. If you need help with some of the things that happened to you, the real hard reality the recruiters don't ever tell you about, then you're smart to get it. That's all I care about. And if I can help you in some way, anything you need, then I will do my best for you."

Williams put her glasses back on to hide the sudden wetness in her eyes. These days she seemed to struggle so much to control her emotions. She hated it. But Christina simply shrugged again.

"You can cry," she said flatly. "I don't mind that either."

Williams choked on a mouthful of beer. *Yeah, for sure*, she thought. This one was made of the right stuff. She slapped her companion on the shoulder, grinning, and touched the side of her glass with her bottle.

"Cool as ice," she approved. "Just what I thought."

She saw the woman's eyes light up in pleasure.

"Oh, yeah," she exclaimed. "Nice! I like it!"

"Good. And Spiller?"

"Yes, Major?"

It was obvious that Christina was never going to get the hang of calling her by her first name, and actually, it had been a stupid idea for her to suggest that she did it in the first place. Williams shook her head, and she ordered herself another cold beer.

"Nothing," she smiled. "Everything's perfect."

CHAPTER SIX

The good news was that she did not have to see her therapist until the second day. So, it gave her and her new buddy ample time to finish their lunch, go for a walk on the beach, and explore the town a little. When Christina dropped her off at the resort a while later, Williams spent some of those rare, and usually unwanted idle hours that she had discovering her new quarters.

Luxurious was the only way to describe the apartment. You could have held basketball games in the lounge, easily. The kitchen was vast, all dark chrome and sleek appliances. She quickly located the microwave in the corner, which was the only piece of equipment she intended to use on the rare occasion that she would not eat out. The bedroom situated at the back contained a large, comfortable-looking bed, and sweet-smelling, dark-blue silk sheets to go with it. Williams walked into the bathroom, ignored her reflection in the mirror, and smirked when she saw the shower room. It was bigger than the entire female communal showers on the ship.

"Too bad I don't care about all this stuff," she reflected.

As she went through each room, getting used to the extra space, from time to time one of her old friends' voice would pop up inside her head.

'Look at the size of that fucking TV!', Edwards would probably have exclaimed as soon as he walked in.

She stopped in front of it, and trailed a light finger along the side of the screen, smiling faintly. She could picture the tall, ex-football player who had been born on Earth just as clearly as if he had been standing there by the side of her. She could see the grin on his face, and the little scar on the side of his mouth that always made it look as if he were amused, even when he was not. She shook her head, and the image disappeared. So real... But Sergeant Edwards would never again appreciate a good game of football on the TV. Edwards had been killed in the science lab explosion. He ended up caught in the fire just like his best friend Collinson.

Williams gave a bitter shake of the head at the thought of him. Collinson would have enjoyed himself in this cavernous kitchen, for sure. Nicknamed *'Le Chef'* because of his love of French food and cooking, he always used to say that he would open a restaurant after the Marines. It was Collinson who had cooked her chilli that night, and got drunk with her after she had learned of her sister's death.

The L5 officer felt the familiar tightening in her chest, and the little hitch in her breathing that signalled a panic attack was not far off. She was letting her thoughts run away with her again, doing exactly what she knew that she should not.

"Stay in control, damn it," she said out loud.

Knowing that the best way to deal with this sort of thing was to keep moving, she threw on a pair of shorts and a sports bra, no shoes, and headed for the beach. Ice had said that it was twelve miles long, and great for running, so it was about time she gave it a try. Turns out it was perfect, much better than the running track onboard the ship. Nice and steady, she ran halfway across the vast expanse of sand before she stopped, did a series of push-ups and stretching exercises, and turned back around. She felt better when she ran, as always, although it seemed to take longer and longer for the endorphins to kick in these days. A few lengths in the swimming pool outside her apartment completed her training schedule that evening. And as a much more settled Williams sat on a lounge chair afterward, drying herself off and thinking about food, Sergeant Holson suddenly materialised in front of her. The woman looked a little smug. A little hot, and a little annoyed too.

"Well, it took me a while, but I did manage to find you at last," she exclaimed.

"Congratulations," Williams replied with a wry smile.

Holson dropped onto the chair next to her, and draped a comfortable arm around her shoulders.

"So. Miss me?"

Williams politely took hold of her fingers, and lifted her arm off. She stood up.

"No," she said, and started to walk away.

"Oh, please don't be like that," Holson protested. "I spend all day looking for you, worrying about you, and that's all the thanks I get when I finally manage to track you down? Come on!"

Williams paused for a second, looking surprised.

"Worried?" she asked, frowning. "Why?"

"You looked a little unwell this morning. Are you okay?"

"Yes. And don't worry about that."

"Oh, I'm certainly not concerned about you now, Major," Holson replied, with a lazy grin spreading all over her lips. "I can see you look... Well, you look..."

She made a vague gesture toward her, and Williams glanced down at herself, her frown deepening in obvious wonder.

"What?" she muttered. "Something wrong with me?"

Holson rolled her eyes at her. Williams did not even seem to realise why she and half the other women onboard the ship always struggled to take their eyes off her. She took her time observing her now.

There was an impressive array of new scars on the woman's body, and some of them still looked a little raw. Holson knew that her right arm and shoulder had been replaced with synthetics. She searched for differences, imperfections, but could not see any. If she had not known, she would never have been able to guess. The commando officer was tall, slender. Her body was well-muscled, chiselled to perfection. Long blond hair, currently wet, a few strands clinging seductively to the side of her neck. She had been gifted with lean, sharp, intelligent features, just like she was; and a pair of limpid blue eyes to complete the package. If anything, the scar across her cheek added even more allure to her otherwise perfect looks. Holson shook her head a little pensively. Major Williams, she reflected. No wonder the military had decided to stick posters of her all over the damn planet.

"Holson?" the object of her musings suddenly called.

The operator shook herself.

"No, nothing wrong at all," she replied, smiling. "You look good, Williams."

She also appeared to be one of those people who could spend just one day at the beach, and end up with the perfect tan. The sweetest thing about Williams was probably the fact that she had no idea about any of those things. It was cute, Holson decided, how so little self-aware she was. And she wanted more.

"Have you eaten yet?" she asked.

The L5 started to say that she was not hungry, but her stomach chose that unfortunate moment to issue a loud rumble.

"Great," Holson exclaimed.

She jumped to her feet, looking pleased, and came to hang her arms around Williams' neck. She leaned against her, and met her gaze. She gave her the sort of shy and gentle smile that not many people could resist. Williams would have liked to be the one who found it easy, but she obviously struggled not to return it in earnest.

"What are you doing?" she murmured. "Don't, okay?"

"I'm not doing anything," Holson said. "Relax, will you?"

Williams smelt strongly of swimming pool, sunshine, and something else that was entirely hers, and quite delightful. She remained standing still, right where she was. She did not return the light embrace, but neither did she try to move out of it. She felt solid, hard, like a lump of granite. Under such unyielding, unrelenting control. Holson wondered what it would take to break it.

"Let's go to dinner," she invited.

"Uh…"

"Come on. You need to eat, and so do I. Okay?"

Presented in this way, it did seem like a pretty easy decision to make.

"Okay, I just need to change first."

"No problem. I'll come along. You lead the way."

Williams threw a wry look over her shoulder.

"Worried I'll make a run for it?" she asked. "Try to lose you again?"

Holson seemed to find the suggestion highly entertaining.

"You are welcome to try, Major," she said. "But two things for you to keep in mind."

"What's that, Sergeant?"

"One, it's a small resort; and two, I don't give up easily. Just so you're aware."

Williams grunted, but she was not really annoyed. *Yeah, tell me something I don't know,* she reflected.

"Is that a threat?" she joked, and her companion laughed easily.

"More like a promise," she grinned.

She was extremely impressed with the size of the apartment, and she insisted on walking through every single room, admiring the surroundings. She flashed a slow, sizzling smile when she spotted the bedroom.

"Wow. Nice," she commented.

"Don't get any ideas, Holson."

The operator chuckled, and she handled the comment like a pro.

"Who, me?" she grinned. "As if."

Williams smirked in reply. She locked the bathroom door behind her while she showered, just in case the woman did get the wrong idea, and emerged out of it wearing the new clothes that she had bought in the resort's shop. Above-the-knee shorts, a fitted tank top, and something that looked suspiciously like military desert boots on her feet. Her dog tags were dangling from her neck. Holson flashed her an amused smile.

"Not much of a girly girl, are you?" she remarked.

"Hell, no."

"Well. It suits you. You look amazing."

Williams shrugged, and she finally allowed herself to glance at Holson, whose body was tightly clad in a sensuous black dress. It was designed with a plunging neckline that highlighted her perfect breasts. Skin creamy and delicate, the sort that would certainly be delicious to kiss. Short black hair expertly sculpted into a fashionable style, and full lips made even more inviting by a subtle layer of red lipstick. She wore high heels that night that made her appear as tall as Williams.

She went to stand in front of her, shifted her weight on one leg, and rested her hands over her hips.

"How do I look?" she asked, eyes smouldering. "Okay?"

Williams had a nicely thoughtful expression plastered all over her face, and she blushed when she realised that she was staring straight at the woman's breasts. Said woman seemed extremely happy that she was doing so.

"Yeah," Williams replied. "Uh... Yeah."

She swallowed.

"Good," Holson nodded, satisfied.

This soldier might be a little damaged, she reflected, but there was life in her yet. She linked her arm through hers, and flashed her a brilliant smile.

"Shall we?"

∞

A sharp knock on her door the next morning startled Williams out of a deep and difficult sleep. She checked the time. 7 a.m. She had overslept.

When she moved, she was reminded of some of the heavy drinking she had done the night before. Still dressed in the same clothes that she had fallen into bed with, she got up and stumbled over her boots lying across the floor. She padded into the kitchen. *Where the hell is the coffee machine in this place?* Another knock on the door reclaimed her attention, and Williams glanced at the monitor above the wall.

"It's open," she yelled.

"Good morning, Major," Ice greeted her brightly as soon as she walked in.

Williams flashed her a distracted smile in response.

"Hey. Morning."

She carried on banging around the kitchen, opening and closing cabinet doors. Her young visitor refrained from asking her if she had slept well, or had a good night, which was the clever thing to do. Williams was swearing loudly under her breath by the time she pointed her in the right direction.

"Uh, is this what you are looking for, Major?"

"Yes!"

Williams rolled her eyes as she finally spotted the coffee machine, tucked away inside a clever little compartment hidden inside the wall.

"Damn it," she exclaimed. "Who'd do a stupid thing like that?"

Ice was laughing.

"Some clever designer, probably."

"Yeah, probably," the marine muttered.

Nothing clever about that, but whatever.

"Coffee?" she offered.

"Yes, please. I brought you some groceries, too."

It was Williams' turn to laugh when Ice unloaded her bag of so-called groceries all over the counter. It was all packets, ready-made, and protein bars. She liked that kind of 'groceries'. She ripped the wrapping off a Powerbar, and took a large bite out of it.

"Help yourself," she invited. "How much do I owe you?"

"Nothing. Remember it's all free for you here apart from..."

"Apart from the booze, I know," Williams grinned.

Ice took a sip of her coffee, winced at how strong it was, and then she stared at her with a slightly hesitant look on her face. But it was intense. You could almost see the questions rolling around her head.

"What's up?" Williams enquired, amused.

The woman instantly turned bright red.

"Uh, you've got a… Uh… A Thing."

"A what?" Williams frowned.

"A Thing, like, right on the side of your neck," Ice informed her, caught it seemed between the urge to laugh about it, and total embarrassment.

"What do you mean?"

Williams rubbed a finger over her neck, puzzled. And then she groaned, suddenly realising the reason for her young friend's discomfort. *Holson,* she remembered.

They had spent the whole evening together at a quiet restaurant in town, with magnificent views of the harbour. Sampling the delicious sea food, and drinking margaritas like there was no tomorrow. It turned out the operator was really good company when she managed to talk about something other than sex for five minutes; or how *'fucking sexy'* Williams looked, in her own words, and not ones that had been received too well by the major.

But Holson had also made her laugh with some hilarious stories of her early years with the Marines, when she was still trying to find her feet. And from time to time, she had even managed to help Williams forget what she was there on Mars to do. They both had way too much to drink, which did not have much of an effect on the L5 initially, but certainly did on her companion. Holson was slurring her words quite badly by the end of the night. And she was struggling to keep her balance by the time Williams walked her back to her room. Taking one step forward, and two steps back. It took them a little while, which Holson quite enjoyed in a way, because it was an opportunity to get her hands all over the woman she wanted, and not get shoved back the way she normally was. She may even have exaggerated her condition a little. When they got to her room, and before the startled officer could do anything about it, Holson had grabbed her around the waist, and laid a kiss on her that had made Williams' legs tremble. Then, she had sunk her teeth into the side of her neck, hard enough to hurt, and whispered, '*Stay tonight, and I will make you scream in pleasure.*' Williams had pushed her inside, got her safely to her bed, and beaten her retreat.

"Sorry," she muttered. "I ran into my Martian fan club last night, and they were all over me. It's those damn posters, you know?"

Strangely enough, this seemed to make perfect sense to Ice.

"Yes, ma'am," she agreed. "I know."

Williams looked down, and she smiled.

"What are you doing here so early, anyway?" she enquired. "Or were you just delivering a bunch of food to me? It's nice, by the way."

"Good. There was something else, though."

"Spit it out, Ice," Williams encouraged when the woman hesitated.

"Well, you know I'll be starting basic training soon, right?"

"Yep. Got your dates, yet?"

"No, but it should be fairly soon."

"So, what is it you want to ask me?"

Whatever it was, the young woman had obviously been wanting to ask it for a while. She was almost squirming with excitement.

"I was wondering if maybe you'd have some time to train with me a little," she said quickly. "Just to help boost my fitness levels in prep for when I go in. I know you probably have more important things to do with your time, and that this is not a holiday for you. And I know I'm just supposed to drive you around, and help you with shopping and stuff... But I just thought I'd ask..."

She looked like she could not wait to get started, Williams noticed, and also more than a little apprehensive at the same time, which was understandable. Obviously, checking out videos of Level 5 officer trainings would tend to make one feel a little nervous.

"Are you looking for a beasting, Spiller?" she asked.

She just managed to keep a straight face, and sound threatening enough to achieve a result. Christina swallowed hard in response, but she also stood a little straighter. Her answer came through sharp and clear.

"Yes, ma'am!"

"Good," Williams decided. "If you want to train with me, you are more than welcome. How about a run/swim to warm us up, and then we can spend some time in the gym? There's a few things I can show you."

"Great!"

CHAPTER SEVEN

It was all incredibly nice, but five o'clock had to come around eventually. The therapist's practice was only a few miles away from the resort, and Ice dropped her there on time.

"Don't wait for me," Williams told her. "I'll walk back when I'm done."

She was not sure what sort of a mood she would be in after an encounter with Dr West, but if previous appointments of this kind were anything to go by, happy and relaxed was probably not an option. There was no need for the young woman to witness her at her worst.

"Okay, no problem, Major."

Williams gave her a friendly pat on the shoulder.

"Nice work in the gym, by the way. Just a little more, and you'll be able to ace that basic training without even breaking a sweat."

Ice responded with a tired, yet contented little smile. She had thrown up once on the run, and once more in the gym, but then she had impressed Williams with her stamina, and almost managed to keep up with her until the end. Of course, the L5 had only been at 50% of her capacity.

"Same time tomorrow?" she asked.

"Looking forward to it."

Williams nodded, satisfied, and she started to walk away.

"Hey, Major Williams?" Ice called back.

There was no doubt from her expression that she knew exactly how much her officer friend did not want to go in there. She gave her an encouraging look.

"Good luck, okay?"

Williams flashed her a thumbs-up and a smile in reply, and she watched her drive off down the street. Then she exhaled slowly, and allowed her smile to fade.

She was feeling sick to her stomach at the thought of another round with a shrink. Still, spurred on by the thought that she would be back on active duty soon, she braced herself, and walked right in. Since there appeared to be no one at reception, she wandered down toward the office at the other end of the hallway. The door was wide open, and she risked a glance inside. A woman sat behind the desk. Dressed in black slacks despite the weather, a white blouse, sandals on her feet. Mid-fifties, probably. She wore a pair of thin, wire-rimmed glasses on her nose, and her hair was tied up in a bun. She looked like a school teacher. She appeared every bit as conservative and strict as Williams had worried she would be, and it made her wince inside. *Just my luck*, she sighed. *Well. Here we go.* She was just about to knock on the door when the woman spoke. She was on a call, obviously, and had not caught sight of her new client standing there.

"I have to tell you darling, sometimes people don't need therapy," said therapist declared. "Sometimes they think they're depressed, but I think they would do well to check they are not in fact surrounded by a bunch of freakin' assholes."

Williams could not help but chuckle out loud. It was what the woman had said, combined with the language she used, and the fact that she even subscribed to such a point of view that did it for her. It also happened to perfectly match her opinion on the matter. Immediately, the therapist swivelled in her chair, and fixed her with an enquiring stare.

"Sorry. There was no one at reception, and the door was open."

The woman glanced toward the clock up on the far corner of the wall. She appeared a little irritated.

"Listen, Jennifer, I will call you back later," she said, and ended her conversation abruptly. "It is definitely I who should apologise, Major Williams," she stated then. "I am late. And you are most welcome. My name is Doctor West, and I am looking forward to working with you."

Williams nodded, and she even managed to flash her a quick smile, despite the butterflies in her stomach. She was an L5 marine, after all. A trained assassin. She ate Scythian soldiers for breakfast. But all the same, shrinks seemed to have a special, dark power of some kind. She was hoping that she did not look half as desperate as the way that she truly felt inside.

"Thanks," she said. "And I think you're right, Doctor. I am surrounded by a bunch of freakin' assholes. Funny how that is, uh?"

West stood up, and she walked over to shake her hand.

"Nice try, Major," she observed. "But you are going to have to do a lot better than this if you want me to sign your release. I happen to know Colonel Ary quite well. And she is definitely not one of those."

Williams' fake enthusiasm disappeared. This woman would be harder to manipulate, she realised. She would probably not be as gullible as some of the other shrinks. Those ones she could normally lie to quite easily, and get away with it to her satisfaction. But this West character knew Ary, too, which was not good news. The way the therapist stared at her, unblinking and intense, also reminded Williams quite a lot of the colonel.

She shrugged.

"Worth a try," she muttered.

West did not seem particularly impressed.

"Please, have a seat," she offered.

The marine went to lean against the windowsill on the other side of the room. She crossed her arms over her chest, her legs at the ankles, and she waited. The doctor returned to her desk, and they both looked at each other. *Now what?* Williams seemed to be thinking.

West had gone through her files and service records with a fine-toothed comb. The L5 officer was impeccable in every sense, both on and off the stage it seemed. And the military surgeons had obviously done an outstanding job of putting her back together. West had discussed her new case with Ary, and she knew that some of that medical stuff was part of the issue, but she did not believe it was the root cause of the problem. The real damage, the one that could not be fixed so easily with a handful of synthetic implants, was probably a lot deeper on the inside with Williams.

There was something clearly missing from her eyes too, which the counsellor was not surprised to notice. And there was none of the veiled hope that she was used to seeing in some of the people she treated. Those who pretended they did not need her, but were secretly desperate for help. The ones who burst into tears after only ten minutes in the office, and admitted to her that they were not coping. West quietly assessed her new client in the first few seconds of their encounter. The woman appeared tense to the point of breaking. She just stood there returning her silent stare, smiling faintly, but the smile never touched her eyes. She seemed a million miles away, and the only thing that she appeared to have in common with West's usual clientele was that she genuinely did not want to be there.

The therapist waited a few seconds longer, just to see what would happen. Williams did not disappoint.

"See something you like, Doctor?" she suddenly snapped.

West flashed her an appeasing smile which did not appear to have much effect.

"Only doing my job, I can assure you."

"You think staring at me like this is going to help?"

"Do you need help, Major Williams?" West murmured.

Damn it! Williams almost shouted in exasperation. She had fallen right into that trap.

"No," she said, clearly making an effort to calm herself down. "I don't. I'm fine."

"Maybe. But you still failed your return to duty test."

"Just a glitch. I'll pass next time."

"I'm sure you will," West agreed. "I was informed the reason you failed initially was because of elevated amounts of cortisol and adrenaline in your system, which are playing havoc with your autonomic system. Is that right, Major?"

Williams threw her a dark look.

"You read the report. Why ask me?"

"And this seems to be all due to long periods of sustained stress and anxiety. Major Williams? Is this correct?" West prompted her again when she did not offer a reply.

Williams did after a short while, and it looked like it cost her.

"Yes. Right," she confirmed.

"Looking at you now, I would say that it is probably a fair assessment," West remarked. "You seem to be under a lot of pressure. Perhaps it would help you to discuss it with me. I can assure you that everything will remain confidential. Strictly between the two of us."

"Sure, it will," Williams snorted ironically.

West immediately cocked an eyebrow up.

"You don't believe me?" she enquired.

Williams looked at her as if she were trying really hard to decide whether the woman was only playing dumb, and this was just another trap.

"Doctor," she said eventually, "I'm sure you are aware that I was given a layer of neural lace."

"Yes, I am aware of it."

"Against my will."

"I am sorry about that, Major, but it did save your life. You had zero level of brain activity when the shuttle landed back on the…"

"Yes, that's because I was dying," Williams interrupted. "I arrested twice more in the OR whilst they were busy pushing that AI stuff into my bloodstream. You'd think someone would have got the message, right?"

West remained silent.

"But no," the furious officer exclaimed, "they went right ahead over my head, and turned me into a fucking cyborg. Based on this, Doctor, you will forgive me if I do not believe that anything Colonel Ary wants to know about me will remain confidential for very long."

Williams took a deep breath, and tried to bring her raging temper under control.

"Look, I know full well what the problem is, okay?" she added. "I don't need your help to fix it. I have a stressful job, I understand. A few more days on the beach should take care of it. Now, let's get this session over and done with, shall we?"

She was used to being in command, West reflected, and it showed. What she obviously did not realise was that she was not going to be the one in charge here.

"Sure you don't want to sit down, Major?" she asked.

Williams looked ready to explode, but she did drop into a chair. *'See? Cooperating'*, her expression seemed to say. West pushed a glass of water in front of her. From the look of suspicion across her client's face, you would have thought that she expected it to be poisoned. West waited a few seconds, and Williams still did not touch the glass. She avoided eye contact. She seemed to be trying really hard to stay in her seat, and not bolt out the door.

"Tell me what happened during that mission," West requested.

The major visibly bristled at the request.

"You read about it in my file, right?"

"Yes, I did. But I would like to hear it from you. In your own words, please."

Williams blew air loudly out of her mouth. She stared at the form that she could see on top of West's desk. It was the one that, as soon as it was signed, would allow her to re-take the test, and get the hell back to her job. She ran both hands through her hair, and decided to tell the woman what she wanted to hear. With a bit of luck, if she did well, she could walk out of there with a free pass. It was worth it.

"All right," she said, in a slightly more conceding tone of voice this time. "We were sent over to Elesion to free up some Council hostages. Unbeknownst to us, our AI system was compromised by an enemy virus. It completely overwhelmed our comms system, sending bad intel to everyone involved, and it also infected some of our support craft vehicles." *My crew died because of all that shit, you know? It cost them their life!* "We walked straight into an ambush. People got killed. End of story."

"People?" West repeated.

She was watching her intensely through slightly lowered lids. Williams stared right back at her. God, she hated doing this.

She wanted to scream, and throw her chair across the room. She wanted to break something. But she managed to keep it all in. She kept the emotion, the rage, and the fury that she felt locked up tightly on the inside, where it could do no harm. Well, except to herself, and she deserved it.

"My team were killed."

And Maxx, she reflected sadly, remembering the beautiful Cretian officer who had served on her crew for five years, longer than anyone else. The lover who had paid an excruciating price for trying to save her life on that day. She and Maxx had been together for six months prior to that mission. No one but the rest of the team had known about it. Not even Ary, certainly not Ary. It was not in any official report anyone would ever read, and Williams resolved that Doctor *Fucking* West would remain in the dark about it as well.

"How extensive were your injuries?" the woman asked her.

"Benign," Williams shot back immediately. "I said my team died, didn't you hear? Compared to that, losing my arm is pretty light stuff, don't you think?"

"Well. Yes, indeed," West agreed, somewhat reluctantly. "You're right, Major. And now you are..." She glanced down at some paperwork. "50% AI, is that right?"

"I *have* 50% AI," the marine corrected furiously. "It's not what I am."

"And it will be helpful to you on the battlefield, I assume," West reminded her.

As far as she knew, neural lace was simply something that they used to enhance a soldier's brain capabilities. It made them better able to function and communicate with their AI support assets, and faster as well. Probably safer to operate in the field too. Not smarter, which Williams already was, and certainly did not need.

"I personally would tend to view this as a good thing, Major," West commented, and it sounded like a genuine remark this time.

Williams answered it accordingly.

"AI can be highjacked and manipulated," she said. "AI is not human. I wanted to remain human. Not that much to ask, is it?"

"But it saved your life."

"So you keep saying."

"Because it is a good thing," West pointed out to her for the second time. "Or don't you agree?"

Williams stretched out her legs in front of her, and she met the doctor's gaze. She grew impassive. Her brief moment of compliance was over, it seemed.

"Yeah," she said. "It's fucking great. I love it."

West leaned back against her seat, and she poured herself a glass of water. She took a sip, and it was a little while before she spoke again.

"You know, Major Williams, neither Colonel Ary nor I are the enemy here," she remarked eventually.

"I never said you were."

"So, work with me. Let go of your anger. You know it will get you signed back on quicker."

Clearly exasperated, Williams sighed impatiently.

"I am working with you, Doctor," she argued. "I am here, aren't I? The only problem is that I was rated negative TX. But apparently, my wishes count for shit because I am a Level 5 officer. I get it. It's fine, really. I just need a holiday, give my body time to relax, and then..."

"Why don't you talk to me about your other marines, Major," West interrupted. "Uh... Which one was it on your team, hold on..."

She took another glance at a random piece of paper on her lap, as Williams sat gritting her teeth in front of her, sweat pouring down her face. Then, the woman found the name she wanted, and she focused her deep green eyes on her again. *She looks like a fucking snake.*

"Let's start with Gunnery Sergeant Er'Kolbr-Ey-Ahman," West instructed. "The one you used to call Maxx. Tell me about her, Major."

Williams felt like a piece of her heart was being ripped out of her chest at the mention of Maxx. A little sliver of darkness floated in front of her eyes. She took a difficult breath, and tried to focus on something else.

"Why?" she replied.

She almost choked on the word.

"Why not?"

"She's dead. They all are. What does it matter now?"

West obviously picked up on her distress, because she leaned over the desk with renewed interest. Eyes boring into her client like a missile locked onto its target.

"I didn't realise that this one meant so much to you, Major," she reflected a little pensively. "Is that right? Did Maxx mean a lot to you?"

This was the exact moment when Williams went from generally disliking her therapist's approach to full-on hating the person behind the job. She tried desperately to hang on to her composure.

"No," she murmured.

The rest of the crew had nicknamed their Cretian colleague 'Max', because that was the way she always did everything: to the max. She always poured her entire heart and soul into every mission, every challenge. She was one of the smartest, kindest, most generous people Williams had ever met. And a loyal, gifted, outstanding marine as well. Williams had decided to add an extra X to her nickname one day, and when Maxx had asked her why, one fateful night after a few too many drinks in the mess hall, she had simply replied, *'Because I love you'*.

"Major, are you with me?" West insisted.

She was like a dog with a bone, this one, but the marine would not let her come any closer to the marrow. This stuff was personal, it did not belong to the therapists.

"All the members of my team meant a lot to me, Doctor," she replied, forcing a shrug. "Then again, they knew the risks when they signed up. We all do."

"You sound pretty cold about it all."

Williams fixed her with an icy stare. She wanted to put an end to this conversation. She had to convince West that she really was okay. She gave her a little smile, and felt herself grow sicker inside.

"Not cold," she said. "Realistic. You have to be in my line of work, wouldn't you say?"

West nodded approvingly. She appeared thoughtful for a second. And then, she went for broke.

"Tell me, Major, what was it like to watch your lover die?"

CHAPTER EIGHT

Williams ran. She punched a hole through West's heavy, solid wooden oak door on the way out, making dubious use of her new cybernetic arm. And then, she simply ran. Out, away, as far and as fast as she could from that wretched place, and this despicable woman.

What a fucking psychopath! How could she even think of saying those words? She had no right. Shit!

She kept going as hard as she could for as long as she could, in total shock at what had just happened. Her mind was a complete blank. *'What was it like to watch your lover die? What was it like? What was it like?'...* Then, out of breath, exhausted, she suddenly cried out in broken anguish. She came to an abrupt stop. Hands on her knees, leaning forward, and breathing hard.

Maxx. Oh, Jesus, Maxx.

Images of the assault inside the science lab flashed unrestricted through her mind. They had been busy clearing each room, methodically, one after the other. Her team were good at that. They excelled at CQB. But then, they had started finding more and more enemy troops, inside a building that should have been almost empty save for a couple of guards, and the hostages. Williams remembered crouching on the floor, desperately trying to coordinate support, not realising that most of their AI had been sabotaged, and were now working against them. She had failed to spot the enemy soldier crawling along the walkway above her head, getting ready to take a shot at her. But Maxx had seen him. She had tackled him from the side, hard. They both lost their footing. Standing up so high inside that lab, right above a large vat filled with boiling acid...

Don't think about it, don't think about it...

But everything was spinning, and she was too far gone. Simply overwhelmed, Williams took a couple of unsteady steps toward a cluster of palm trees on the side of the pavement. She dropped to her knees, bent over, and vomited. Everything went strangely quiet after that, slow and dreamy. She blacked out.

It only lasted a few seconds, but it felt like much longer when she finally came back to her senses. She was slumped against a tree. Thankfully, she was still alone. It was getting late. Williams was unable to reflect on anything for a while, not even to question why in the world her CO would send her to someone like West. The woman should count herself lucky that she had not simply jumped over her desk, grabbed her by the throat, and squeezed. The usually controlled L5 officer shook all over at the thought of doing it. It was such a pleasing idea, and even though she was appalled at her own reaction, she could not help but feel intense pleasure in imagining it.

"Fuck," she murmured. *What the hell is happening to me?*

She swallowed back hot, painful tears at the thought of Maxx, as well as the overwhelming urge to punch, hurt, and kill something... Or someone. She focused on her breathing, and repeated her usual mantra inside her head. *Focus. It's okay, it's okay, it's okay...*

After a while, she decided to check her comms. She had three messages from Ary already, and a fourth one landed in her inbox as she was watching. That one contained an order to contact her immediately in the reference field, and some bullshit warning about the consequences of going AWOL. Williams ignored all the messages, and she disconnected the device.

"Fuck you, Ary," she muttered under her breath. "I don't belong to you."

She spotted a flickering neon sign across the street, and crossed over. *Perfect.* They would have what she needed there. Quickly, she followed a series of dilapidated steps down to a dented door with a metal bar stuck across the middle. Someone had thrown up in the corner. The whole area stank of booze, and human sweat. Undeterred, the marine pulled the door open, and she stepped inside a dingy, dimly lit room full of shadows. It was hot in there. No air. Men and aliens alike sat hunched over small tables, drinking steadily and silently. Not many noticed her walking in, and those who did could not have cared less. She walked up to the bar, and slapped some money down onto the counter.

"Whiskey," she muttered.

Her voice shook when she spoke. It sounded raw and hoarse even to her own ears. Williams brushed her fingers over her mouth, and she used the back of her hand to dry the sweat off her face. Not that it worked. It was like a sauna inside the bar.

"Make it a double," she added.

The woman who served her was a Pleiadian. Beautiful, a combination of Asian and Nordic-looking. She had large blue eyes set a little too far apart in her lean face to allow her to pass for a human. Very pale white skin. There was an intelligent, inquisitive aura about her. She looked clean, and tidy. With long, shiny black hair. Williams did not bother to make eye contact with her. Under different circumstances, she might have wondered what someone like her was doing, working the counter in such a dive. Then again, if the circumstances had been different, she probably would not have found herself in one.

"Here you go, honey," the woman announced. "Double-shot as requested."

Almost frantically, Williams downed three of them in a row in rapid succession. It seemed to help a little with the shaking. Then, she pointed to the shelf behind the counter.

"Give me some of that," she ordered.

The Pleiadian reached for a bottle of vodka.

"No," Williams snapped. "Give me the Ichor."

Ichor was the Cretian equivalent of absinthe, except that it was even stronger. It was the stuff that Maxx always used to warn her fellow human colleagues about. Ichor meant trouble. Serious trouble of the sort that landed you six feet under the ground. Well, Williams was clear on what she wanted. She repeated her order. Only this time, the bartender arched a quizzical eyebrow in her direction. She threw her a wry smile, and shook her head no. Williams immediately felt her temper rise.

"Problem?" she snarled.

"No problem," the Pleiadian replied calmly. "Except I can't sell you that stuff, honey, and I think you know it too. Now, how about some food instead? You look like you need it."

She spotted the immediate flash of fury that sizzled in the human's sparkling blue eyes. She took in the vivid red scar on her face, and the network of fresh-looking ones crisscrossed all over her shoulder. She sensed deep darkness, and certain danger blistering all around her, but it was not enough to worry her. It would not be the first time that she would turn down a broken soldier's request for the strongest, most lethal liquor known in the galaxy. And she was convinced beyond a shadow of a doubt that the woman in front of her was both of those things; a soldier, and breaking apart at the seams too.

"I'd like a full bottle, please," Williams said, as if she had not heard her. "Now."

Several men at the back of the room looked up at that precise moment to glance in their direction. As if they were equipped with a sixth sense. The Pleiadian knew there were at least two reasons they had started watching. One, they were hoping for a fight; and two, this was one soldier who was hard to ignore for very long. Despite her general dishevelled appearance, she was still beautiful in a broody, devastating sort of way. Williams herself ignored all the eyes burning at the back of her head. She knew they were there, and if anyone wanted a fight, she would be delighted to oblige. She dropped more money on top of the sticky bar counter.

"Hey, did you hear me?" she barked at the bartender.

The woman eyed her steadily.

"I heard you just fine, soldier," she replied. "But I'm afraid I can't serve you that stuff."

"I don't need you to serve it. I want you to sell me a bottle."

"Uh-uh. No way. I mean, Ichor? You want to kill yourself or something?"

"That's none of your fucking business," Williams shot back in anger. "Now, are you going to pass that thing over, or do I have to come and take it myself? You got about two seconds to decide."

The Pleiadian gave a soft laugh. Just like Ary, she could do all sorts of tricks with her energy-mind if she wanted to, including sending the soldier flying across the room, or slamming her head down against the bar if a harder solution was needed. She appreciated her boldness, but not the idea of a confrontation. She leaned forward, and stared deeply into Williams' eyes.

"Look, why don't you go sleep it off for a while, uh?" she suggested. "Come back tomorrow if you want, and I'll buy you a beer. How about that?"

There was a gentleness in her voice that gave the confused officer pause for a second. It even held her back from storming behind the bar, and grabbing what she wanted. She almost dropped her defenses then. Almost. But soon, she felt someone sidling up to her, and a scrawny arm coming to rest around her waist. A raspy, unpleasant voice whispered into her ear.

"I got whatcha need, my darling," the voice said. "You want Ichor? Alien comfort? Sex? Don't worry. Whatever you want, my lovely, I can get it for you. Or provide it myself if you prefer."

Williams broke eye contact with the Pleiadian, and she looked to her right at the much smaller, older man. Now, this one was all too human. Missing half his teeth, a clear sign of drug abuse, and he reeked of old urine. But all that the desperate marine saw, or heard for that matter, was a promise of release. She grabbed her money off the bar.

"It's your funeral, soldier," the bartender stated quietly.

You're damn right, it is, Williams thought.

"Let's go," she muttered.

She bought a bottle of Ichor from the old dealer. It had some dodgy labels on it, written in a language she did not understand. She knew for sure it was not Cretian. But she ignored that obvious warning, paid him the extortionate amount he asked for, and walked back out into the street. A mile further down the road, she veered off the path, and headed toward the beach.

Inky black clouds had gathered over the town, and the wind had picked up. The sea had turned stormy and grey, and heavy waves foamed at the shore, as if trying to tear big angry bites out of the beach. There was no one around. Williams spotted the red flag stuck on a pole next to an empty lifeguard station. She switched her comms device back on. Not sure why. Maybe a little desperate for some kind of connection. Slightly afraid of it too. Unexpectedly, there was a message from Ice, and she immediately clicked on it. As she read though the email, she could almost hear the young woman's voice, and see her excited smile. Ice wrote emails in exactly the same way that she spoke. It was cute, just like she was.

"Hey, Major Williams, I got selected for advance commando training! I'm leaving for Earth this evening! I am so sorry I won't see you before I go!!! Hey, can I call you sometime? Tell you how it's going? Damn, I'm nervous... But EXCITED!!!!!!!!! Right, I gotta go pack. Call me, okay? I mean, if you want to... Sorry, I guess I'm kind of nervous!!! Talk to you soon. I hope you get this! Bye! – ICE xx. PS: thank you for letting me train with you!! I won't let you down, I promise!!!"

Williams shook her head, and she bit down hard enough on her lower lip to make it bleed. Tears streamed down the sides of her face as she re-read the message over and over again. She hit 'Reply', stared out at the churning sea in front of her for a while, and cancelled it. What would she say? *'Don't go, or you might end up like me?'* She could not think of anything else to write. If she responded right now, she would end up saying all the wrong things. So, better not to. Better to cut all ties.

"Leave it be," she murmured.

She reached for the bottle instead, took a single mouthful, and swallowed quickly before she could taste it. She shuddered all over as the fiery, disgusting liquor hit the back of her throat.

"Argh, shit," she gasped.

She coughed. Her stomach contracted. She twisted to the side, and immediately threw up again. Still intent on doing this thing though, she took another determined swallow, and managed to keep it down this time. She resumed walking toward the pier. Over there, she could see the resort in the distance. No doubt Ary would be on the war path by now, looking for her all over the place. She spotted another red flag fluttering wildly into the wind. She remembered Ice's warning to her. *'The rip tide will swallow you up, and we will never see you again, Major.'* Williams nodded, and she took another long sip of the dreaded Ichor.

"It's not so bad once you get used to the taste, Maxx," she murmured in a trembling voice. "I miss you. I can't wait to see you."

She climbed onto the pier. It was old, she could tell. A little rusty in all the places it should not be. The stricken commando officer drank some more, and she started to make her way toward the end of the walkway. A flash of lightning hit the beach. A clap of violent thunder made the air shake. She kept going.

CHAPTER NINE

Whatever the hell Williams was doing, Sergeant Holson reflected, and whatever the reason for it, she was going to kick her ass when she found her. Forget rank, her L5 rating, and other stupid stuff like that. This time, Williams had it coming. Holson trudged all the way up and down the beach that evening, looking for her, yelling out her name and trying to figure out what on earth was going on. Two other things were on her mind specifically.

One, she had just received the fright of her life. Holson had been in her room, getting dressed for the evening, when there was a knock on the door. She opened it with a smile on her face, expecting to see her date for the night, only to find Colonel Ary standing there instead. In full dress uniform, and looming over her, the Cretian looked beautiful as always, and about a million times scarier; she appeared a little worried too, and massively pissed off. Thinking that she was there because of some mistake she might have made in her recent work almost caused Holson to faint in shock. Thankfully, it had nothing to do with her, but with Major Williams. *Find her,* Ary ordered, and Holson had simply swallowed hard, saluted, and jumped into her boots.

The second thing that bothered her was the way the woman in question had simply abandoned her the other night. It should not have stung so much, and yet, it did. Holson was a little worried about that. Also, it was raining, and cold, two things that she hated; especially when she was on leave in the so-called *'Martian Key West'*. She was wet, uncomfortable, and her night had been ruined. Williams was going to hear about it for sure. All these things were running through Holson's head as she approached the pier. Not sure why she was looking there, to be honest, but it seemed like somewhere that she would go if she wanted some privacy. Obviously, never in the middle of the night, or when a storm of epic proportions was brewing. Then again, the woman was a commando. Holson knew that these weird people tended to enjoy being cold, wet, and miserable.

"Williams," she shouted. "WILLIAMS!"

It was hard to make herself heard over the howling wind. Holson climbed onto the pier, staring down toward the other end. When she spotted her, she snapped right back into soldier mode.

"Fuck," she muttered under her breath.

This was the worst possible scenario.

"Major Williams?"

The pier jutted out half a mile into the sea, and the officer had taken herself and her bottle of poison, as Colonel Ary would have called the Ichor that was brewed on her home planet, over and beyond the security barriers. She was standing close to the drop, swaying into the strong wind. She had her back to Holson, and her eyes were fixed onto the churning, cold waters fifty feet down below.

"Hey, Williams!" Holson bellowed.

She started running toward her.

"HEY!" she screamed.

Her shouts finally managed to pierce through to the marine's consciousness. Williams turned around, slowly, as if she were in a trance. She was standing dangerously close to the edge, and clutching the half-empty bottle of Ichor in her right hand. That she had drunk so much of it, and was still on her feet, was a miracle. That she would not be able to keep it up for very much longer was also a given. Holson came to a stop a safe distance away from her.

"What are you doing?" she asked, trying to keep her voice light. "Doesn't look very solid where you are standing, Major. Want to get back over here maybe?"

Williams stared at her for a second or two. She glanced back toward the ocean, and then at Holson once more when the woman repeated her request a little louder.

"Stay back, Sergeant," she warned.

Holson made an open, calming gesture with her hands.

"Sure thing, Major," she nodded. "Sure thing..."

She was trying to sound like this was no big deal, but in fact she was feeling more than a little scared. No wonder Ary had looked so worried, she reflected. *Damn. She could have warned me that this was what I would run into...*

"I'll stay right here, no problem," she added.

Her tone was reassuring now, and gentle.

"Hey, are you okay?"

The L5 did not reply, and she returned her gaze to the water. She took another swig of the dark liquid inside the bottle, shivered all over, and Holson saw her fight to maintain her balance against another vicious gust of wind. This was really bad. She needed to get her attention, and keep her talking. Bring her back toward safety before something really terrible happened.

"Come on, talk to me," she repeated. "What's wrong?"

"Nothing," Williams muttered. "Go away."

"Hey, I missed out on a scorching hot date tonight because of you, stud," Holson replied, joking lightly. "So, I think you kind of owe me."

Williams glanced back over her shoulder once more, and Holson's smile instantly faded when she realised that she was crying. She had never seen her in such a state before. She had never seen the major cry. Ever. And yet, there she was now, eyes full of tears, scar burning, wet tangled hair falling all over her face. For once in her life, the mighty Special Forces officer appeared less than invincible. She looked vulnerable, extremely confused, and heartbreakingly sad. In Holson's words, this would have translated as *completely fucked up,* and it was not something that she would have expected from Williams. She was shocked to be witnessing such a thing.

"Major, you are standing too close to the edge. Please, get back," she pleaded.

"Go away, Holson," Williams repeated.

Her tone had suddenly turned threatening.

"No. Not until you tell me what's wrong."

She took an impulsive step forward, sensing that she probably did not have a lot of time left before Williams got tired of talking, and did something unbelievably stupid. Eyes wide, her heart pounding, Holson walked a little closer to her, feeling the loose planks of wood under her feet flex a lot more than she was happy with.

"Don't," came another warning.

But it was only a whisper this time, caught by the wind, and quickly lost. Williams looked exhausted. Holson hesitated. She came to a stop.

"This is really screwed-up," she remarked. "Don't you think?"

She was shaking her head, almost pleading. Trying to convey the absurdity of the situation to the distraught officer, desperate to get through to her, and make her listen. But the other woman seemed unreachable, completely lost in a world of her own. A painful, unforgiving universe. Holson was not a quitter though.

"Come on, Williams," she insisted. "Let's get out of here, okay?"

The marine's response was to take another long swig, and to lean over the edge.

"Get back!" Holson yelled at her, really frightened out of her wits all of a sudden. "Look, if you jump in there, I will jump in right after you. You know that, right? I can't let you do this. I can't let you kill yourself in front of me! Major Williams!" she screamed. "I am fucking talking to you!"

This finally seemed to give Williams cause to re-think her options. The instinct to protect, and to care for others was hard-wired inside of her, deeper than any layer of neural lace could ever reach. One thing she would never, ever be able to do was put someone else's life at risk. Willingly, like this. For no good reason, other than her own selfish needs. Holson did not report directly into her, but Williams was still a superior officer. She was responsible for her. And the woman had brilliantly hit on the one single nerve she still had left to feel. A soldier's life was not something that Williams would ever be able to simply rationalise, and file away as irrelevant. She glanced back toward the sergeant, as if to ascertain her true intentions. She saw determination in her eyes, and a little anger there as well. There was fear, and something else that she could not quite grasp. It was getting harder for her to think, and even harder to remain on her feet. She had been almost ready to let go when Holson had shown up. And now…

"Just go," she begged her. "Just walk away, Holson, this has got nothing to do with you. Please."

"No. I won't. If you jump, I'll jump."

"Just leave."

Holson shook her head no. She took another step forward.

"It's not safe over here," Williams snapped. "Go away, Sergeant!"

"I'm not going without you. Never without you. Take my hand."

"I can't!"

"Sure, you can. Evan, take my hand. Please."

Holson was standing very close to the edge now, within touching distance. The wind was getting stronger, and the force of the waves pounding against the pier structure was making it shake and shift with every devastating gust. Thunder reverberated in the distance. She could hear the water rumbling and echoing down below, sucking and hissing at the pillars, hitting violently against them. Death was down there, waiting for one or even both of them to make a mistake. Holson took a deep breath to steady her nerves. Williams was a few steps in front of her, tears streaming down her face. She looked completely wasted, and almost ready to give up.

"I screwed up," she muttered. "I lost her..."

And then, just at the point of absolute no return, she startled, and her eyes grew wide. Holson was there, standing next to her, fingers wrapped safely and reassuringly around her wrist.

"Her?" she asked.

She was smiling gently.

"You mean Maxx?"

Shocked at the unexpected question, Williams stared into her eyes, as another wave of despair rocked through her body.

She let out a strangled, wounded cry in response, and she fell to her knees.

"Evan, it was not your fault..."

Holson kept one hand wrapped around her wrist, and she rested the other one on her back. She knelt down. There were tears sparkling in her eyes now, too. Shining with sympathy, compassion, and deep understanding. She had caught sight of the two women hanging out together in the mess hall a few times. Even though they had been careful not to advertise their relationship, it did not take a genius to recognise the signs, and figure out what was going on between them.

"I'm sorry," she whispered. "You know, I lost someone too. Her name was Kate."

There, that did it. She finally managed to get through to her. Williams suddenly looked up, and she gripped her shoulders hard, as heavy rain pelted both of their faces in the dark, and made it hard to see.

"You?" she cried into the wind.

"Yes." Holson nodded, smiling sadly. "She was a medic. She got shot down trying to drag a wounded colleague off the field, and to safety."

Williams squeezed her eyes tightly shut. She leaned forward again, and her entire body shuddered. Grief shook her hard.

"I'm sorry," she moaned. "I'm sorry..."

"Me too. But for now, come with me, Evan. Please. It's cold and dark up here, and it's really dangerous. Let me take you home, okay?"

The L5 hesitated, but now it was only because she was not entirely sure which way to go. The Ichor was fast catching up with her.

"Okay..." she murmured. "Okay."

Her mind did not feel like it was her own anymore. She was afraid the neural lace was doing something to her. Something bad. Every muscle in her body had started to hurt. The liquor bottle slid from her grasp, shattering into pieces as soon as it hit the deck. She allowed Holson to take her by the hand.

"I'm sorry," she repeated.

She felt pressure on her fingers. Warm, reassuring pressure.

"Don't worry. You're going to be just fine. Just follow me, okay?"

But it was too late. Before Williams could answer, the rotten wooden deck they were standing on finally gave way, and they both went hurtling down into the void. She smashed her forehead against a pillar. She heard Holson yell. When she hit the water, the force of the impact was such that it completely sucked the air out of her lungs. Unconscious, she sank fast below the deep structure.

CHAPTER TEN

In the quiet, eerie darkness that followed, images floated and drifted through Williams' mind, as she was tossed and pushed underneath the waves. Memories of her crew. Good ones, for a change, and one in particular. Must have been the water that brought it back.

They all sat together in the mess hall that night, celebrating a particularly successful mission. Collinson had used the ship kitchen, out of hours and without permission, to make pizza and a round of nachos for his colleagues. Williams had managed to get her hands on a case of premium-quality tequila.

"From Colonel Ary's private stash," she claimed, and everyone cheered.

It had been weeks since the team had enjoyed an opportunity to relax like this. And now, everyone sat around the table, laughing and joking, in various stages of drunkenness. Williams had chosen a seat directly opposite Maxx. She was holding a large slice of pizza in one hand, and a bottle in the other. Her blue eyes were sparkling. She was smiling, in high spirits. Maxx, who never drank, was happy to just kick back and relax. She enjoyed listening to her lover, as the marine regaled them with tall tales of her L5 training.

"Are you making all this shit up?" Sanchez complained after a while, enjoying provoking her a little.

Williams threw him a pointed look. She clearly appreciated his little challenge, even though she pretended not to.

"Of course not," she shot right back, grinning. "Now shut up, Sanchez, and listen."

Maxx flashed a quick glance toward Edwards, the team medic, who was sitting on her right. She smiled when she spotted the goofy look on the man's face. He was listening to his boss intently, eyes wide, and with his mouth hanging open. Obviously loving every second of all this stuff, Maxx reflected. Good for him.

She returned her gaze to her lover, and became distracted by the alluring flush of colour that had spread all over her cheeks. Williams excelled at telling stories, and she was clearly enjoying herself tonight. She looked at ease, completely in her element. Her timing was perfect. She had a gift for words, and a knack for teasing her audience into a frenzy. This was something else the Cretian officer had found out she could do quite well in the bedroom. To Maxx, Williams was nothing less than absolutely brilliant, hugely entertaining, and she loved watching her. She caught her eye, and sent her a little private wink. Williams laughed, and made a show of returning it in front of everyone. Then, she launched into a detailed description of a training exercise she had once taken part in. Curiously, it involved having your ankles bound with tape, your wrists tied in front of you in the same way, being loaded with weights, and shoved head-first into a deep swimming pool.

"Fuck that crazy shit!" Collinson exclaimed immediately. He looked disgusted. "Those L5 instructors are deranged, man," he declared. "Anyone who'd do this kind of crap has got to be wrong in the head somehow. No offence, Boss, but that means you too."

"Yeah."

Williams nodded, looking pleased, as if he had just paid her the highest compliment. Maxx giggled.

"So, then you gotta do some lengths," Williams carried on explaining to her troops. "The pass rate is twenty. Anything less than that, and you get kicked out of the programme. You know you won't get another invite either. Like, not *ever*. This is it. Level 5 training is all or nothing, guys. It's all day, every day. High adrenaline, high stakes."

"How many lengths did you do?" Edwards asked.

He was visibly shaking with excitement, and Maxx had no doubt that if somebody had offered to tie him up and throw him into the pool, right now, it would probably have made his day. *Humans,* she reflected, staring at her lover with a thoughtful smile on her lips. *Can't help but love everything about them. Especially this one.*

"I did thirty-one," Williams replied around a mouthful of dripping cheese. "The second guy could only manage twenty-four," she added, her voice heavy with contempt. "Also, I drowned on my last lap."

"Drowned?" Maxx repeated, alarmed. "What do you mean?"

"I mean, I drowned," Williams replied with a brilliant smile aimed in her direction.

She even looked proud of it. Maxx could not help but laugh, even though she did not believe a word of it.

"You're kidding me," she said.

"Nope. It's all true, I promise. I finished my last lap, passed out, and sank to the bottom. I was not breathing when they pulled me out. Officially dead for 3 seconds. But I won the race, so..." Williams beamed, as if it were a badge of honour. "Then I threw up all over my drill officer, which was another great thing about that day. He was an idiot."

Edwards appeared ecstatic.

"Wow," he drawled. "Wow… I so hope I get called up."

Williams held his gaze, and she reached for another bottle.

"You will," she promised. "You're an awesome marine, Ed. Won't be long before you're the one in charge of your own team. Now, there was this other time when I…"

"Hey, we really gotta listen to your exploits all night, Captain?" Sanchez yelled at her, teasing as always. "Cos it's getting kind of boring, you know?"

Williams smiled knowingly.

"Well, I would really love to listen to yours, Jorge," she replied. "Shame you ain't got any."

The entire table erupted in whistles and shouts. Sanchez laughed, and he threw his empty bottle at her, missing her head by only about an inch. Maxx glared at him.

"Hey. Watch it," she warned.

"See what I mean?" Williams chuckled, unconcerned, as the glass bottle exploded against the wall behind her. "What's wrong, buddy? Can't hold your drink anymore? Getting old? Or do you need glasses?"

"Ask me again when you're passed out from too much tequila, L5, and you need someone to carry you back to your digs."

"She won't," Maxx interrupted, grinning. "That's my job."

Her lover threw her a drunken, lazy smile.

"Yeah. Like she said," she murmured.

She leaned in for a kiss. Sanchez rolled his eyes.

"Aw…" he groaned. "You two get a fucking room."

Williams deepened the kiss, just because, and Maxx flipped him off. Everyone laughed. It was the last night they got to spend time together like this. As a family.

∞

A flash of lightning hit the water, and Williams broke through the surface at the exact same time, wheezing and coughing her lungs out. She sucked in a painful breath, and spun her head around.

"Holson!" she shouted. "Holson!"

She spotted her, drifting with her face down not too far away. Williams swam quickly over to her. Slipped underneath her body, flipped her onto her back, and started to swim toward the shore. She did not allow thoughts of that rip tide to interfere with her concentration. It would have been welcome before, but definitely not now anymore.

She kept Holson's chin tilted well back, and protected from the waves, allowing her to keep breathing... Of course, she had no way to know for sure that the woman was still doing that, but she could not afford to waste any time trying to find out. Every second counted. She had to get her out of the water, and fast. Williams kept her arm wrapped tightly and safely around her chest, she kept her head down, and she swam harder than on any L5 test she had ever taken. As soon as she felt solid ground under her feet, she lifted the unconscious soldier into her arms, and ran with her toward the beach. She rested Holson on the wet sand, just out of reach of the crashing waves, and knelt down next to her.

"Can you hear me?" she enquired anxiously.

The woman's lips had turned blue, and her face looked grey. Williams pressed her fingers against the side of her neck. She waited for a couple of seconds, holding her own breath in anticipation. Nothing. There was nothing there. She pressed her ear against her chest. Same result.

"Come on now, Holson, come on," she muttered under her breath.

She made a fist, and she hit her in the chest, once, as hard as she could. There was no reaction. Williams breathed air into her lungs, and she performed CPR on her intensely for several anxious seconds. Still, the soldier remained motionless, unconscious, and dead.

"Wake up!" Williams screamed at her.

In desperation, she pounded on her chest, even harder than before.

"Wake up, damn it!" she yelled.

Just as she was running out of options, beginning to think that she was really going to lose her, Holson's eyes flew wide open. She jerked forward, gasping. Feeling relief flood through her, Williams immediately pushed her over onto her side.

"Breathe," she instructed.

She held her head, as the woman threw up a huge amount of sea water onto the sand.

"It's okay," she murmured against her ear. "I've got you now, Sergeant, and you're going to be just fine. Keep breathing, all right?"

Exhausted, panting, Holson lay there without speaking for several long seconds. Williams pulled her up against her own body, trying to shield her from the worst of the wind. A million goose-bumps rode over the operator's naked arms, and every bit of exposed skin. Williams rubbed her hands over them, and all over her back, trying to bring some much-needed warmth into her limbs.

"Are you okay?" she asked after a while. "You're freezing, we need to move."

"Wi... Williams?" Holson mumbled.

"Yes. I'm here."

Holson twisted around to face her. She spotted blood from a cut on her forehead running freely down the marine's pale face, and the black bruising around her left eye that was growing darker by the second.

"Are *you* all right?" she gasped.

"I'm fine. I'm just glad you are," Williams smiled weakly.

Holson's eyes slowly filled with tears as she stared at her.

"Don't ever do that again," she cried. "Do you fucking hear me?"

She threw herself at her, and locked her arms around her shoulders. Wrapped her fingers around the back of her neck, felt the soft flesh there, and she started to sob.

"Don't ever do that again," she repeated, her voice breaking. "Please. Promise me right now."

The first moment of surprise over, Williams returned the embrace. She allowed Holson to rest against her, and she even squeezed her a little harder. She felt startled, shaken by the woman's outburst. But she understood. It made her shiver.

"I won't," she murmured. "I promise. I'm sorry."

Holson pulled back. She gripped the bleeding woman's face in both her hands, and she looked deep into her eyes. Up until that night, she had not realised the magnitude of her own emotions, or the depth of her feelings for the L5 officer. Now she did, and it was all way too big and too strong to keep contained.

"Even though you may not think it would matter when you have lost so much already," she murmured intently, "you're wrong, Evan. If anything happened to you, there are people out there who would miss you terribly."

Williams returned her gaze. She spotted that flash of emotion again that she had noticed before. What was it? It looked familiar. She was intrigued, but could not quite figure it out.

"I mean people like me," Holson enlightened her, eyes burning. "*I* would miss you terribly. I know I may have quite a clumsy way of showing it, and that you may not like it very much at all, but I really am extremely fond of you."

And just like that, Williams realised exactly what the emotion was.

"Damn, Holson..." she murmured.

Taken aback, puzzled, her immediate reaction was to pull the woman back into her arms. She was not sure how she really felt about the sudden admission, but still, the unconscious impulse to respond in kind was undeniable. She buried her face into Holson's shoulder. She allowed her to rub her fingers gently through her hair. It felt so good, but... *Shit. What the hell am I doing?* Williams' heart was beating so fast inside her chest that it felt like it might burst. There were too many conflicting emotions raging inside her head to allow her to be really clear on what was happening. The alcohol she had consumed earlier did not help with any of that either. Hugging Holson seemed like the only thing that made any sense. And so, she did.

"I won't tell you the number of times I felt like doing exactly the same thing after Kate was killed," the operator admitted to her. "For months, all I kept thinking about was the cargo bay airlock area. How I could just sneak into it, hit the button, and eject myself out into space. End the suffering."

Williams instantly tightened her embrace on her. She shivered violently at the thought.

"I never realised..." she murmured.

She spoke to control room personnel all the time when she was on a mission. When she was on the ground with her team, and during operations, it was often Holson who would offer helpful updates to her regarding enemy tactics and positions. Williams had never detected anything different in her attitude, or the quality of her work. Unlike her, Holson had done an excellent job of keeping it all locked down, and under complete control.

"You probably think I am some sex-crazed idiot with a big problem," the woman added, forcing a chuckle as she pulled back.

This was something else Williams had noticed about her. Self-deprecating humour, and a tendency to always hide behind a joke. Now, she knew why. Without thinking, she caressed the side of her cheek with her thumb.

"No, I don't think that. I wondered about it, that's all."

Holson took a deep breath, and she exhaled slowly.

"I go out with a lot of women," she replied in a tiny voice, "because I feel so alone. It also reminds me that once upon a time, even before Kate, I used to be happy to just be alive. I want to feel that way again. I think I'm getting there."

She smiled at Williams, eyes full of tears, and with a sheepish expression on her face.

"But when I asked you out the other night, it was for a different reason, you know."

"Well, I..."

Williams had been about to ask a question when a bright, intense light shone into her eyes, effectively blinding her. She raised a hand in front of her face, and immediately pulled Holson against her side to protect her from whatever was coming at them. It turned out to be a friendly threat.

"Major Williams," the MP officer said to her.

"Who's this?" she snapped.

She was still squinting in that glare, trying to identify who the male voice belonged to, and he helpfully averted the beam of his powerful flashlight so that she could see him, and the two armed officers standing on either side.

"I need you to come with me, ma'am," he stated.

"What?"

"Colonel Ary's orders."

"Why? What's going on?"

"You are under arrest, Major. I have instructions to escort you back to the ship immediately."

Under arrest? *Damn Ary,* Williams thought. She should have felt angry, but she was fast running out of steam. She stood up, pulling Holson gently to her feet with her.

"It's all right," she murmured to her. "Don't worry about it."

Of course, Ary would do this, she reflected. It made sense. She must have thought that her precious soldier was about to go AWOL on her after all. She needed to bring her back in line before she lost her little investment. The L5 actually chuckled when one of the officers walked up to her, and cuffed her wrists behind her back. The need to retaliate, to drop him with a good kick, was almost impossible to resist. She channeled the urge into something useful instead.

"Sergeant Holson here needs medical attention," she informed the guy in charge. "I want one of you to take her back to the resort, and make sure that she gets seen to. You got that?"

"Yes, ma'am."

"But I'm fine," Holson protested. "It's you who needs medical attention. And what the hell are you idiots saying, she's under arrest?" she yelled, turning on the three MPs. "Are you fucking out of your mind?"

"Sergeant Holson," Williams said quietly. "That's enough."

Looking shocked, dejected, and hurt, Holson stared at her in complete silence. Wounded tears welled up in her eyes, which almost got Williams herself started again.

"Give me a minute," she ordered the MP.

He nodded, and she turned to her companion. She wanted quite badly to take her in her arms again, but even if the handcuffs had not made it impossible, she still would not have allowed herself to do it in front of them.

"Look," she whispered. "I have been breaking rules left, right, and center. Ary's pissed off with me. That's what this little show is all about."

"But you're hurt," Holson protested.

Williams flashed her a gentle smile.

"It's just a scratch, and I'll get it sorted. Go back to the resort, and have a doctor look at your lungs."

The sergeant appeared reluctant.

"Please," Williams insisted. "Trust me, it's important."

"Okay. All right, I will."

"Thanks. I'll see you back on the ship then."

She walked away before Holson could think of anything else to say.

"Officer," she called. "Ready to go now."

"Yes, ma'am."

Two of the guys got on either side of her, holding tightly on to her arms as if they were afraid that she would try something. Williams sneered. She felt way too tired for that. She risked a quick glance over her shoulder, back toward the beach and where Holson was standing, watching her go with an anxious look on her face. She flashed her a reassuring smile, and the woman impulsively touched her fingers to her lips, and blew her a kiss.

CHAPTER ELEVEN

Williams was not terribly surprised when Ary decided to throw her in jail for a few days. Her boss was obviously out to send her a message, and she was making herself understood, loud and clear. The marine suspected, and she hoped, that the sentence would not last for very long. And it did not feel much like regular jail duty, anyway. It was more like an intensive training camp designed to help her body heal. With a good dose of obedience thrown in, obviously. *Whatever,* Williams reflected. There was no mention of her seeing a shrink this time, which she would have flat-out refused to do, no matter what the consequences to herself, or her career for that matter.

Ary did not come to see her at first, but she kept her busy from 6 a.m. until 6 p.m. every day, through a series of gym and pool exercises, runs, more gym, medical tests, more swimming, stretching, massage, and then back to her cell for dinner, and an evening of quiet reading. Or at least this was clearly what the colonel hoped that Williams would choose to do in her downtime. When the L5 officer was delivered back to her temporary home after her first day, she found a pile of books on neural lace and human/AI interface waiting for her on top of her bed.

"Awesome," she sighed tiredly.

But with nothing else to do, she devoured the first one on that very same night, and ultimately carried on with all the others. The last one that she read was called, *'Merging Biological with Digital: Applications of Neural Lace in Military Combat Situations.'* She had to admit that she found it interesting. Fascinating, even.

She sat on her bed after finishing it, leaning against the wall with her legs crossed, and she stared pensively into space for several long moments. The jail was situated just above the engine room, and she could hear the low rumble of the ship's turbines through the walls, which often lulled her to sleep at night in her cabin. Despite the luxuries of Mars, she was glad to be onboard again. And even if she would have preferred to be allowed back to her own quarters, this jail thing was strangely okay all the same. It gave her time alone, time to think, and recover. It was an opportunity to read some books, too, which she always used to enjoy, but had not done in years. Williams rubbed her fingers across her forehead as she reflected on her situation, which was a habit she had developed after they had given her the lace.

The previous version of neural lace around the 2017 era had been about allowing human beings to wirelessly connect to a computer, and then, later on, AI. In the year 2252, quite a bit more had been added to the technology. Neural lace these days drew on some latent processes in someone's DNA that would allow them to develop ESP capabilities. And God knows what else, which Williams had more or less decided not to think or worry about anymore. There was just no point in doing so.

She stared at the ceiling for a while, which gave her a feeling of space above her head, very welcome in her current dwelling. Her cell was impossibly tiny. It just contained a small bed alongside one wall, a toilet affixed to the other one, and a sink. She could almost touch both sides of the walls if she stood up, and spread her arms wide.

"Good thing I'm not claustrophobic," she remarked ironically to herself.

She glanced toward the sink now, and her toothbrush standing on the side. She stared at it, focused all of her attention onto it. She allowed her mind to float, like they said in the books. She emptied her brain of all thought, except one. *Rising... Rising and floating. Higher, and higher...* Amazingly, it only took about five minutes for something to start to happen. The toothbrush suddenly quivered, and it began to lift. Williams' eyes widened in surprise.

"Shit," she exclaimed.

She kept her focus going, and she continued looking at the thing, moving her head just a little bit until the toothbrush was floating right in front of her eyes. Just by concentrating on it, she could make it go down, up, sideways.

"Well, fuck me..." she muttered under her breath.

She grinned. She made the toothbrush twirl and wriggle in front of her. She chuckled to herself. Then, a sharp voice at the door that she had not heard open due to being so deep into her practice suddenly shattered her concentration.

"Having fun, Williams?"

The toothbrush promptly dropped to the floor, and Williams turned her head to discover Ary standing there, leaning against the doorway with a frozen smile on her face. One eyebrow raised in obvious disapproval. Watching her intently, like she normally did. Williams stood up. She came to attention, and saluted smartly.

"Colonel," she said. "It is good to see you, ma'am."

Ary snorted, rolling her eyes at the blatant lie.

"Yes," she muttered. "I'm sure you must be absolutely delighted. So, levitating toothbrushes now, are we? How very creative of you, Major."

Williams kept her eyes fixed onto the wall opposite.

"There is not much else to do in here at night, Colonel," she pointed out.

The Cretian officer shrugged, and she threw a quick glance around the cell.

"No, I guess there isn't," she admitted. "Well. I thought seven days should be long enough for you to cool down. Didn't want you to use your newfound skills to try to punch me in the face again."

Williams was not entirely sure what the best reply to this would be. She thought it safer to remain silent. Ary turned around, and gestured for her to follow.

"Come," she invited. "Let's go for a walk."

They ended up in the deserted mess hall, and they sat together at a table in the back, where the L5 demolished a steak the size of a cow in record time. Then, she proceeded to drown her chips in mayonnaise and chilli flakes. She did not look up until she had finished her second portion.

"I thought I had left instructions for them to feed you," Ary observed, watching her with a slightly puzzled expression on her face.

"Well. They do, sort of," Williams replied with her mouth full. "They give me all that quinoa nonsense. Protein shakes and kale smoothies at every turn. No steak allowed. Or cheesecake. Or beer, for that matter."

She laughed, used her steak knife to stab a few more chips, and started hungrily eyeing up a rack of desserts on the counter. She ignored the lump of mayonnaise stuck to the side of her mouth, knowing that it would annoy Ary, who was nothing but elegance and poise in everything she did. The colonel seemed unimpressed.

"It is all for a good cause, Major," she replied evenly. "And you've only got yourself to blame for this, really. I sent you to paradise to get better, and you chose to make a total mess of the opportunity. So, I decided a little tougher regime would be in order for you this time."

Then, she said something else that almost made Williams fall off her chair in surprise.

"I am sorry about West. It was the wrong approach with you, and not something I would have wanted any of my officers to have to go through. She has been spoken to accordingly. And I offer you my sincere apologies."

Williams eyed her a little warily. Ary was such a difficult woman to figure out, she thought. One second brutal and sharp, the next all warm and friendly. One minute reminding her in no uncertain terms that she was just property, and then only a few days later, looking at her with such immense compassion in her eyes that it was hard not to respond. But she knew only a small portion of these pretend emotions would be truly heartfelt with someone like Ary. Maxx had been different in that way. She had embraced her feelings. Williams thought it had made her a better soldier. But, still...

"Thank you, Colonel," she murmured.

She felt tired suddenly. Truth be told, she did not like being at war with Ary. She had never had a single issue with the woman before, until the neural lace episode, of course. And Ary had always been fair to her in the past. Sharp, by the book, but fair. If Williams was really honest about it, she knew that the colonel had allowed her to go quite far over and beyond the line before she had pulled on her leash. She was lucky that her behaviour over the previous weeks had not got her thrown off the ship, and stripped of her rank. Oh yeah, she was an L5. But there were plenty of other ways they could have used her, without allowing her any of the privileges.

"No need to thank me, Major," Ary remarked in typical fashion. "It is nothing personal."

It suddenly occurred to Williams that the jail was probably the only place the Cretian officer could figure out that would be really safe for her. Forcing her to spend some time alone was good, something that she needed. Putting her on a crazy vegan diet, allowing her zero alcohol, and keeping her focused and busy with hard, grueling training sessions was also the best way to bring her back to full fitness. As punishments went, it was pretty light, Williams reflected. Pretty helpful, too. She wiped her face with a paper towel, leaned back against her seat, and met the woman's gaze.

"Is Sergeant Holson doing okay?" she asked.

Ary nodded.

"She's fine. I checked on her myself that very same night at the resort. I have spoken to her a couple of times since. She asked about you."

Asked what about me exactly? Williams desperately wanted to know. *And what did you tell her?* But once again, and even though she had thought about Holson a hell of a lot over the past few days, she decided that it would be wiser not to express too much interest in the matter. As always, the less she gave Ary to play with, the better it would probably turn out to be.

"Thanks for the books," she said instead.

Ary finally allowed herself a small smile.

"Found them helpful, did you?"

"Yes. Very much, thank you."

The colonel relaxed a little more.

"Good. So now you can levitate things, right?"

Williams grinned. Yeah. That was pretty cool, actually.

"I have only just started," she admitted. "But I like it so far. I was hoping there may be some specific training I can do to develop those abilities a bit more. Is there?"

"Absolutely."

Ary looked pleased with the request.

"We have a specialist on board who can help you with that. I would have suggested him to you before, but I did not think that you were ready then."

It was true. She had not been. But she was now. Maxx had saved her life. She would have wanted her to do the best she could with it. And stop being such an idiot about all this, too. Williams smiled faintly at the thought of her. She could picture it. *'What's with the histrionics?'* used to be one of her lover's favourite comments. They could be pinned down under heavy fire, stuck in the middle of a bomb field, or planning a delicate op in the war room; and whenever people started to get a little hot under the collar, Maxx would simply shrug, flash a quick smile, and say, *'Hey, what's with the histrionics'*? It never failed to help break up the tension. Williams was pretty sure that she would have told her the same thing about the neural lace.

"So, am I reinstated then?" she asked.

"Not yet. But as soon as your HRV numbers get back to normal, and when it is safe for you to return to duty, I promise that you will be."

Williams suppressed a disappointed sigh.

"And how are those numbers doing now?" she enquired.

"Getting better with every passing day. Should reach optimum level soon."

"Right. And I assume I have to stay in jail until they do?"

"That is correct," Ary responded.

Williams reached for a forgotten chip on the side of her plate, as if to prepare herself for a long separation. Ary rolled her eyes at her.

"Come on," she instructed. "Break over, let's go."

She walked the reluctant prisoner back to her cell in mostly complete silence. It was only when they got to the door that she spoke to her again.

"There is something else I have to tell you, Major," she said, stopping there for a moment. "When they brought you back from that mission, half-dead, and I saw the negative TX form flash up on your records..."

She paused. Williams waited patiently, sensing that she should probably remain quiet.

"Well, let's just say I had my orders from up high, but all the same..."

She stopped again.

"What is it, ma'am?" Williams prompted her then.

It was extremely unusual for Ary to show hesitation of any kind, and she was curious to find out what was causing it.

"Well, I was glad they made that decision," the colonel confessed eventually. "Because letting you die when I knew there was something I could do to stop it, even if it was against your wishes... I don't think I could have done it, Major. *You* are one of *my* crew, after all." She shrugged. "And for all I knew, you might have forgotten all about that form, and not even want it anymore."

Williams was silent for a moment, just staring at the floor, reflecting on the statement. When she looked up, she was surprised to see real emotion burning in Ary's deep brown eyes. So, the woman could feel something after all; from time to time... Too bad that she did not have anything nice to say to her in response.

"If I could," she murmured, "I would still not choose to have the lace, Colonel. I would still decide to let go at that point. Just so you know. Just because I am on your crew doesn't mean that you own me. You never will."

Ary nodded stiffly. Her eyes became expressionless, and hard.

"Noted, Major," she replied. "You have made your point. Now get back in your cell."

"Wait," Williams added quickly, before the woman could shut that stupid door in her face again.

Ary raised a suspicious eyebrow.

"Yes?" she asked. "What is it?"

Williams held her gaze. She gave her a small conciliatory shrug.

"Well," she said. "When I landed on Mars, there was this smell in the air, like bougainvillea or something. Still not sure what it was. But it was nice to be able to smell it. So. There you are."

Ary looked at her for a few more seconds.

"That is good to know, Major," she smiled eventually. "And I thank you for sharing that with me."

Feeling encouraged by her warmer response, sensing that perhaps some sort of truce had been established between them, Williams tried a little bold move.

"Hey, maybe I could go back to sleep in my own bed tonight, Colonel," she suggested, smiling. "I feel a lot better. And I'm sure my numbers would benefit from it too."

But it was like hitting a brick wall. The interlude had been sweet, but short, and now the Ary that she was used to dealing with was well and truly back.

"Negative," the Cretian snapped. "Get back in there."

With another big sigh, Williams stepped in, and she watched the door swish immediately shut behind her. *Ary,* she thought. *What a complicated, infuriating, yet interesting woman...* Realising that she had forgotten to ask her for something, she threw herself against the door.

"Hey, Colonel!" she shouted. "Will you get me some more books?"

For a couple of seconds, there was only silence, but then the response floated through. It made her want to laugh, and slap the woman across the face. Both at the same time, and in equal measure.

"This request will be granted, Major," Ary said. "Now get back to your toothbrush."

CHAPTER TWELVE

Williams threw herself into training with renewed vigor, especially where all the mindfulness and psi stuff was concerned. It was an area that was new to her, something she had never been interested in before, and a challenge to say the least. Standing still, letting her mind grow quiet, and meditating for an hour or more at a time every single day was not her style, nor something that came easily to her. But when she saw the progress it allowed her to make with the neural lace, the things that she could do, and how much easier it became to control it, she let go of any doubts she may have had.

"The mindfulness exercises will have a positive impact on your HRV, too," her instructor promised.

"Great," she approved. "Just tell me what to do, and I'll do it."

She buried herself into her studies, and listened to her coach. She took the advice, and acted on it. She did everything she had to do to get herself out of jail, and reinstated. Because it may have felt like a relief to her at first, a refuge even, but now living out of a cell was beginning to really get on her nerves. If nothing else, it was another clear sign that she was ready to get back to action. Three days later, not surprisingly, she aced her return to duty test.

"Well done, Major," Ary commented. "I knew you could do it."

"Thank you, Colonel."

"Now, if you ever try to hit me again, I will break your legs. Are we clear?"

Williams knew that she was serious.

"Clear," she agreed.

She sat alone in her quarters on her first night back, going through a pile of paperwork, and several pages of emails she had received in her absence. When she was done with that, she walked over to the window, and leaned her forearm against the glass. She rested her head against it, and sighed. *What now?* she thought. Staring into space this way made her think about Holson suddenly, and her crazy admission about the cargo bay airlock. *She asked about you,* Ary had told her. Williams wondered if the operator was back from her R&R yet. Probably not, she suspected. Still, it was worth sending her a quick message, just to make sure that she really was okay, at least. She kept it brief, and to the point.

'Holson. Ary said you were doing fine. Really glad to hear - I hope that's true? I've been reinstated. Not sure what you're doing, or where you are, but feel free to drop by for a chat anytime you want. My quarters are located on the Officers' Deck, section C34-S.'

She hesitated, and finally signed it, *Evan.*

Then she thought about Ice, and a thoughtful smile came to her lips at the memory of the young woman. Her new friend was probably freezing cold on some hellish training exercise right about now. Face covered in cam cream, feeling wet, tired, living off disgusting field rations, and learning exactly how many push-ups she could really do before she passed out. The next message was for her.

'Hey, marine. How's it going down there? Hope you're doing well. I want you on my team, so keep working hard, okay? Get strong. I know you can do it.'

This one she simply signed, *Williams.*

She checked the time, then. It was just after midnight, and she was nowhere near tired. She knew Ary wanted to discuss soldier applications to form a new team with her first thing the next morning. It was true, they were hiring. Well, it had to happen sometime, she told herself, even as a fresh wave of apprehension and regret blew right through her. But they had to. She needed to go on operations again, and she had to have people for that. She needed a crew. It did not have to mean anything other than that. *No histrionics, Williams,* she reminded herself. She settled down on top of her bed for an impromptu meditation session. Hopefully, it would help her to get to sleep quickly, and there would be no dreams. She closed her eyes, and she relaxed her body. But only a second later, a soft knock on the door announced a visitor.

"Screen," Williams ordered, curious as to who it would be.

One side of the wall immediately showed her the outside corridor in front of her cabin, and Holson standing there. *Well, that was quick.* Feeling unusually happy all of a sudden, the marine jumped off the bed, went to the door, and pushed a button on the side. The door slid open, she said '*hi*', and Holson burst into tears.

"What's wrong?" Williams exclaimed, taken aback by the soldier's unexpected reaction.

Holson hiccupped a couple times, then started laughing through her tears. Williams grew increasingly confused.

"Sergeant Holson, tell me what's going on," she insisted, frowning.

"Nothing," the woman assured her, smiling now. "Sorry. I just... I was just really worried about you when Colonel Ary wouldn't let me see you. I tried, you know? I started thinking that maybe you were injured, or even dead, and I..."

"Come in," Williams interrupted.

She did not want to have this conversation in the middle of the hallway. She pulled Holson in after her, shut the door, and almost went dizzy. There was that awesome smell again, she realised. *Damn, if this is not the absolute best thing in the entire universe...*

"Those are for you, Major."

And Holson effectively solved the mystery of the scent by gently placing a small bouquet of delicate white flowers into her hands.

"They are called lily of the valley," she explained. "My favourite flower. I brought them back from Mars for you, and I managed to keep them alive for long enough."

"Gosh," Williams murmured.

She closed her eyes, and she concentrated on the smell for a few seconds. This was the sweetest thing. It sang of joy and happiness to her.

"I love this stuff," she declared. "How did you know?"

"I didn't," Holson replied, beaming. "But I'm glad you do."

"You think we can grow them on ships?"

"I don't see why not."

"Great," Williams sighed.

A meditator, and about to turn herself into a gardener as well. One of these days, she thought, Ary was going to really struggle to recognise her fierce L5 assassin. She lost herself in the scent of the flowers again. Remembered that she was not alone after a while, and she turned toward Holson. She spotted the redness in her eyes, and instantly grew concerned about her all over again.

"All right, tell me why you were crying before," she ordered. "Are you okay, really?"

Holson nodded quickly. She even blushed a little.

"Yes, all good," she confirmed. "And it is just like I said. I wanted to bring you those in jail, and Ary said no. She said you were fine, and busy, and I wasn't sure if that was the truth or not. So, when you opened the door, and I saw you standing there... Well, it was a huge relief, that's all. I cry at the drop of a hat. It's just how I am. Don't worry about it."

She did not wait for Williams' reply, and pointed at the flowers in her hands instead.

"Before you crush these, Major," she said, smiling sweetly, "would you happen to have a vase we can put them in?"

When the marine looked puzzled, she immediately pulled a little flask from her pocket.

"It's okay. Didn't think you would, so I brought you one. And water, too."

"I've got water," Williams groaned.

Okay, she was a commando. Did not mean that she was this rough around the edges. She poured some liquid into the flask, settled the flowers into it, and brought them up to her nose again. *Hmm. Delicious.*

"Thank you, Sergeant," she said as she settled them on her desk. "I was just..."

She was startled when Holson threw her arms around her neck, and pulled her close. Automatically, she responded in the same way. Holson's embrace, the warmth of her body against hers, and the smell of the flowers... Well. She could not help but think it was a wonderful combination. It made her brain swim a little, too. It had been a long time since anyone other than a bunch of doctors had touched her. This was... Well, it was badly needed, and over a little too soon, she had to admit.

"My friends call me Nic," Holson said as she released her.

"Okay, Nic. My friends call me Evan," Williams replied.

She rolled her eyes, thinking about Ice.

"Well, those who can manage to forget the rank, anyway," she added.

"What rank?" the operator chuckled.

"Exactly. Would you like a drink? I only have fruit juice, I'm afraid, or protein recovery aid if you're into that sort of thing. I am not doing alcohol anymore."

Alcohol interfered with the neural lace. Also, since she had started the meditation exercises, Williams found more comfort in doing that then drinking. Another good thing about it was that she had noticed her nightmares were definitely getting less and less. This was priceless to her, and she intended on keeping it going.

"You're looking better," Holson remarked.

Definitely not dead, she thought. Her eyes drifted to Williams' forehead, and she was pleased to notice that the injury she had sustained when falling through the pier was healing well. Her other scar looked a lot less inflamed as well. Williams went to sit on her bed, and Holson followed her there, since there was not a single other place to sit in the small cabin. Close enough to touch, Williams noticed. She did not comment on it.

"So, how long have you been back?" she enquired.

Holson sighed rather longingly.

"Three days," she said. "I really miss the beach, and the sunshine."

"I'll bet. Thank you for the flowers."

"You're welcome."

Williams held her gaze, and she spotted the rather intense and focused way that Holson was watching her. She was obviously trying not to let it show, and not doing a very good job of it. Yet, although she was not very subtle, there was a little hesitancy in her eyes as well, and some hopefulness maybe. It made Williams feel quite warm all of a sudden. Nervous, too.

"Thank you for helping me the other night as well," she murmured. "I am sorry about the whole thing. I wasn't myself. And I am especially sorry about almost getting you drowned with me."

Holson gave her a little smile. It was gentle, and full of warmth.

"You didn't. And anytime."

"Hopefully, never again," Williams reflected. "But thanks. And if you ever need to talk to someone, about anything at all, Serg... Nic," she corrected herself, grinning. "If you ever need me, my door's always open."

"Thank you, Evan."

Williams gave a self-deprecating smirk, and she raised a reflective eyebrow.

"Well. Unless I'm in jail, or something. You know."

Holson started to laugh at the comment.

"Yeah, right," she giggled. "I'll keep that one in mind, for sure."

She could not stop herself from laughing after that, and pretty soon, tears were running down her face. Williams joined in with her. She could not really remember the last time that she had laughed like this. It felt pretty amazing to her.

"Hey, Nic?" she offered. "Want something to eat?"

She levitated a packet of crisps over to the bed, amused and pleased at the flabbergasted look on Holson's face.

"Are you doing that?" the woman exclaimed.

"Yep."

"How? I thought only Cretians and some alien species could levitate stuff!"

"It's the lace," Williams said. "I studied its applications when I was in jail. Began to do some psi training with one of the on-board specialists, too. I am starting to see the benefits of it."

Holson returned her eyes to her, watching her intently.

"It will make me faster in battle. I can do some of that energy stuff that Ary does now, too. Create a shield, and throw energy balls. Things like that. I still need to work at it, but it is coming along fine. It'll make me more efficient when I need to be."

"And safer?" the sergeant enquired.

That was definitely the most important thing for her.

"Yeah," Williams replied with a smile. "Safer. And better able to protect my team, too."

"Then I'm glad. It's a good thing."

"It is."

A silence fell over them. Williams was suddenly reminded of what Holson had said to her, down on the beach that night, right before she was arrested and taken back to the ship. Something about a reason for asking her out. It did not take a rocket scientist to figure out what it was, and she was not sure that she could really go there. Not now, not so soon. And yet, there they were, sat together on her bed, shoulders almost touching. The gentle smile on Holson's lips, and the tender expression in her eyes every time that she looked at her made Williams feel even more afraid to ask. Her nervousness returned. But she should really be saying something, all the same. *Fucking say something,* she ordered herself furiously.

"Hey, Evan?" her visitor asked her before she could figure something out.

"Yeah?"

Holson had noticed the sudden tense, fierce look on the officer's face, and the way that she seemed to struggle with something deep inside her head. She could guess what it was. She could sense it even now, the heaviness between them, loaded with meaning. But there was no need to go into it. Not now, for sure, maybe not for a long time. She was used to pushing her way into women's arms, but she had gone far enough with this particular one. Now, Evan would have to make the next move if anything else was going to happen between them.

Because she was different, Nic realised. Different, and incredibly important. That was the reason why, for the first time since her lover's untimely death, she had felt herself moved to bring a woman some flowers. Even though she was at that stage, ready to get involved with someone emotionally again, and with Evan specifically, she suspected that the other woman was not there yet, not by a long way. And so, if friendship was all that she could get for the time being, then it would be fine with her.

"I should probably go," she remarked. "Let you get some sleep."

"Hmm…"

It was all that Williams said. She did not move. She did not look like she wanted Holson to go. She appeared lost in thought, but not in a dark place this time. Just thinking really hard about something.

"Evan."

Nic touched her arm briefly, and she flashed her a crooked smile.

"Only if you're not sleepy, I could tell you about the second time that I almost drowned on Mars, only three days after you left."

Williams frowned.

"You're joking, right?"

"Nope."

"What did you do?"

"I tried to learn to sail. It's actually quite a funny story, especially seeing as I didn't drown. Want to hear?"

Williams smiled. She grabbed a pillow, and stuck it behind her head. She stretched her long legs out in front of her, and made herself comfortable.

"Oh yeah," she said, eyes sparkling in anticipation. "I sure do."

CHAPTER THIRTEEN

She opened her eyes slowly, knowing instinctively that it was too early to get up. She was not sure what had woken her, but whatever it was, it was not a nightmare, and Williams was so thankful for that simple fact she could have cried.

In the darkness of the small cabin, she gradually became aware that she was not alone. She had fallen asleep on her back, on top of the covers. Still fully clothed in her combat trousers, a training shirt, a pair of heavy boots on her feet. Not unusual for something like that to happen, but now there was also one additional, puzzling fact to consider. She had one arm wrapped around a sleeping woman's body. Said woman was all tucked in against her side, head resting comfortably on her shoulder, fingers tight around a handful of her t-shirt. Williams took a careful, quiet breath, and she dropped her head back against the pillow. *Nic,* she reflected. The woman who appeared completely transformed from the way she used to be before, when it seemed that everywhere Williams went, there she was, trying to tempt her into bed. Well, now she had reached her goal, it seemed. Maybe even one better. She was on her bed, and in her arms. *Does it matter?* Williams wondered fleetingly.

She knew full well that the night before, she had not wanted to be alone. But specifically, it was Holson's company that she had desired. Not someone else. Just her. Maybe that was the important matter. And the evening had been fun, really. It was great to be able to sit back, and listen to someone else's stories for a change. Funny ones, too. Good stuff. The sergeant had made her cry with laughter, and even now, Williams could feel herself smiling at the thought.

"Humph..." Holson mumbled suddenly.

"What?" Williams murmured.

The operator whispered something in her sleep, flung her leg over her body, and tightened her grip on her, everywhere that she could. Then she gave a contented sigh, and settled back down again. Her right hand had dropped to Williams' breast. Doing nothing but resting there, nicely heavy, and the marine felt a trickle of sweat suddenly running down the side of her face. Holson's right knee was pressing into her crotch. *Fuck,* she thought, only to immediately decide it was entirely the wrong word to use. But still. *Fuck. What do I do now?* Not that she lacked experience in that department, but sex had been the last thing on her mind, and now... *Now,* she thought, sinking her teeth into her bottom lip, *now Holson is getting me all triggered, and she is not even awake!*

Williams wrapped her fingers around her wrist gently, tried to lift her hand, and drop it to the side. Holson did not seem to like that very much. Still asleep, she pressed herself harder into Williams' body, and dropped her hand onto her stomach this time. Low, very low, down below her belt line. Her lips came to rest against the side of her neck, as soft as a feather. But to Williams, they felt like a hot branding iron being applied to her skin. A strong pulse of arousal flashed through her body. This was torture, pure and simple. Nice, and extremely enjoyable of course, but...

I wonder what time it is, she thought, and immediately, a set of numbers flashed in front of her eyes. *04:30 a.m.* She had forgotten about that AI link stuff. Of course, she could now communicate with her system directly, without needing to use her voice. It helped to take her mind off of Holson for a second or two, but not when the woman suddenly shifted again, and more or less simply climbed on top of her. She produced another one of those happy sighs. The insane thing about it, Williams noticed, feeling herself breathe a little harder at the thought, was how they fit together so perfectly...

Enough, she suddenly decided. She could not take much more of this, and 04:30 was a perfectly good time to get up and hit the gym. She wrapped her arms around Holson, and gently rolled her over onto her back. For a second, the temptation to just lay there, to rest her head against her chest and close her eyes was almost too strong to deny. She flinched when an image of her lover, smiling, floated in front of her eyes. *Maxx...* But Maxx was gone, Williams forced herself to remember. Gone, and never coming back. She, on the other hand, was alive. Whether she liked it or not. And she was beginning to like it again. Something felt wrong about that, somehow.

Feeling disturbed all of a sudden, she pulled herself up and off the bed, grabbed her gym kit, and stopped at the sight of the flowers on her desk. She took a step over to have a smell. Closed her eyes for a second. She smiled.

"Evan..."

Williams' eyes snapped open.

"Evan?"

"Yes, right here."

Lights, she thought, and the overhead lighting suddenly activated. Holson sat on her bed, rubbing her eyes. Face a little flushed from sleep, hair sticking out. She looked a little worried, a little unsure. Beautiful, Williams decided. The thought startled her.

"What's wrong?" the woman asked.

"Nothing. I need to get to work, that's all."

"Is it the middle of the night?"

"No. It's almost five."

Holson made a face that clearly indicated it was the middle of the night for her.

"Oh... Okay," she murmured.

Williams busied herself with her gym clothes, looking everywhere around her quarters but at Holson. She spotted a bottle of water on the side, grabbed it, and shoved it into her bag.

"Evan?"

"Yes."

The operator was up suddenly, and standing right in front of her.

"Sure everything's okay?" she enquired.

Williams finally met her eyes. She tried not to stare, and failed.

"Fine," she said.

She wanted to... *What?* she thought. *What do I want?* Holson smiled at her, and cocked her head to one side. Looking like she was waiting for something more. Williams took a trembling breath. She opened her mouth to speak, but nothing came out. Heart pounding in her chest, ears buzzing. She just *wanted*, that was all. Badly.

"I have to go," she mumbled.

"Okay. Well, thank you for last night. I had fun."

"Yeah. Me too."

She fumbled with her bag again, and finally managed to get her legs to work.

"You can stay if you like. I, uh... There is no food in here, but I've got coffee."

"Thanks, Evan," Holson said gently.

She knew what was going on, she could recognise the signs. But she was going to stick to her promise, and not make the first move, or any move for that matter. If she remembered correctly, they had ended up lying side by side on the bed the previous night, swapping stories. Williams had been the first to drift off, and Holson had closed her eyes then, too. For just a second. Quite a bit of time must have passed, she reflected, before she opened them again, and found herself more or less completely fused against the side of the marine's body. It had felt incredibly too good for her to want to move a single inch away from her. Was this what was causing Williams' uncharacteristic fluster now? Probably.

Good, Holson decided.

"Do you mind if I take a shower?" she asked.

Testing her theory, and the officer's face instantly turned crimson. Okay, not making a move... But not making it easy for her either.

"Sure. Go ahead. Do what you want."

"Thanks. See you later, Evan."

"See you later, Nic."

∞

Williams was surprised to find a small crowd clustered inside the gym when she got there.

"What's going on?" she asked a marine who was standing by, looking excited.

"Ary is fighting," he replied.

She raised an interested eyebrow.

"Fighting regular?" she asked.

He grinned.

"Yes, Major!"

Well, this could be fun to watch, Williams decided. It was not often that Colonel Ary spent time in the gym. She was a Cretian after all, and a master of all this mind stuff that her L5 was trying so hard to learn. She did not need to practice like everyone else.

From time to time though, Colonel Ary decided to make an appearance, and fight *regular*. Meaning simply using the weapon every other marine had access to. Their body. A couple of times, she had found herself well and truly beaten by one of her troops. Williams had given her a good lesson in dirty street fighting once, and sent her home with a broken tooth. The next time, she discovered that Ary had integrated every dirty trick in the book, and then some. She ended up on her stomach, being asphyxiated by the colonel after only ten seconds on the mat. She managed to free herself, somehow, only to get dropped by a kick to the head that earned her three stitches, and a couple of hours in the hospital.

"Is that all you've got to give me, Captain?" she heard the colonel shriek now, as she made her way toward the front of the enthusiastic crowd.

Poor Captain Ellis James tried to say something through a mouthful of blood. Williams frowned. Blood was not allowed in the gym. Obviously, it was not Ary's concern currently. Standing there with her fists raised, dressed like everyone else in a pair of fatigues belted at the waist, boots, and a simple t-shirt, she looked magnificent.

"Who's next?" she laughed.

A young marine instantly stepped in. He dodged her first hit, grabbed her by the waist, and wrestled her down onto the mat. Ary fell back, and there was a nice 'whoosh' when all the air was pushed out of her lungs.

Williams found herself grinning from ear to ear.

"Who's that?" she asked the man on her right, who was busy taking bets.

"Tom O'Neil. New recruit, fresh off commando training. He's got some balls, stepping in like that! Hey, Major, wanna bet?"

She chuckled. Yeah, that guy was all right.

"Give me twenty on him," she said.

And then, she yelled a warning at the man.

"Watch out for her, marine! This one fights dirty."

Ary's eyes flashed onto her, and she looked like she was going to bark something nasty in reply. But just at that same time, the soldier shoved his knee into her face, and pushed her down onto the dusty floor.

Williams laughed out loud.

"Nice," she approved.

"No worries," he grunted. "I got this."

Or so he thought. Because in the next second, the blood drained from his face, and he howled out in genuine pain. Ary had just grabbed a handful of his balls, and squeezed. Merciless, she made him scream like a little girl. Quite a few of the men present shuffled and muttered uncomfortably. When he was just about ready to pass out, she released him, and sent him crashing into the crowd.

"Next!" she yelled. "Williams, get up here!"

Finally, Williams thought. She jumped in, feeling searing hot adrenaline flood through her body. This would take her mind off of Holson, no doubt.

"Looking for punishment, Colonel?" she teased.

They started dancing around each other, both aware that one or the other was going to end up regretting this. Both convinced that it would be the other one.

"Going to try to break my legs, are you?" she challenged.

Quick as lightning, Ary attempted to land a kick against the side of her head. Williams dropped to the floor, rolled, and sprung up right behind her back. She landed her booted foot in the middle of her bum, and shoved her forward.

"What's up, Colonel?" she laughed. "Feeling tired?"

The marines in the back all whistled in delight. Ary regained her balance, grinning dangerously. She looked like she was enjoying herself, and this was always a warning sign of painful things to come. Williams kept her eyes locked on to her, and her guard safely up.

"You know what your problem is, Major?" Ary growled.

"What's that, Colonel?"

"You talk too fucking much."

In the next instant, a powerful ball of energy hit the L5 right in the centre of her chest. It felt like someone had punched her with a giant glove, and the force of three fighters. Winded, she fell to her knees. Disappointment rippled through the crowd.

"Hey, you're not supposed to use that shit!" someone yelled.

"Fucking out of order!" somebody else agreed.

Ary ignored them all. Eyes flashing, smiling in anticipation, she stood in front of Williams.

"Get up," she ordered. "Show me what you..."

She was surprised when the marine shot to her feet and threw herself at her with a volley of clever kicks and punches. Staggering backward under the assault, Ary managed to deflect most of the strikes. But the last one, a high, fast, well-aimed kick caught her right underneath the chin. It knocked her head back painfully, and sent her flying. She hit one of the pillars, and struggled to keep her balance for a second.

"What was that, Colonel? Want to see more?"

Williams slammed her right fist into Ary's stomach, grabbed her by the throat as she doubled over, and threw her back into the centre of the mat. She landed on top of her, as heavy and dense as she could make her body feel, and she was pleased when she coaxed a reluctant grunt from the colonel.

"What? Can't hear you," she laughed.

All the same, she knew that she was playing with fire. Ary never allowed anyone to mess with her like this for very long. But hey, she had asked for it, and…

"Williams, watch out!"

What the…

A concentrated ball of energy hit her right between the eyes. Ary got to her feet, raised her hand, and generated two more.

"What I mean, Major," she snarled, "is use your fucking lace to fight me with."

One ball of light rushed toward her at the speed of light, too fast for Williams to see it coming. It punched her in the stomach. Hard, but not hard enough to incapacitate her.

"Come on. I'm waiting," Ary said.

Another ball hit Williams in the jaw. It rattled her teeth, but again, not hard enough to break any. She tried to raise her own energy. She was feeling clumsy. Slow. Not at all like she did in training. During practice, she could throw energy balls like nobody's business.

"It's different when you're being pounded," Ary remarked nonchalantly, before hurling another one at her. "Isn't it? And I guess your toothbrush doesn't fight back either, does it?"

Yet another ball hit her in the face again. This one hurt. It busted her lower lip open, and fresh blood dripped onto the mat. Williams was still trying to form a single one.

"Fuck," she muttered under her breath.

Ary was getting closer. She raised her hand again, twirled her fingers in the air like a fucking magician, and unfurled a wave of still unformed stuff to float high above her head.

"If you don't want a broken leg, Major Williams," she threatened, "I suggest you get your shit together. Now."

The flustered officer suddenly remembered something her instructor had told her once.

'If you ever find yourself struggling in combat, when you're under pressure and have no time to think, don't. Gather your emotion, and send it. Don't wait to see it form. Don't wait for confirmation. Just fucking do it.'

"Come on, L5," Ary sneered. "Let 'er rip, for crying out loud…"

Williams thought of her crew. She thought of Sanchez, staring into her eyes just as he was about to let go. *Hell, no.* Quickly, she raised her hand, closed her eyes, and gathered all the rage that she could muster. All in all, it took less than a split second, and Ary never saw it coming. She did not hear it either. Before she had any clue that it was headed her way, a rush of energy so powerful it made her skin burn and prickle slammed into her body. She fell backward, hit the wall, and collapsed on the floor. Down for the count. Silence followed. The marines around the room all stared at Williams in awe.

"Shit, Major," someone commented flatly. "Now you're dead."

CHAPTER FOURTEEN

But Ary did not want to kill her, far from it. She was much too pleased with Williams' rapid progress with her energy work to want to do that. Too happy to even be tempted to punish her for smashing her lights out in such spectacular fashion. What she did instead was treat her L5 to a magnificent steak dinner in the mess hall that night, and then she kept her working late inside the war room, going over application forms until the marine could barely see the ink on the pages.

"So, any suggestions, Major?" she asked eventually.

Williams leaned back against her seat, nodded, and handed her the first form that she had selected.

"Tom O'Neil. Ah, the young marine from this morning," Ary commented wryly, staring at the form. "But do you really want a rookie on your team?"

"Why not? He applied, and I like him."

Ary snorted.

"You liked the way he jumped on me?"

Williams gave an honest shrug in response.

"Yeah," was all she said.

Ary allowed herself a small smile of agreement.

"I must admit," she remarked, "so did I. I hope I did not hurt him too much. Okay, he's a possible, but I would prefer a more heavy-duty soldier to back you up when it matters. Who else you got?"

Williams produced two more forms, including one for the heavy-duty soldier that Ary wanted. His name was Ernesto Velez. He had already served ten years in the Marines, and been involved in several Special Forces operations. He had an impressive background in communications, had trained as a medic, could fly a transport craft, and his records were impeccable in every way.

"I worked with him once," she explained. "He's solid. He's done it before. And he's been on the waiting list for a while. Every op that comes his way, he's game. So, he clearly wants the job, and to become a regular. I think we should give him the chance."

"Agreed," Ary nodded. "I like this one. Next."

The following form held application details for a physical training instructor going by the name of Joanne Binks, who had only five years with the Marines under her belt, but who was an expert tactician, and a seasoned survival instructor to boot. Williams enjoyed surrounding herself with people who were used to toughing it out as much as she was.

"Experience?" Ary queried.

"Not with SF. But she scored the highest marks on her sniper training three years in a row. I like a good shooter on my team."

"Hmm. Okay, we'll see. Next?"

"That's all I've got. But it's all I need, right?"

"No, you need three more."

"Three?"

"Yes. O'Neil and Binks don't cut it as far as I'm concerned, and so I need you to come up with a few other options in case they fail the interview."

Williams stared at the forms, and she suppressed a groan.

"I hate doing this," she complained.

Ary smirked.

"Of course," she agreed. "I know you do. But I am not simply going to select them for you, Major. I need your input on this one, since you know what you are looking for better than me. It makes sense. So, how many forms have we got here?"

"57," Williams replied.

"Don't tell me you can't find three other potential crew members out of 57 entries. You've got until 7 a.m. tomorrow morning. Meanwhile, I am heading off to bed. It's been a long day."

"You're telling me."

Ary shrugged, clearly unconcerned.

"See that it is done. Happy trawling, Major."

Williams watched her go, sighed, and got up to pour herself another cup of strong coffee. *Payback for this morning,* she reflected. *Well, at least I got a nice steak out of it...*

She sat down again, and went through all the forms once more, one by one, diligently. Eventually, she settled on another Cretian officer, a female who had significant experience with Special Forces, and a specialty in electronics. She also chose two other soldiers with previous achievements of the kind that were sure to satisfy Ary. Williams then rubbed her eyes, and she stretched. She crossed her arms over the table, rested her forehead onto them, and breathed out. *Just for a second,* she promised herself.

It was the way Holson found her fifteen minutes later when she walked into the war room. Dozing with her head down on a pile of important paperwork. She approached her quietly, and rested warm fingers against the side of her cheek. She allowed them to drift over the back of her neck, and go up into her hair. Williams lifted her head slowly, looking confused, blue eyes hazy with sleep.

"Oh. Hey," she said. "Sorry, I was... uh..."

Holson gave her a soft smile, nodded, and she removed her hand.

"Thinking of going to bed, I hope."

Williams shook the sleep out of her eyes.

"No. I was just taking a quick break."

Holson threw her a questioning look. She caught the shadows under her eyes, the fatigue reflected in her demeanour, and she shook her head in instant disapproval.

"Nothing wrong with calling it a day, I'm sure," she remarked. "It's late. And I know you were up extra early this morning."

"Well, what about you? It's almost midnight."

"Oh, I'm fine. I went back to sleep in your bed after you left," Holson replied casually.

From the stunned look on Williams' face, it was clear that she got a specific, meaningful picture out of it. Before she could get any deeper into it though, Holson poked her in the chest to get her attention.

"I was looking for you," she declared.

Williams appeared a mixture of deeply interested and slightly apprehensive at the same time.

"Yeah?" she said.

Holson nodded.

"Yeah," she replied. "I got seeds."

"You got what?"

"Lily of the valley seeds," the operator reminded her.

She produced a tiny packet, reached for Williams' hand, and dropped a few of them onto her palm. She covered it with her own, and she met her eyes. Gave her a gentle look, and a smile of the same ilk.

"For you, Evan," she murmured.

Williams smiled too. It was one of those tentatively happy ones she gave from time to time, totally unconscious, as if something really great had happened to her, and she was not really sure that it was there to stay. It made her look really young when she did that. Innocent, and completely open. In Holson's opinion, beautiful. And Williams appeared genuinely pleased.

"That's awesome," she said.

"I was going to show you what to do with them, but you look tired, so we can do that some other time."

"No, I'm fine. Let's do it now."

Holson hesitated.

"Are you sure?"

"Positive."

"Well, okay then."

Back in her quarters, and wide awake once more, Williams watched attentively as Holson planted the seeds, explaining what she was doing as she worked, and the reason for each thing; smiling often, only pausing to glance back at her from time to time. Each look was a little more pointed, a little more intent. Eyes drifting all over the marine's body with every single gaze, and each private thought that she contemplated.

"Okay so far?" she asked.

Williams nodded.

"Yeah," she lied.

She would not remember a single word of what Nic had said afterward. She would have no idea where seeds came from, where they went, or what to do with them for that matter. But she would remember the sweet timbre of her voice. The precise way her fingers moved over each item, and the gentle yet focused expression in her eyes every single time that she looked at her. It made the back of her head tingle nicely. The familiar, hungry feeling from the morning returned to her with a vengeance.

"And that's all there is to it," Nic declared eventually.

Williams had to clear her throat before she replied.

"Great," she said. "Thanks."

Holson nodded, threw her a little look.

"No problem."

She walked over to where Williams stood. She reached up to tuck a strand of her hair behind her ear, and she allowed her fingers to rest against her cheek for just a moment. Watched her struggle not to close her eyes under the simple touch. She flashed her a gentle smile.

"You look exhausted. Now, I really should go..."

But Williams caught her by the hand.

"Nic. Wait," she murmured.

She raised a hand to caress the side of Holson's face, and she let it drift over the side of her neck and shoulder, coming to rest over her chest. She was breathing a little harder than normal, and there was such a fierce look in her clear blue eyes that it made Holson swallow in anticipation, and just a hint of nervousness.

"Evan..." she whispered.

"Hmm..."

Williams raked her fingers through her short dark hair. She buried her face against her shoulder, pressed herself into her body, and kissed the side of her neck. Holson felt the wall behind her, solid, hard, and she was glad that it was there to steady herself. Williams had found the buttons on her shirt. She gave a little grunt of impatience as she struggled with the last one, got it, and paused. Nic almost screamed.

"Don't stop," she panted.

"Are you sure? I..."

But Holson swallowed the rest of her sentence with a deep, scorching kiss. She felt Williams stiffen against her, and it was not due to hesitation of any kind. Her hand was on the back of her neck, her thumb on the side of her jaw. Tilting her head just so, guiding her into position to allow Williams to deepen the kiss the way she really wanted it. Holson tried to raise her hands to touch her, but that was prevented by the sleeves of her uniform being slid down her arms. Williams cupped her breasts in both hands. She started doing things to her nipples and through her bra that had Nic whimpering furiously into the kiss. This went on for a little while, until she felt that she was going to pass out, either from too much pleasure, or lack of oxygen, whichever came first. And then, Williams dropped to her knees in front of her. She looked up as the operator brought her eyes down. Nic almost fainted at the sight. *Major Williams,* she thought. *L5 commando hero, kneeling at my feet, and about to...*

"Wow..." she mumbled. "You look... Oh, Williams, fuck!"

"Evan," the marine corrected with a dazzling smile. "And soon. But not just yet."

Nic gave a loud, drunken sort of laugh. She started to lower herself down.

"Stay," Williams instructed.

Using her command voice on her, and it had an immediate, peculiar effect on Holson. She almost lost it, right there and then. Williams got rid of the belt on her trousers in one swift movement, and threw it over her shoulder. She started on the buttons, and glanced up again to meet her eyes.

"This still okay, Nic?" she murmured.

Holson nodded.

"Yes," she gasped. "And you can stop asking."

A chuckle.

"Good. I will if you say so."

Nic remained standing with her back against the wall, doing her best not to explode. Williams took her own sweet time with it, but soon she had her standing there in just her pants and bra. And those did not stay in place for very long either. She ran her hands along the outside of her thighs. She licked her lips just once. Holson felt her shiver in arousal.

"Evan, I think we..." she started to say.

But then Williams just grunted, and she put her full mouth on her. The rush of heat and pleasure that shot through Holson was almost enough to make her faint. She gripped a handful of her lover's hair to help her with balance. Williams wrapped a strong arm around her legs, keeping her upright. She looked up just once more.

"I've got you," she whispered. "Relax."

Holson barely heard her. What happened next were wave after wave of pleasure washing over her, never enough to push her over the edge completely, but increasing in intensity until she had no idea if she was still standing, up, down, or even quite conscious.

"Nic?"

Williams was whispering into her ear suddenly, and Holson realised that they were on the bed. *How the hell did we get there?*

"Stay with me, okay? Almost there."

Holson fisted both hands into her hair, and she brought her down for another devastating kiss. She felt Williams try to pull back, but she did not allow her to. She needed to regain some level of control, some semblance of authority. She needed... She felt her lover smile into the kiss, and chuckle. The woman was both infuriating and delightful in her lovemaking. Attentive and focused. Insultingly good at it.

"Evan," Holson gasped. "Oh, God..."

The marine did not respond, and Nic bucked and shivered as her fingers circled on her skin, sliding in and teasing her so expertly, but never far enough. Once, twice, three times… Holson nearly howled in a mixture of bliss and frustration. *I can't take this anymore,* she thought. *I just can't…*

"Please," she panted. "Please, Evan…"

And then, Williams finally gave her what she wanted. She did the things that her partner so desperately needed her to do. All of them, and all at once. Nic screamed. She fought, she convulsed, she tried to drive herself through her lover's body. It was the best orgasm of her entire life, and it was the last thing she was able to think for a long, long time…

∞

She woke up what felt to her like days later, but a quick check of the clock indicated that it was only just after four in the morning. She was lying naked on the bed. Feeling warm, spent, almost liquid with relaxation.

"Evan?" she whispered.

Williams was fast asleep, minus her trousers and socks but still wearing her t-shirt and pants. Head pressing gently against Holson's shoulder, both arms locked tightly around her neck. Several strands of hair had fallen all over her face, almost completely obscuring her features. Holson bent over her, and gently kissed the side of her mouth. She tasted herself on her lips, and she blushed.

"Evan," she repeated. "Hey."

Finally, Williams opened her eyes. A slow, uncertain smile spread over her face.

"Hi," she murmured. "Nic…"

Voice husky from sleep, lips a little swollen. Gorgeous.

"Hi," Holson replied softly. "Hey, what's this?"

Williams' smile faltered.

"What?"

"Come on, get rid of it," her lover whispered, lifting one side of her t-shirt. "It's my turn now. Let me make love to you, Evan. We've got time."

Williams seemed to hesitate. She stared with a strange expression on her face. She looked away for a second, appearing a little stunned. And then she simply turned, swung her legs over the side, and stood up.

"Sorry," she mumbled. "I... I have to go."

Nic's smile instantly faded, and she grabbed her by the arm.

"Wait..." she murmured. "Evan, is something wrong?"

When Williams turned to look at her, she gasped at her sudden pallor. She spotted the sweat on her forehead, and the rapid pounding of her pulse. Her eyes, so bright only a few seconds before, had completely glazed over now, and her breathing appeared totally out of control. *Panic attack,* Nic realised, shocked.

"Okay, sit down," she instructed. "Please, sit down before you..."

"I'm fine, damn it," Williams raged in response.

She tore her arm from Holson's grip. She took a single step forward, exhaled, and collapsed.

CHAPTER FIFTEEN

"Hey there, Major Williams!" Ice greeted her a few days later, grinning at her through the wide screen of Williams' comms device. "Thank you for taking my call. It's great to see you again!"

"Hey, Ice," the L5 smiled in reply. "It's great to see you too, buddy. How's it going over there? You enjoying it?"

"Yes, it's awesome!" came the answer, enthusiastic as ever. "I love basic training, you know, I really do! Well, even though it's tough sometimes, but still…"

You ain't seen nothing yet, Williams thought, but she wisely kept her comments to herself. It was the first time they had spoken since Mars, and she was keen to catch up on the woman's news, not scare her to death. Before she could do so though, Ice spoke again.

"Hey, what happened to your eye?" she asked, curious.

Williams raised her fingers to her face. She felt the bruise there.

"Oh, that." She shrugged. "Training wound. Bloody sand bag decided to fight back."

It was all a lie, of course. The truth was that she had given herself a black eye from hitting her head on the corner of her desk that morning, when she fell. Still, it made Ice laugh.

"Oh yeah," she said, grinning. "I know the feeling."

It had been really hard, convincing Holson that the only reason she had fainted was because she had skipped dinner. Williams blamed it on the lace, too, saying it made her feel tired at times. She put it down to lack of sleep, and a punishing training schedule. Anything she could think of not to have to reveal the true reason for it. Not that Holson had been very receptive to her far-fetched explanations at first. When the marine had opened her eyes, three long and worrying minutes after she passed out, she had been fully dressed, back in uniform, and ready to call for help.

"No," Williams snapped. "I'm fine."

Holson clearly did not believe her.

"Evan, you just dropped!" she exclaimed. "I thought you were dead!"

She was frantic about the whole episode, and then she started to ask questions about a whole bunch of stuff that Williams did not want to think about, let alone discuss with anyone.

"I just need some food," she assured her. "Don't worry about it."

Holson had kept pushing and pushing, and it was all because she cared, Williams understood that. Unfortunately, she could not afford to let it happen. After a while, she realised that she had to put an end to the conversation, for both of their sakes. And so, she did. She could be really convincing when she wanted to be, charming really, and she was an excellent liar. This was one of those dubious talents she had acquired during her L5 training. Three days of resistance to interrogation practice had concluded that eventful part of her life, and it was not something that Williams would ever wish on anyone. It had been awful, and it had almost broken her. Saying the things that she needed to say in order to get Holson to hate her was harder. It almost achieved what seventy-two hours of exquisite physical and mental torture at the hands of her L5 instructors had not been able to do.

"Look," she told her eventually. "I'm tired, that's all. You should go."

Holson was on the edge of tears.

"Evan, please, don't shut me out. I care about you, and..."

"Well, I don't want you to care, all right? Sorry if I misled you."

Williams tasted vomit in her throat as she continued. She forced herself to maintain eye contact with her, as Holson's surprise and confusion finally turned to the deepest expression of hurt.

"I don't need anything from you, Nic. I just felt grateful for what you did for me, and so I wanted to be nice too. It was just sex, okay? Glad you enjoyed it, and now we're even. No need to make it into something it's not."

Struggling not to burst into tears in front of her, her lover fled the room without another word. Gritting her teeth, Williams took a cold shower, ran to the gym, and she punched that sand bag in rage and in frustration until she could not lift her arms anymore.

Over the following days, thankfully, there was plenty for her to do. Welcome some of her new team members on-board the ship, train with them, work with Ary, avoid nightmares, and practice her energy work. She was getting better at it with every passing day, and better at controlling her flow as well. But she could still not create any good shields.

"Why can I do everything else, and not that one simple thing?" she exclaimed one day, hissing in annoyance after her instructor managed to get through her defence once more.

"Two reasons," he said.

"I'm listening," she replied, massaging her shoulder.

Not only had he managed to get through, but he had also delivered a nice hit with it. Williams was irritated beyond belief at her own exceedingly poor performance.

"Okay," he stated. "One, you're a fighter. It's always all-out aggression with you. Protecting yourself does not come as easy as the urge to throw a good punch. Or an energy charge."

"That may be true, but it's just an excuse," Williams pointed out. "Ary is a fighter too, but she is excellent with both."

"Well, keep practicing."

"What's the second reason?" she insisted.

Her trainer shot her a long, lingering look in return.

"In order to create a really good protective shield around yourself," he said eventually, "you have to believe that you are worth protecting."

Williams stared at him in complete silence. She could find nothing whatsoever to reply to that. He was right. He had hit the nail on the head absolutely perfectly.

"When you really need to, in the field, I'm sure you'll manage it. So, don't worry about it too much, okay, Major? Now, come on," he added, squeezing her shoulder in sympathy. "Let's meditate."

She had done poorly at that too on this particular day, fighting tears all the way through the session instead of being able to relax into it. *Not worth it,* she kept thinking over and over. *I am not worth it.* The feelings of self-hatred and guilt that she had first encountered after her last mission instantly made a cruel and devastating return. She had failed to bring her team back. She had allowed her lover to die. Now, she had feelings for someone else. And she had hurt that woman, too, badly. Of course, she was not fucking worth it!

Her thoughts turned back to that first morning with Holson. She had realised the truth the second she had woken up, and spotted the tender, loving expression in her eyes. It was too much. She did not deserve it, and she could not allow herself to receive it, or even feel the same. Ever. Because in the next second, Nic's beautiful face had morphed into that of Maxx, screaming as acid burned through her skin, and her face melted away in a horror of mucus and blood. This was the real reason Williams had panicked, and fainted.

"... and I'm looking forward to that, too."

Ice was still on the comms link, still talking to her. *Focus, damn it!* Williams made a huge effort to shake the dark thoughts out of her head, and return her attention to the screen.

"Uh, sorry, I didn't catch that," she admitted.

Ice did not seem to mind.

"I said my squad is going to be included in this big exercise that's taking place next week on Sanar," she repeated. "Really can't wait for it."

Sanar was a relatively new planet where the Council had started holding training simulations in recent months. Williams had never been there, but she had heard a lot of good things about it. This, in commando speak, meant that the weather was challenging, the topography rugged and hard, and the sea always cold and stormy, no matter what the season. All in all, it was the perfect place for military training of any kind.

"Exercise Crimson Peak," she said, nodding. "You're involved with that? How come?"

"I'm going to be a casualty," Ice replied, sounding proud.

This made Williams chuckle in spite of everything.

"Oh, really?" She grinned. "So, is that how they use the nods these days? Painting them with fake blood, and using them as props?"

144

A 'nod' was a term applied to any marine undergoing basic training. Because they were made to feel so tired all the time they were there, on purpose, that they always nodded off at the first opportunity. Woe betide anyone who did so without permission. Ice herself looked suitably exhausted.

"I hope I get a chance to do a bit more than that," the young soldier declared.

Williams shook her head at her, smiling knowingly.

"I wouldn't if I were you," she remarked. "It's not often that you get a chance to lie down quietly and be still and comfy during trainings, so make the most of it. Anyway, my whole ship is going to be involved in this exercise too, so maybe I'll get a chance to see you."

"Great!"

"No promises. Keep working hard, okay?"

Ice grinned.

"Yes, Major!" she declared, and threw her a perfect salute.

Williams disconnected the link, and went out in search of her team. She had secured the people that she wanted in the end, and she was happy with that. O'Neil and Binks both aced their interview, and Ary let her keep them. Velez had been a given anyway. Now they were only waiting for the Cretian officer, nicknamed 'Red' on account of all the enemy blood she had spilled in her illustrious career, to join them from her previous assignment.

"Should be interesting," Ary had commented, looking pleased.

Williams found her new crew sitting together in the mess hall, eating burgers, downing energy drinks, and discussing the latest news about CP-EX, as the Crimson Peak exercise had already been dubbed. They made space for her, and pushed food and a drink in front of her as soon as she joined them.

"Thanks," she said.

"Hey, Major, you think that we're going to see action soon?" O'Neil enquired. "All this training is good, don't get me wrong, but I am itching to get my feet wet."

"In what?" Velez grunted.

As a seasoned operator, he knew that sometimes you had to be careful what you wished for.

"There is no way to know if or when a job is going to come up," Williams remarked as she took a bite of cheeseburger. "And the best way to deal with that…"

She intentionally kept her sentence open, to see if anyone would jump in.

"The best way to deal with that is to always be ready," Binks finished for her immediately.

"You got it," Velez approved.

Williams smiled.

"Yep," she said.

And just at that precise moment, her comms device came to life. It was Ary. She flicked it on, and set it on the table in front of everyone.

"We've got a seemingly unresponsive vessel drifting way too close to us, Major," the Cretian officer announced. "Be good if you could go take a look."

"No problem, Colonel," Williams replied.

"Be ready in the cargo bay in ten."

"Yes, ma'am."

The rest of the team were already up and running. *Good stuff,* Williams thought, as a shiver of excitement ran down her spine. It was her first shout since that disastrous mission. The first time that she would be back in armour at all. The first time with her new crew, and also… As she went barrelling around the corner, going down the list in her head, she ran straight into someone who had been running the other way. The woman bounced off the marine's solid frame, and landed on the floor with a sharp gasp. It was Holson. *Damn it,* Williams thought. She immediately offered a hand up to her, which the sergeant pointedly ignored.

"I'm on a call," Holson explained tersely. "Sorry, didn't see you there."

Meaning that she was running to the control room because a combat team was about to go out on a job. Williams suspected that it might be hers.

"The unidentified vessel?" she ventured.

"Yes."

So, Holson would be their comms liaison, Williams reflected. Well, it was both good and bad. Good, since she was great at her job, and bad because she would be in her earpiece the entire time.

"That's my call," she commented flatly, and turned to go.

"Evan, wait..."

Williams paused, and she met her gaze. She realised how much she missed hearing Holson call her by her first name. It always felt like a caress to her whenever the woman did. But hey, she had made her bed now. And so, she would lie in it, and stop being so pathetic. *No histrionics.* She clenched her teeth.

"Yes, Sergeant?"

The look that Holson gave her made her legs go weak. It was a mixture of angry and understanding, sad and tender, loving and hard all at the same time. Williams felt herself irresistibly drawn to her. Everything else around them suddenly seemed to simply melt away, and disappear, until all that she could see was her. The urge to stop fighting, to simply step forward into the woman's arms, and to lose herself into her embrace was so strong that it almost stopped her breathing. She nearly started to cry. She blinked, clenched her fists, and she had to take a sharp breath to steady her nerves.

"What?" she asked.

Holson shook her head, hesitating. Williams' heart was in her mouth. *Don't say anything,* she thought, a little desperately. *Please, don't say anything...* It had been her fault, going for something that she wanted so badly in spite of the consequences. Making love to Holson had reopened old wounds, it had made her feel again. Turns out her heart was still beating after all. Allowing the woman to see how much it really hurt was not an option.

"What is it, Sergeant?" she repeated impatiently.

She made her voice tough, emotionless, and cold. She knew she had hit the right tone when Holson simply shrugged, and looked right through her. There was no anger there. Certainly no tenderness or compassion in those quiet brown eyes now, either. It was all just blank, gone, and never coming back. *I am not worth it...*

"Nothing," Holson replied. "Good luck with the mission, Major."

She spotted both huge relief and immense sorrow flash through Williams' eyes at her words. She wanted to touch her hand. She wanted to kiss her, and beg her to be careful. She wanted to tell her that she loved her. Instead, she just nodded once, turned her back on her, and kept going.

CHAPTER SIXTEEN

"Still no response from them?" Williams enquired.

She and her team were standing at the entrance to the drifting ship, weapons drawn, ready to go in. Holson's voice in her ear was calm, and controlled when she responded to her. Williams herself was finding it a little difficult to concentrate on the task at hand.

"Negative, Major," the operator confirmed. "Still nothing. You are cleared to proceed."

ICU officers could board any vessel, at any time. They could do it anywhere in space, and under any circumstances. It could have been to search for illegal drugs, weapons, refugees, terrorism-related activity and the likes. Sometimes, they just did it for training purposes, and often they went ahead with a boarding simply because they sensed that something fishy was going on. Not receiving any response from an unmarked spaceship, no matter how many times they tried, or how many different frequencies they used definitely qualified as fishy. And today, it also provided a nice little warm-up intro for the L5 commando new team.

"Okay. Velez, you're on," Williams ordered.

She trusted her most experienced soldier after herself to enter the ship first, quickly followed by O'Neil, and Binks. Williams kept a position toward the rear, a little distance away from them but not dangerously so, just where she could keep eyes on everything. They found themselves in the cargo bay of a tiny transport ship where it would be difficult for any crew to hide for very long. Yet, it seemed empty for now.

"Stay alert," she advised.

They made their way alongside the corridor that led to the engine room.

"Want me to check in there, Major?" Velez asked.

"Yes. Binks, go with him. O'Neil? You're with me."

Williams and her escort carried on toward the bridge and crew quarters. They walked with their weapons at the ready, safety off, finger on the side of the trigger-guard.

"So quiet," O'Neil remarked.

Williams nodded.

"Yeah. Must be a reason for that."

The bridge was also empty. O'Neil sat in the pilot's seat, and he punched a bunch of coordinates into the control system. Rows of numbers flashed quickly in front of his eyes.

"Seems all is in working order," he remarked.

"Then why the hell are they drifting all over the place like that? Doesn't make any sense at all. Velez, you got an update for me?"

Williams heard him chuckle as he responded.

"Yep. Looks like they ran out of fuel, Major. Simple as that."

"But who's 'they'?" she replied, frowning.

Her pair went on to inspect the crew quarters next. All empty as well, except that when they walked past a door marked 'Maintenance', they heard a small noise. Williams immediately flattened herself against the wall on one side of it, with O'Neil on the other side.

"Velez, Binks. Get back up here," she murmured into her comms device. "Holson?"

"Go ahead, Major."

"We found something. We're going in."

"Roger that, Major Williams."

Williams looked at her partner, one hand poised to hit the push entry button.

"Ready?" she mouthed.

He nodded. Eyes fixed on the door, rifle well-balanced against his shoulder, finger on the trigger and ready to go. She hit the button, and the door slid open.

"Shit!" O'Neil exclaimed.

Williams' eyes widened at the sight. The room was large, well-lit, and full of kids. Pleiadian children, all in various states of panic and fear, sat on the floor chained to each other. There must have been something like twenty-five of them, ages ranging from six to ten years old. All dressed the same in what looked like white prison uniforms.

"Damn, it's a trafficker's ship," O'Neil said.

"Looks like it."

"I hate those motherfuckers."

"Me too."

Williams quickly relayed the information to Holson, then she shouldered her weapon, and squatted down next to one of the older kids.

"Do you understand me?" she asked.

He nodded, fear still shining in his eyes but not as much.

"Good." She smiled. "Don't worry, okay? We're here to help."

As she spoke, she fiddled with the chain that kept him bound. It was heavy, padlocked, but no match for her new synthetic hand. She snapped it in half, and quickly got him out of handcuffs. He surprised her by clinging to her with all the strength he could muster. His little body was shaking. And he was crying.

"Thank you," he murmured. "Thank you for coming to help us."

Williams kept her arm wrapped safely around him as she instructed her team to free the other children. A lot of them were crying now, with relief, obviously, and delayed shock as well. Some looked even younger than six, she realised. She was filled with disgust at the thought of anyone sick enough to practice this kind of trade. Unfortunately, species trafficking was flourishing in these parts, and kids especially were prized targets.

"Don't worry," she reassured the little boy who was still attached to her leg. "You're safe now. We won't let anything bad happen to you."

She got down to his level, and allowed him to sit on her lap. The boy said something to the other kids in his language that seemed to calm them down.

"Are you hungry?" Williams asked him.

His eyes widened, and he nodded vehemently. She flashed him a bright smile.

"Okay, then. We'll take you back to my ship now, and you can have something to eat there. Anything you want. And then, we'll get you back to your family. All right?"

Once again, he pressed himself against her armour, closed his eyes, and held tightly onto her neck. Williams managed to understand from what he said that they had been on a school trip to Earth when the transport craft they were travelling on was hijacked. The kids were taken. He missed his parents. She did not press him with any more questions, and just allowed him to rest against her for a moment longer.

"Holson," she announced over her comms, "we're getting the kids out now. Make sure we have a medical team on stand-by, and plenty of food for them. Like the good stuff, all right?"

"Understood, Major," Holson replied.

There was a smile in her voice, Williams could tell without a doubt. Rescuing kids in need, hey, that was everyone's favourite part of the job.

"O'Neil," she asked, "can you coordinate transport?"

"Sure thing, Boss."

It startled her a little, the way he used that word. Maxx always used to call her 'Boss' when they were in the field. Sometimes, she did it after hours too, but in a different way. Williams shook her head to chase the memories away. She was pleased when she was able to do it quickly.

"Velez," she enquired. "Am I right in thinking that all three emergency escape pods were still there in the cargo bay when we arrived?"

"100%," he replied.

"Then where the hell is the crew?" she whispered.

"You think hiding someplace?"

"Well. Don't you?"

His face grew hard. He nodded, watching O'Neil and Binks as they helped the little kids file out of the room, quickly, and mostly quietly. Williams was reluctant to send one of her team back with them. The craft would fly itself, she thought, and Holson would make sure that good people were at the other end to welcome the Pleiadians on board.

"Guys," she murmured when O'Neil and Binks walked past her. "I want you to get the children loaded, and then come back here. Both of you, okay?"

Binks nodded, looking serious. So did O'Neil. No one spoke, which let Williams know they were thinking the exact same thing that she was. They were not alone here. And they were being watched.

"Holson," she said.

"Yes, Major Williams?"

"We'll be coming back after the kids."

"Roger that, Major. Is the ship empty then?"

"Yes, seems totally empty," Williams said to whoever else may have been listening. "The crew probably abandoned it when they saw us coming."

As she spoke, something in her mind was becoming clearer. She felt a little separate from her own body all of a sudden. *It's the lace,* she thought. The neural lace was doing something inside her brain. Accepting the impulse, Williams took a deep breath, and she went still. Her trainer had started to teach her the art of remote viewing recently. The idea that her mind could detach from her physical body, and go roaming somewhere to get her the information she wanted was so alien to her that she had struggled with the practice at first. Now, though, it all started to make sense to her. She was still conscious, and yet a part of her mind was flying through the ship. So fast it would have made her dizzy if she had stopped to think about it. But she relaxed, kept breathing nice and slow, and she allowed the viewing to take place. When she felt it, she grabbed onto Velez's arm.

"What?"

Looking up, she stared at the panels in the ceiling above her head. She raised her eyebrows. *What a great hiding place.* He followed her gaze, and his eyes narrowed. Looking back to her, he nodded his assent. Williams climbed on top of a table, stretched herself out, and she pushed her fingers over the top of one of the panels. It seemed solid. She carried on with her slow exploration, letting her fingers drift all over it, looking for something... *There.* There was a spot there that showed a little weakness. She put more weight onto it, until a small space appeared in between this panel and the one next to it. She reached for her sidearm, and glanced back toward Velez once.

"Okay," she murmured.

He was ready. And so was she. She used her right synthetic arm to push hard over the panel. In the very next second, and without any warning, the entire section collapsed on top of her, pushed down by a large number of tall, grey, screeching creatures.

"Contact!" Williams had time to yell, before she fell off the table, and onto the floor.

She had no idea what the entity that landed on top of her was. It was an alien for sure, the praying mantis type. She had never seen that particular kind before, but if it was like all the others… There, she was not disappointed. The thing pinned her down underneath its body, and a metal rod appeared from in between its mandibles. Skewered Marine for breakfast… *Oh no, you don't,* Williams thought. She used a strong pulse of energy to send the alien flying backward. She was impressed. It seemed to have come from nowhere, simply rising out of her before she could even think about it. *Good.* She raised her weapon, and pulverised the creature before it could come at her again. Then, more of them started to leap from the ceiling.

"O'Neil, Binks, I need you here now!" Williams shouted into her comms.

She and Velez got busy blasting a bunch of violent aliens into oblivion, but several of them managed to slip through the net. And they kept on coming.

"Major Williams, do you need backup?"

Holson was still in complete control. Not for the first time, Williams was reminded of how good the operator was at what she did. There was something extremely reassuring about Holson being so collected, and so focused during a fight. It made her want to go harder at it. She gathered all her strength.

"Negative," she replied. "We've got…"

She suddenly heard gunshots in the main corridor, and she paused.

"O'Neil? Binks? Talk to me, guys."

"We found more crew," O'Neil responded.

He was breathing hard, and yet sounding like he was having a good time.

"They're pissed off we're here," he added. "Hey, good shot, Binks!"

Those things were jumping out of the ceiling endlessly, just like balls in a dispenser at the baseball practice ground. Williams and Velez backed up slowly toward the door. They were still managing to keep most of them at bay it seemed, at least for now. The two marines finally made it back out into the corridor, and she slammed her fist over the door lock. One alien's arm, or whatever else it may have been, got cut in half by the heavy door, and landed at her feet. It instantly attached itself to her ankle, and started to crawl up her leg. She tried to pull it off without much success, and the thing was halfway up her thigh in almost no time at all, squeezing hard. She started to feel her leg go numb.

"Damn it, Velez!" she yelled. "Get it off me!"

He grabbed his knife, and sliced the thing to pieces. They dropped to the floor, but it took a while for them to stop twitching. Velez barked out a laugh, and stomped the remains under his boot.

"Stay," he growled.

Williams got her racing heart under control.

"Thanks."

She did not mind the fighting, but that thing crawling up her leg had been freaky.

"A little help?" Binks suddenly enquired.

"Be right there," Williams replied.

With one last look at the door, which was being pounded from the other side by a bunch of angry mantis, she and Velez ran through the ship, and they burst into the cargo bay to find Binks and O'Neil firing all they had at a wall of the same creatures.

"They just keep on coming," O'Neil announced. "Where the fuck do they all fit in?"

"Every time I kill one, another one seems to take its place," Binks remarked.

She was hunched over behind a cargo crate, sniper rifle balanced expertly on it. She was taking shot after shot, and never missing once.

"Having fun, Binks?" Williams asked her.

"It's the absolute best," the talented shooter confessed, grinning broadly. "But I'm going to run out of ammo pretty soon at this rate, Major…"

"Roger that," Williams acknowledged. "Holson, where's my transport craft?"

"Docking for you as we speak, Major."

Williams shot a quick look out of the airlock, and saw it indeed attaching itself to the mantis ship's mainframe. The door opened. It was directly behind them. She glanced at her team, busy firing at the enemy, and quickly assessed the distance between where they were standing and the safe haven of their craft. Then, she made her decision.

"O'Neil, Velez," she ordered. "Get on board."

Without their firepower output, the number of creatures coming at them instantly seemed to double.

"Binks. You're next, go."

The sniper spared a single glance at her. As far as she was concerned, Williams' order made zero sense. If she left her now, the marine was not going to be able to keep those things at bay.

But questioning orders was not Binks' style, and so she simply shouldered her weapon, and sprinted past her superior officer toward their craft.

"What's the boss doing over there?" O'Neil enquired, as Binks jumped on board, and the L5 remained standing at the other end.

Velez shook his head.

"No idea," he muttered darkly. "But I don't like it."

Then, Williams dropped her weapon.

"WHAT?" Binks shouted.

In the very next instant, a buzzing swarm of disgusting creatures fell on top of her... and instantly bounced off of an invisible barrier.

"Ha!" O'Neil exclaimed, grinning excitedly. "She's got a shield. No worries. She knows what she's doing."

They all observed her, as she stood behind the protective energy field for a few seconds, absorbing the vibrations from the assault as creature after creature tried to break through it. Unfortunately for her, and pretty quickly too, several large cracks started to appear. The entire shielding mechanism began to crumble.

"Major Williams!" Velez shouted in alarm.

The shield collapsed, and in the next instant, Williams disappeared from view.

"Oh, fuck..." Binks murmured.

But then she watched, breathing hard with relief, as a wave of energy blasted all of the aliens up into the air, away from Williams, and across the cargo bay. They all screamed in unison. It was a horrible, chilling sound. But they appeared to pause for a split second, and it gave Williams just enough time to run to the craft, and jump onboard.

"I'm in!" she shouted. "Go!"

O'Neil hit the door switch, and it slammed shut behind her. A bunch of writhing creatures crashed against the side of the window, and started pounding on the frame. The vibrations from that were pretty intense. Those things seemed to be getting stronger all the time.

"Let's go!" Williams ordered. "Velez, get us out of here."

Not needing to be told twice, the man immediately fired up his engines, and within seconds, they had left the mantis ship way behind. Williams went to lean against the side of the cockpit wall, catching her breath and brushing bits of alien blood off her armour.

"What was that all about, Boss?" the old marine enquired, taking his eyes off his control panel long enough to shoot her a dark look.

He sounded a little outraged. She shrugged.

"Just a test."

He did not look happy about it. Neither was she.

"Sergeant Holson," she called. "Do you read?"

"Affirmative, Major Williams."

"I want you to blast that ship," she ordered. "Just blow it up. There is nothing in it that we want."

CHAPTER SEVENTEEN

During their evening meal that night, which Williams shared with her troops in the mess hall, Velez took great pleasure in recounting one particular, and rather unusual aspect of the day's mission.

"Tell you what, guys, that thing was crawling up the boss's leg like, like…"

She threw him a wry smile.

"Like what?" she challenged. "Go on, spit it out."

"Well, like it knew where it was going."

"And where do you suppose that would be?"

Velez looked embarrassed, but young O'Neil did not have the same problem.

"Where it would do the most good, Major," he replied, and made a lewd gesture at the same time.

Binks shivered at the thought.

"Shit, you're disgusting," she winced. "What were those things, anyway?"

"Not really sure," Velez replied, "but I'm glad they didn't have weapons."

"You think they didn't?" Williams countered. "When that one landed on me, it produced a metal rod about eight inches long. Pointed, and sharp too. You get one of those through the neck, that's going to hurt, believe me. I think they…"

She stopped when she spotted the amused look Velez and O'Neil exchanged, and the way they suddenly both turned crimson as they tried not to burst into laughter. Binks clearly caught on to what was going on as well, because she rolled her eyes, and delivered a hard punch to Velez's chest, who was the closest to her.

"Ouch," he complained.

"You guys are hopeless," she declared.

"Oh, come on, Jo. You've never watched alien porn?"

"Fuck off, O'Neil."

"You mean really? You never?"

Binks suddenly appeared a little hesitant, but interested. Williams decided it was time for her to call it a night. The need to be alone again was making itself known, especially when the conversation turned to alien porn, and it would be good for these three to bond without her.

"I'm going to the gym," she announced. "You're on your own time until 05:59 tomorrow morning. Prep for Crimson Peak starts at 06:00 in the war room. Everybody got that?"

They all nodded, smiling.

"Yes, Boss."

"Got it, ma'am."

"Wouldn't miss it."

"By the way," she added, just before she left. "Good job today. All of you."

She made her way to the pool instead of the gym, feeling in the end that today's efforts on that mantis ship had left her simply wanting to spend some time doing lengths. Swimming on her own like that, just staring at the black line underneath her as she went, was something that she had always loved doing. Getting into a nice rhythm, and just repeating the same movement over and over was also useful meditation practice.

She had done well today, and she knew it. When some people needed others to appraise their performance, and tell them if and when they needed to improve, Williams was pretty self-sufficient at it. She always knew when she performed adequately, above average, or below par. Today, she had done everything right. With her crew, and with the kids. She had made good use of her neural lace as well, and although she was disappointed with the result of her shield, she was sure that she would be able to improve on it. And it had been a worthwhile test anyway. The remote viewing thing had been the icing on the cake.

Williams got to the end of her lane, and flipped over. She landed her feet firmly on the pool wall, and pushed off. She kept her hands locked out in front of her, arms extended straight, legs together. She dolphin-kicked the entire length under water, turned at the other end, and did it again. Then, she resumed her slow front crawl, breathing every four strokes, nice and controlled. She kept it going, lap after lap, feeling her body respond in a way it had not done in a long time. No surprise there, of course. The synthetic graft of a new arm and shoulder, although not considered a major surgical intervention these days, was serious business all the same. And then, over the following months, her body had been working overtime to absorb the changes, and merge with the synthetic implants. The lace as well, just a microscopic mesh of electrodes at first, had to be assimilated into her brain. Despite what the surgeons and the specialists had to say about this particular process, Williams was convinced that it did not happen without a certain number of unwanted side-effects.

Still, the more she used it, the more her initial fears about the technology abated. The odds that the AI part of her brain might one day overcome her biological processes, and assume total control of her entire personality seemed more like a crazy fantasy scenario to her now than a real possibility. She was finding herself again, reconnecting with more of who she was with every passing day.

Williams ducked under water again, and executed another perfect turn. She started down another length, and suddenly thought about Holson. Immediately, she tensed, missed her timing, and swallowed a big mouthful of water. *Damn it!* She was choking now, and anger was not far off. She recovered quickly, but her peace of mind had been shattered. Another couple of untidy laps later, she finally decided to call it quits. She climbed out of the pool, shook the water out of her hair, and went to shower. *Never mind,* she thought. It was time to get back to work, anyway.

The restless officer wandered down to the war room, and spent some time familiarising herself with every detail of the upcoming exercise. She checked out duty assignments for everyone onboard the ship, and when it came to the control room specialists, she realised that Holson was listed as team leader. So, she was taking part as well... The only difference for her was that she would be inside a dark room, surrounded by radar, computers and electronics, whilst Williams and her team would most likely spend their entire time out on the ground, freezing cold or melting hot, depending on what the weather had in store for them on Sanar at this time of year. But still, Holson would be there. Perhaps they would bump into each other at some point. And maybe, they...

"Stop screwing with yourself," Williams muttered out loud, feeling irritated.

She rubbed her fingers over her forehead, and for the second time that evening found it incredibly difficult to concentrate on what she was doing. It was ironic, she reflected, how she could hold several thousand dollars' worth of neural lace implants inside her head, and yet struggle so much to control her emotional thoughts. *Ironic, but good,* she decided. AI did not have feelings. And even though she could have done without those particular ones, it was still better than the alternative. She finished reading the brief on the CP-EX, and decided that a hot cup of coffee and possibly even a piece of cake before bed were in order. The mess hall was empty, save for the kitchen staff. She got herself an espresso from the machine, and grabbed a piece of chocolate cake off the counter.

"Freshly made, Major," the cheery kitchen assistant informed her. "Want some custard to go with it?"

"Sure. Hey, you got any ice cream?"

"What flavour would you like?"

"How about rum and raisin?"

He laughed.

"Yeah, nice."

He dropped a large scoop of it onto her plate, and drizzled crushed almonds and golden syrup all over the lot. Going over the top, but hey. Williams had a sweet tooth, and this looked just like what she needed right now.

"Here you are, Major," he announced, looking proud of his creation. "What do you think?"

She stared at the plate with a genuinely dreamy look in her eyes.

"I think I'm in love," she declared.

"Lovely. And thanks, but I'm taken."

She snorted in amusement.

"I meant with the food."

He pressed both hands over his chest, and pretended to be fatally wounded. She shook her head at his antics. Could not help but laugh at them, though.

"Appreciate the extras," she thanked him.

"Anytime, Major," he saluted.

She found a seat with her back to the wall and a good view of the rest of the mess hall, including both regular and emergency exits. It was force of habit, nothing less. She liked to be able to feel safe when she ate, and see what was coming. Although given the choice, she probably would have preferred not to see the next person who walked in, because it was none other than Sergeant Holson herself. Williams swore under her breath. She looked down, and immediately hunched her shoulders, as if it would make her invisible. She should have known. Everywhere that she turned today, there Holson seemed to be. *Should have gone straight back to my cabin,* she thought. *Should have...*

"Hi."

Williams swallowed a mouthful of cake, and glanced up reluctantly. Holson looked tired, she noticed. This morning, she had appeared fine. Angry, disappointed, but fine. Now, she simply looked sad, and vulnerable. Williams felt the sudden urge to get up, and pull her into her arms. She gripped her plate a little harder, and tightened her fingers around her dessert spoon.

"Sergeant Holson," she nodded.

She did not offer a single other word of acknowledgment, and she quickly returned her attention to her food. Pretended as if she were not dying to talk to the woman, and find out how she was. She certainly did not feel like eating anymore, but she forced herself to make it look like she did anyway.

"Major," Holson started, "I just wanted to let you know that the kids from the trafficker ship are on their way back to Earth, where their parents are waiting for them even as we speak."

"Great. Thank you."

Williams felt genuine relief and immense satisfaction at the thought of her little Pleiadian friend, home safe with his family once more.

"One of the kids asked me to give you this."

Holson slid a piece of paper across the table. She stayed to watch what would happen, as Williams glanced at it once, apparently uninterested, but then seemed to suddenly change her mind when she spotted what it was. She let go of her spoon, and picked up the single page. Leaning back against her chair, she stared at it in complete silence for several long seconds.

It was a typical kid's drawing. Pleiadian, Human, Cretian, no matter who they were, kids always tended to draw in the same sort of way when they were little. Williams loved children, although not many people knew that about her, or would even have guessed. In this particular picture, stars and spaceships had been painstakingly drawn up in thick white crayon against a background of heavy black. At the bottom of the page, there was a figure standing there, equipped with four straight black sticks in lieu of her arms and legs, along with a cloud of bushy yellow around what was supposed to be the head. The soldier was in black and red armour. An almost imperceptible smile floated over Williams' lips.

"He told me you were nice to him," Holson said.

This kid was good, Williams thought. He had captured the markings on her armour really well, and even attempted to reproduce the design of the ICU patch on her chest. It was nicely done. Next to the tall figure stood a much smaller one. Obviously, a Pleiadian. Obviously, a child. Beaming a huge smile up at the marine standing next to him. The two were holding hands. They looked happy.

"He said that you gave him a big hug, and made him feel safe."

Williams examined the symbols scribbled underneath the two figures. She deciphered them easily. In Pleiadian, there was an expression that combined both *'Thank You'*, and *'I Love You'*. It was gratefulness and appreciation together, and that was what the child had written for her. The L5 swallowed hard. She exhaled slowly, and still did not utter a single word. But Holson spotted colour spreading fast over her cheeks, and the soft glistening of tears on her eyelashes. Something was happening. Definitely something significant, a rush of powerful emotions, and painful ones by the look of it. She was dying to put her arms around the woman, and comfort her, but something told her that such a gesture would be far from welcome.

"He wasn't scared after that," she murmured. "Ev…"

But before she could finish saying her name, Williams suddenly dropped the drawing on the table. She blinked hard a couple of times, and then stood up abruptly.

"Glad we could do some good," she replied. "Was there anything else?"

Now, she looked irritated, Holson realised; almost angry, and she was startled by the sudden change. Why Williams was feeling that way was the million-dollar question.

"There's nothing else, Major," she replied. "I just wanted to tell you. And I… Wait," she cried, as the marine started to walk away, even before she had finished speaking.

"What is it, Sergeant?"

She sounded a little too loud, clearly exasperated. Holson picked up the drawing from the table. She made as if to hand it to her, but Williams did not move.

"Don't you… Don't you want this?"

She looked stunned, and it made Williams want to punch something.

"Why would I?" she snarled.

She chuckled, except that her tone was glacial, and totally devoid of any humour. She had grown a little pale, and her voice sounded terribly hollow. Holson felt tears welling up in her own eyes in response.

"Why?" Williams repeated, her tone bitter. "So I can pin it to the wall above my bed? Stare at it in the morning, and feel good about myself?"

Holson stared at her, speechless. There was venom in those words, and seething anger underneath as well. Williams stood there for a second longer, as if she expected an answer. When she realised that none was forthcoming, she simply shook her head, made a slashing gesture that seemed to signify, *'Just let it go, will you?'*, and disappeared down the hallway.

CHAPTER EIGHTEEN

Two days later, Holson found herself on a transport craft bound for Saran. Exercise Crimson Peak was about to begin, and her team were being dispatched ahead of some of the combat troops in order to help with the setup. Normally, she enjoyed taking part in these things. As a tactician analyst and control room operator, it was not often that she got to travel anywhere off the ship, and so, training exercises were always good for a change in the routine. Especially since she would get to lead her own team this time. If she did well, maybe she would get promoted. This meant more money, more interesting jobs, better R&R... It was win-win all the way.

But despite all this, her thoughts kept returning to Evan often. Because that was how she thought of Major Williams now. She had become Evan, the woman who had saved her life that day on Mars. Okay, probably caused her to need to be saved in the first place, but still... Evan, who always closed her eyes, and smiled so sweetly when she smelled her favourite flowers. Evan, who had made love to her so passionately. The commando marine had become the lover who held Nic safely and reassuringly in her arms while she slept, and she had done so more than once... She was gentle, attentive. Caring, and protective. But now, she also seemed so angry with her. The more Holson thought about it, the less it made sense to her. There had to be something else, and a deeper problem.

After their conversation in the mess hall that night, which she suspected had only been one word away from turning into a full-blown argument, Williams had gone into hiding it seemed. In actual fact, she had been splitting her time between the war room and the gym, always choosing odd hours for her workouts, hoping it would make it harder to bump into Holson. The strategy had proved effective. And the sergeant had felt it would be wrong, somehow, to just go and knock on her door. She had thought it may be too soon, and that perhaps Evan needed some time on her own to cool off. Now, she regretted not doing it when she had the chance. It was blindingly obvious to her that they needed to talk, and clear the air. Holson resolved to do that at the first opportunity, as soon as this exercise was over and done with, and whether the marine wanted her to or not.

"Hey. What was that?"

As she sat in the back, frowning over the paperwork she was supposed to memorise, and could not even see, it was this off-hand comment from one of her colleagues that brought her back to reality.

"What?" she asked, curious.

She glanced out of the small window on the side. They had entered the Saran atmosphere now, and they were flying through a bunch of clouds. From time to time, she could glimpse long stretches of blue skies in between them, and a vast expense of light-brown desert underneath. Thankfully, there had been none of the turbulence that Nic hated so much.

"Uh… Nothing. Just thought I saw something outside…"

In the next second, there was a loud boom followed by a massive tremor crashing through the craft. Like some giant hand had seized hold of it, and was shaking it about. Nic's paperwork flew off her lap across the aisle.

"Shit," she mumbled.

Of course, since the craft was full of highly trained and experienced soldiers, everybody remained calm, although some worried glances were exchanged. And only a couple of seconds after this, Holson suddenly heard the pilot sending a series of rapid maydays over his comms. What was happening? Had they been hit by something?

"Mayday, mayday, we are going down."

Down? she thought, horrified.

"Mayday, mayday…"

"It's a Scythian fighter!" somebody suddenly yelled. "Fuck, the Scythians are here!"

"What? We got shot?"

"We're being attacked by a Scythian jet!"

Holson's heart jumped out of her chest at those words. Scythian? She felt confused. This was Saran. A friendly planet. A Council station. It was safe! There could not be no Scythian forces here… The guy who was sat next to her started to panic. He grabbed her arm, and squeezed it so hard it hurt.

"Let go!" Holson exclaimed, and she pushed him off her.

"We're going to get slaughtered!" he shouted.

"No, we won't."

She flashed him a quick, reassuring smile, and then she stood up, and started walking toward the cockpit. Not sure why, really, but she could not just remain in her seat like this, and wait for whatever was coming next. Just then, another violent hit, worse than any turbulence she had ever encountered before in her life, threw her to the floor. A high-pitched noise sounded at the back. Now, some people were screaming in fear. Holson heard her friend and colleague, Janet Burton, a talented analyst, muttering prayers under her breath. She was not one for prayers herself, and it was Evan that she thought of, as panic rose inside her chest. What would Evan do in a situation like this? She heard her voice inside her head. She saw her smile that gorgeous smile of hers. *It's okay, Nic...*

But it was not, far from it. Holson heard the pilot yell out a set of coordinates over the net. The entire frame of the aircraft vibrated, threatening to disintegrate at any second. Smoke started to filter through the cabin, and she spotted flames outside the window. *I have to do something... Anything!* But before she could even stand up, she felt the craft suddenly become almost weightless, and then start to plummet. *We're going to crash.* She was puzzled. Disappointed. And yes, scared out of her mind too.

I don't want to die!

During the next smoky, disorienting seconds, Holson had ample time to wonder what it would be like to lose her life. Thankfully, everything else happened very quickly. When they hit the ground, she did not feel a single thing.

∞

Williams and her crew were due to fly in at midnight, get dropped thirty miles away from the main base, and make their way to it across difficult terrain. Further combat orders would await them at base. It was just a gentle warm-up for such an elite group of marines, and she was looking forward to it. She was craving action, and something to keep her mind engaged. That evening, she decided that it might be wise to take a nap in preparation, and for once, she managed to slip quickly and easily into a slumber. She awoke with a start a couple of hours later. Not sure what had caused it. It was all silent and still in the cabin, and she had not been dreaming. She thought she had heard a scream. With a sigh, she discounted it, and allowed her head to fall back onto the pillow. Maybe she could get another hour or so... But the sudden, urgent pounding on her door quickly ruined that idea. Williams checked her screen, and spotted Ary standing outside her door. She rolled off the bed and rushed to open it, still just wearing her briefs and a t-shirt, barefoot, heart beating fast.

"Colonel?" she asked.

Rarely had she seen such a furious look on the Cretian's face. The markings on her head appeared darker, which the L5 recognised as a sign of stress. Not something that she was used to witnessing very often in Ary. Never, in fact.

"Get your team, Major," the colonel barked. "Then meet me in the war room."

She was gone before Williams could ask her any questions. Getting dressed took her less than two seconds, and then she ran to the level below, and the crew quarters to collect her people. The Cretian soldier nicknamed Red had made it to the ship only a few hours previously, after travelling all day to get there. She had obviously been fast asleep when her new boss knocked on her door.

"Sorry, gotta go."

Red was good at getting dressed quickly too, Williams noticed.

"This part of CP-EX?" O'Neil enquired, looking suspicious.

"No," she replied as they ran.

He had asked a good question. It would not be the first time they were given one scenario for an exercise, and then thrown into a completely different situation. Nothing like a bit of confusion thrown in, unknown parameters, and a good dose of extra stress to spice things up. But Williams had seen the markings on Ary's head.

"Trust me," she assured him, "this one is for real."

They all burst into the war room to find Ary staring intently at some wreckage on a screen. Williams narrowed her eyes at it. It was a transport craft of some sort. All broken up into a couple of pieces, half buried in sand. Smoke was still rising from the metal frame. *So, this is recent,* she reflected.

"Exercise Crimson Peak is cancelled," Ary blurted out as she turned to face them. "The Scythians have launched an attack on Saran. We have Council casualties at the main base. This," she added, pointing at the screen, "is one of ours."

Williams swallowed hard. *Ours,* she thought. People she would know. People who were stationed on board the ship with her. A sudden image of Holson flashed through her head. She shivered.

"What we know so far is this," Ary continued. "Three soldiers blew themselves up inside three different areas of the main base. Another one tried to do the same thing inside the mess hall. Fortunately, a couple of off-duty pilots noticed him acting suspiciously, and they brought him down before he could detonate his charge."

"Terrorists, ma'am?" Binks enquired.

"Yes. They were Scythian infiltrators, all of them. At the same time that this happened, and capitalising on the confusion that followed, a couple of Scythian jets invaded our air space, and shot down one of our crafts."

Velez and O'Neil uttered a murderous grunt at the news.

"We have reports of more enemy activity in the mountains near our permanent training area, and also on the island where we hold our amphibious tactical ops. Reinforcements have been despatched from Earth. Now, I'll give you an update on the casualties," Ary said.

Her voice was tight as she delivered the next set of bad news.

"A whole batch of new recruits were supposed to take part in the exercise, along with some commando hopefuls going through basic training. All 150 of them were assembled inside the sports hall for a welcome brief when the first guy hit."

Ice, Williams thought. *Fuck.* She clenched her teeth, but she remained silent.

"Current reports indicate 21 killed, 63 injured, 12 missing."

Williams knew what *'missing'* meant in the case of a bombing like this. It was a way of saying that those soldiers were dead too, but in so many tiny pieces that they could not be identified right away.

"Those bombs were powerful," Ary reflected, her eyes on her. "They were detonated at the right time, and in the exact best place to cause maximum damage."

Next, a series of pictures flashed up on the screen. All close-ups, ten of them in total. The smiling faces of people the L5 officer knew quite well. Soldiers for the most part, but also a couple of technicians, two pilots...

"These guys were on the craft that got shot down."

And Nicole Holson. Williams suddenly remembered the scream that she thought she had heard just before waking up. *Nic,* she thought wildly. *Jesus.*

For the first time since the briefing started, Ary noticed, the commando soldier had started to show some external signs of stress herself. She spotted the way her eyes suddenly widened, and how she blinked a couple of times when she looked at the screen. The distraught look that flashed across her face, and the drop of sweat that rolled down the side of her temple. The rest of the team looked on, not happy of course, but they were too new to the ship to have met or even made friends with many of those guys. Not so for her, Ary reflected. And the L5 was breathing hard.

"Major Williams," she snapped.

Despite her obvious emotion, the marine did not miss a beat.

"Yes, Colonel," she replied.

Her voice was strong. She sounded in complete control. Ary kept her attention focused on her, but she relaxed a fraction.

"You and your team are being sent down to support our crews from Earth. I want…"

No one but Williams could dream of interrupting Ary when she was in the middle of delivering marching orders, and hope to get away with it.

"What about survivors?" she blurted out now, her eyes still fixed on the screen. "Have we sent a craft over there? Heard anything yet? What is being done to get these people out?"

Ary would allow her this one little act of rebellion.

"Obviously, we have done so, Major," she replied. "An AI drone was sent over immediately to investigate."

She saw fury in Williams' eyes at the mention of an AI being used, but she did not give her a chance to voice her opinion about it.

"I was informed that there were no survivors. Of course, a team will be sent out there to retrieve the bodies as soon as it is feasible to do so. And safe. Believe me, I am as anxious as you are to recover our people."

Like hell, you are, Williams thought, fuming.

"*You,*" Ary repeated, emphasizing the word as if to dare her to cut in again, "are being sent to the mountains with your team to assist with whatever is needed over there. Is that understood?"

"Understood, Colonel. May I just make a suggestion?"

Ary stared daggers into her.

"Not really," she replied, "but let's hear it anyway."

Williams glanced at the screen again.

"Before we head to the mountains," she said, "we could go check out the transport craft, ma'am. It wouldn't take us long. Just to be absolutely sure that everyone is…"

"No," Ary said. "We are sure, Major. Everyone on board was killed. I'm sorry. It's hard for me too. But I have my orders, and I have just given yours to you. I expect you to follow them to the letter. Are we clear on that, Major Williams?"

Williams was too clever to argue a direct order, especially at times like this, and particularly in front of her team. She stood at attention, and she met Ary's gaze.

"Clear, Colonel," she said.

"Team, dismissed."

Ary looked surprised, Williams noticed, as she watched her leave the room with her crew. Surprised, but pleased. *Good,* she decided. She needed her relaxed, trusting, and off her back for a goddamn minute.

"Guys," she instructed, "you can run back to get what you need from your quarters. Then straight to the armoury to suit up, get your gear, and head planet-side. Velez?"

"Boss?"

"Pilot duties."

"Yes, ma'am."

Whilst everyone ran back to their digs, Williams herself paid a quick visit to the control room. She was glad to find it empty, and she made sure that no else realised that she had been there. It was just too bad, she thought a little ruefully, that she was about to break Ary's rules all over again, and ruin her happiness. But she was not going to allow anything, or anyone, whether it was her, direct orders, or a bunch of Scythian soldiers intent on mayhem and destruction, to stand in the way of what she needed to do this time.

CHAPTER NINETEEN

At first, it was so hot in the desert that she found it difficult to breathe. But then, when night came, it turned cold. So cold that she worried it might kill her.

Control room operator Sergeant Nic Holson regained consciousness in the middle of a smoking wreck, probably not too long after the final impact. Trembling still, from shock, and fear, she slowly got up onto her knees. She raised a hand to her face when she felt something warm dripping down her nose, and realised that it was blood. She searched for the wound, and discovered a massive cut on the top of her head. It hurt when she touched it. It felt sticky. She had a really bad headache, but her vision was clear. Hopefully, no concussion. She checked the rest of her body. No broken bones. She was alive, and she could move.

Nic stood up, and she turned to inspect the rest of the craft. It had broken up in two on impact, and the back end of it was almost unrecognisable. Just a bunch of twisted metal, bits and pieces of seats and fuselage here and there... And bodies. She spotted bodies in there too, all blackened up and charred. She forced herself to look closer, to make sure that none of them were still alive. Some of them she recognised. There was Sam, a soldier who loved to read philosophy books in his spare time. Terry, one of her tactician colleagues who had just gotten engaged to his girlfriend. And the guy who had grabbed her arm so roughly earlier, whose name tag read Joe Quirk. Nic suddenly realised something. Had she not stood up, and made her way toward the cockpit when the whole thing started, she would be amongst them by now. It brought tears to her eyes.

"I'm sorry, guys. I am so sorry..."

Next, she checked the rest of the craft. Only four people were at the front, including the pilot. A thick piece of glass from the cockpit window had lodged itself into the side of his throat, severing his carotid artery. She winced at the sight. He would have bled to death in seconds if the shock of impact did not get him first. Maybe the smoke had killed the two other people on the front seats. Nic had been lying on the floor. She remembered finding it really hard to breathe, but perhaps being so low had actually saved her. And Janet...

"Oh, my God," Nic exclaimed, as her eyes fell on her, and she noticed that her chest was still moving. "Janet? Janet, can you hear me?"

The woman was alive. Barely breathing, but alive. Nic frantically looked around for some water to give her. She found a full bottle under one of the seats, and she used some of it to gently dab over her friend's face. She pressed some on her lips, and into her mouth.

"Janet," she called, "open your eyes. Come on, you can do it."

But there was no response from her, and the woman showed no signs of stirring. Nic decided to save some of that precious water for later. She stood up, staying close to her unconscious friend, and she cast a worried glance all around her. Desert on one side, but in the other direction, and not very far at all, she could see trees, and hills in the background. Under normal circumstances, she would have remained with the craft, made herself and her wounded mate as comfortable as possible, and waited for a rescue team to reach them. *But will there be any rescue here today?* she wondered. Was it not strange that no craft had come to help them already? And when someone did come, would it be friend, or enemy? She stood there for a little while longer, frowning, thinking hard. Could she carry Janet all the way to the tree line in this heat? Well, if it was a matter of survival, yes, she thought she could. And she damn well would do it.

"Janet, if you can hear, don't worry. We are going to make it through this," she encouraged.

Resolutely, Nic went back inside the craft to gather a few things she might need. She found someone's rucksack, filled with manuals and notebooks but also more water, a couple of energy bars, and a jacket. She got rid of the paperwork, kept all the rest, and paused next to her colleague again. The woman was deathly pale, her breathing just a faint rattle in her chest. Nic rested a hand over her forehead, and she gently stroked her hair.

"It's all right, Jan," she murmured. "You're going to be okay."

Next, she squeezed herself into the cockpit area, and tried every which way she knew to activate the comms systems. But it, too, was dead. She found more food, and one more bottle of water. She allowed herself the luxury of several deep swallows from one of the ones she had, and even though she was far from hungry, she ate one of the energy bars, too. She would need that fuel. It was baking hot inside the remains of the craft, pushing a hundred degrees or more. Outside, a gentle breeze blew, but it was hot, dry, no help at all. Nic shouldered her rucksack, and she struggled for a few seconds under the weight of Janet's body. She practiced fireman carries every year when she took her battle aptitude test, and she kept herself in shape. Still, she was no combat marine, and it took her a while to settle the woman over her shoulders.

What if this is hurting her? she thought. *What if I am making things worse?* As she stepped onto the thick, burning sand, and immediately sank a little, she realised how difficult it was going to be to reach those trees. She hesitated again. Could she stay? Could she wait here? Oh, it would have been so tempting to remain! And what if rescue finally did come, and the two of them were gone? What then? Would they be left behind?

No. No, that won't happen, Nic reasoned. There had been ten people on-board the craft. When they discovered that she and Janet were missing, they would surely attempt to find them. For now, Nic reflected, the situation was really quite simple: they had been brought down by an enemy jet fighter. She had to assume that rescue would not come. She had to take action, and get to cover.

"Just get on with it," she muttered, and she started walking.

Williams boarded her own jet for transport at around the same time that Nic started on her journey. This one was used for inserting Special Forces teams into what they called 'hot' areas, and as such it was heavily weaponised, armoured, and equipped with state of the art radar and electronics. She went to sit next to Velez, and she watched him program their final coordinates into the system. They were bound for the mountains, and she had already spoken to the officer in charge on the ground there, a Lieutenant-Colonel she had only met once before, and who appeared a little green. His team had not come under attack, he informed her, but it was hard to determine what the Scythians would decide to do next. Was it intimidation? Would they retreat after a while? The reinforcements from Earth had still not arrived yet, and the Council forces on the ground were seriously outnumbered. Things were not looking terribly good at this point.

"I can't wait to see you and your guys, Major," he added.

Williams had winced at that comment. No matter which way she looked at what she wanted to do, it still struck her as crazy, and a huge gamble. But she had calculated the time it would take to divert, and it only came down to thirty minutes extra. Of course, if the Scythians decided to attack, it could all be over in less than thirty minutes. Nevertheless, as soon as they were in space, she requested the systems override.

"Override?" Velez repeated, frowning.

"I want to make a quick pit stop before the mountains."

She had used her neural lace to connect to the ship system's mainframe. When she was in the control room, she had accessed the recording of the downed craft. To be fair, she had been surprised that she could do this so easily. It was like thinking up requests inside her head, and having the computer respond. Like she was inside of it instead of out. Everything she wanted, she had been able to download straight to her own brain. She had listened to the pilot's last transmission, and memorised the set of coordinates he had been able to send. Now, she reeled them out to Velez, and she asked him to change his initial input. She saw him hesitate.

"Uh... Permission to speak freely, Major?"

"Sure. Go ahead."

"I'm kind of thinking this pit stop you're talking about involves going to check on the downed transporter. Am I correct?"

"Correct," Williams replied.

She sounded calm, relaxed, and in complete control. She was hoping that if she pretended for long enough, maybe she would start to feel that way...

"Uh-uh." Velez nodded. "Also, kind of thinking this goes against the colonel's orders."

"Correct," she said again.

"Right..."

He appeared thoughtful for a moment, just staring at the new coordinates, obviously working out the consequences of doing what she wanted him to do inside his head. Williams sighed.

"All right," she declared. "Guys, gather round."

One thing she could not, would not do was compromise her team. They all formed a tight circle around the console, and she explained to them what her plan was.

"All an AI drone can do is circle the wreckage, and record video. I know how good these things can be, but one thing it can't do is touch someone's neck, and check for a pulse. Before they can say for sure that there are no survivors, any survivors there may be could be dead."

Everyone nodded, listening intently. Only one decided to challenge her. And of course, it was the Cretian officer who did it.

"Did you have friends onboard this craft, Major?" Red enquired.

Williams nodded. She met her gaze.

"Yes," she said. "I knew them all, but there is one in particular."

"So... Would you want to go and check on these people, even if you did not?"

She was blunt, to say the least, and Williams liked her for that. She was grateful for the question as well, because it allowed her to clarify her own motivation for doing this. The answer was yes, she decided. She would want to go and check for survivors, even if Nic had not been amongst them. Even if they had been total strangers to her. She sighed. *Enough to disobey Ary, put my own people at risk, and make the ground troops wait a little longer?* she asked herself.

"Absolutely," she replied. "In my world, we don't leave injured people behind. We don't put them second. So, what do you say? Ary will be pissed off when she finds out, but she'll take it out on me. Frankly, I couldn't care less. Be aware we might bump into some Scythians though. It might not be as easy as we think. So, consider all that stuff before you answer me. If only one person is against, we don't do it. And that'll be fine by me, so be honest, okay?"

The Cretian officer was smiling broadly now.

"Well, I knew there was a good reason I wanted to be a part of your team, Major," she commented with a chuckle. "Let's do it."

"I'm in," O'Neil replied immediately.

"Binks?" Williams asked.

"Damn, I'm with you," the sniper replied, shrugging, as if offended that her boss would even consider she might decide otherwise.

Williams nodded, relieved, and then she turned to Velez, who was already punching the new coordinates into the jet's GPS system.

"Hell," he muttered under his breath, "I'm in too, no need to ask. If I'd survived that crash, if I was injured, and hurting, I'd want my people to come and get me."

He flashed a thumbs-up at the rest of his crew.

"Let's do this thing, guys," he announced. "I'll do some crazy flying, and make up the time on the way back. Might make you throw up your lunch, but whatever. Don't worry, Major, you won't have to take any flak from the colonel. She won't even know we've been there."

"Thanks, buddy," Williams smiled.

O'Neil was a little quiet after this, and it was obvious that something was bothering him. He pulled her aside as they went back to their seats.

"You know, Major," he remarked quietly. "I really don't like it that they didn't make this our first priority. Why wait to go and make sure, uh? Damn. Imagine if someone's made it through that crash alive... It must be terrifying, thinking they've been abandoned like that. Especially for a bunch of analysts and shit."

He looked extremely disturbed at the thought, and Williams herself reflected on it for a little while. Yes, she thought, there had been non-combat specialists onboard that craft. Like Nic. And yes, she knew this would be terrifying for somebody like her, who was not trained to cope with life-and-death fighting situations on the ground the way that her team were. Her heart tightened at the thought of her. *Nic,* she thought. *I hope you're okay...*

"You heard Ary," she said eventually. "Whatever was on that AI footage must have made it very clear that everyone onboard is dead."

"But you don't think so."

"I don't know. Could be. But I tend not to trust AI very much."

O'Neil shot her a piercing look.

"Yeah, I, uh... I heard what happened to your last crew. I'm sorry about that, Major. That was really fucked up. And I'm proud to be on your team, you know."

Williams nodded, and she threw him a grateful smile.

"Thanks, Tom," she said. "I'm glad to have you."

She went to stand by the door, staring out of the window as Velez flew them hard and fast to *'the major's quick pit stop'*, as people had called it a couple of times. She tried to quiet her mind, and she focused everything she had on Nic. Out of all her ESP skills, telepathy was not one that she had practiced at all. But she did not feel like the woman was gone, dead, like she was no longer a part of this world. And her thoughts turned back to that scream she had heard... Well, heard was not the right word. *Sensed* was a much better one. Now, the more she thought about it, the more she grew convinced that it was linked. It might not have been Nic herself, of course. Perhaps it was just the passengers' collective fear at that instant, manifesting through her neural link. Whatever it was, she sent a clear message toward her lover now.

I'm coming for you, Nic. Don't give up. I'll be there soon.

CHAPTER TWENTY

Night came a couple of hours after the crash. And with it, debilitating cold. Weather patterns and information about how many hours of darkness the planet went through each day was not something that Nic had bothered to check before leaving for her assignment. She would be in a control room, after all. On base, safely inside. She did not need to know these things, unlike Williams, of course, who was well aware of the fact that Saran went through five hours of darkness each night cycle. And that it tended to be extremely hot during the day, with temperatures averaging ninety degrees, and freezing cold at night, with something closer to thirty-two.

She also knew how to survive in the forest, and how to make fire out of almost nothing, which was something that Nic had been shown only once during her basic training, and had never practiced again after that. Not that she should make a fire, she reflected, as she stared at the way her breath clouded up in front of her face with every exhale. It was too dangerous, and she could not risk giving away their position. But she would have attempted a small one if she had known how to do it, for Janet's sake and well-being if not for her own comfort.

Nic went quite far up into the trees to seek shelter that night. Her intuition, some instinct deep within herself kept telling her that she should be careful. And so, she endured the darkness and the cold for five long and painful hours, holding Janet tightly in her arms and against her chest, and whispering gentle words of encouragement into her ear.

"Help is on the way. I am sure it is. And we are going to be okay, trust me."

She did the best she could to keep her warm, and hydrated. She told her little stories. She described the places that she would like to go visit on R&R, all of them hot, beautiful islands with miles and miles of deserted sandy beaches. She talked about the food that she would eat there, and she did mention that when it got cold in the evening, perhaps then Evan would make a fire on the beach, and they would snuggle up together, and watch the stars. The L5 officer crept into her solitary conversation before she was truly even aware of it, but when Nic realised that she had, she found strength in the discovery.

"We've had a bit of a difficult start, she and I; you know, Jan?"

She whispered to her friend, rubbing her hands over her arms, and all over her chest and legs to keep her comfortable. She felt better for doing it, and not just physically. Looking after someone like this helped to take the focus off of her own predicament, and the fear that she felt about the situation. She was immensely grateful for it.

"I haven't felt this way about someone in a long, long time," she added. "And I think that Evan probably does too. I can't wait to see her again."

Nic did everything she could to keep herself going, and take care of her injured colleague. Sadly, during the last hour before dawn finally came, Janet's condition took a turn for the worse. And then, quietly, she passed away.

"Oh, God, Janet... I am so sorry, honey," Nic whispered to her.

As she held the woman tightly in her arms, crying silently, she heard the sound of people, someone, or something approaching through the trees. It was subtle, as if they were being extremely careful not to make a noise, but it was still there, and she could hear them. Unsure of what to do, but still responding to the sixth sense that told her she should not make her presence known, she dragged Janet's body into a cluster of bushes with her. Really, she should have left her there, and walked the other way while she still could. But she could not make herself do it. And so, she hunkered down beside her, hoping and praying that this would be the rescue team she so badly needed.

∞

Williams jumped out of the aircraft's open door before it even landed properly on the ground.

"Everyone stay onboard," she ordered. "I'll go check out the wreck. Keep an eye out for trouble, and let me know the second you spot anything."

She was in full armour, and carrying her rifle. Not feeling the cold, since the Kevlar that protected her when in battle was also designed to heat up or cool down whenever she needed an adjustment. So, she was nice and warm as she ran the short distance toward the wreck, feeling a mixture of anticipation and dread as she approached it. Everything was exactly the same as when Nic had left it, except that the stench of dead bodies and burnt flesh was worse, as the corpses had started to rot in the last few hours under the baking sun. As a combat marine, Williams was more used to the smell of blood than decay. She swore under her breath as it made her gag, and her eyes water.

"Bloody hell…"

Keeping a hand over her mouth as she got used to the worst of it, she made her way inside, and flashed her light over the bodies of the pilot and the two soldiers sat in the front. She checked their tags, and remembered their names from the manifest that she had memorised. These two were not people she had known extremely well, but she had spoken to them a few times in the mess hall.

"Sorry, guys," she murmured.

Heart pounding hard inside her chest, Williams then made her way toward the second half of the craft. She could see the outline of human bodies in the darkness, and she aimed the full beam of her torch over them. Some were so badly charred that it was hard to make sense of what part of their anatomy she was actually looking at. Others were already in the advanced stages of decomposition. *Must be something to do with the air composition on this planet for it to be happening so fast,* she reflected. Anyway, they were dead, for sure. *How many are there?* Some appeared to be fused up together, and obviously, the intense heat generated during the crash would have done that. It was hard to tell, but she thought perhaps four, or even five. Regardless of how difficult it may be, she needed to make really sure of that, and identify them properly.

She counted five, twice, and was convinced that she was right. So, there were two soldiers missing. Survivors? Lost during the crash? Maybe buried under the sand somewhere? She had no way to know this, of course, but she could definitely identify the bodies that were in front of her, and she got to work without wasting another second of her precious time. She looked for and checked everyone's ID tags, terrified that she would come across the one name she did not want to see. But in spite of the tragic circumstances, this was good news, it seemed.

Williams quickly came to the conclusion that the two missing from the wreckage were Nic, and someone called Janet Burton, one of the other analysts. Hope suddenly flooded through her heart. *I knew it,* she thought, exhilarated. *I knew it!* She exited the battered and distorted frame of the former shuttle, and walked all around it with her eyes cast over the sandy ground, looking intently for clues. Would it make sense that only two people out of the ten might have been ejected from the craft, when everything at the scene of the crash appeared so tightly held together? *Not likely.* So, more reassuring news. She checked for footprints, but the breeze was a little stronger now, and every time that she moved, her own footsteps became almost immediately covered up in fresh sand.

"What would you have done, Nic?" she wondered out loud.

One thing was pretty much for certain. If she was alive, and had not waited around for rescue, it meant that she was afraid of something. Williams remembered the recording from the crash, and the pilot clearly stating on the net that they had taken a hit from a Scythian jet. Nic would have known this, and the most logical thing for her to do at that point would have been to find somewhere to hide. The L5 trusted one of the best tacticians in the whole ICU to still be able to think logically, even if she were injured, and fearing for her life. So, where would Nic have decided to go?

"Boss," Velez suddenly called out over the comms.

He sounded tense. Williams immediately froze in place.

"Go ahead."

"We've just picked up a Scythian jet on radar, headed our way. Still a fair distance away from our location, but it's moving fast."

Shit.

"How long have we got?" she asked.

"Before they realise we're here? Two minutes, top. Unless their equipment is as good as ours, in which case we'd better get ready for a fight."

Williams threw a wild look around the wreckage. *Come on, think!* What would Nic have done, which direction would she have headed toward? Not the desert, that was for sure... As Williams heard her pilot start to rev up his engines behind her, she suddenly looked up, and spotted the line of trees in the shadows ahead. She knew from previous research that the mountains were just over on the other side, about twenty miles north, and that this was where the desert ended, and the hills started. She was surprised to realise that they were so close to it. There was some forest over there, thick, dense, and the perfect hiding place. *Gotcha,* she smiled.

"Major, unless you want to make fireworks up in the sky with a bunch of Scythians, we have to go now," Velez informed her loudly.

Getting twitchy now, and with good reason.

"Roger that," she replied.

She ran back toward the hovering craft where Binks and O'Neil were positioned at the door, laser rifles at the ready, both looking alert and incredibly switched on.

"Throw me my bag," Williams shouted up at them.

"What?"

"My rucksack, throw it down."

O'Neil immediately responded, grabbing it and throwing it to her like a football. She caught it in both arms before it hit the ground.

"Now get out of here," she yelled.

"What? You're not coming with us?" Binks exclaimed, eyes wide.

"No, I'm not. We've got two survivors, probably headed into the forest. I'm going after them."

"So, what are we supposed to tell the LT when we get there? And Ary especially?"

"Tell them the truth," Williams shot back. "Tell them that Holson and Burton both survived, and that I am going to find them. Velez, you're in charge until I get back. Now go!"

The craft immediately gained altitude, and then as soon as they reached the proper level, it zoomed out into the atmosphere and disappeared from view. Williams started to run toward the trees. It was maybe a mile away, and it would not take her long to get there. She heard the Scythian jet, just a rumble over her head. It was too dark to see, but she threw herself to the ground anyway, and burrowed into the sand when it got a little too close for comfort. She had an option to cancel out her heat signature when she was in armour, and she activated it immediately. Pretty soon, she caught sight of the enemy jet approaching, flying low and fast over the dunes. The crew were obviously not interested in the wreckage, and they flew over her head, nice and easy, before disappearing into the night.

Where are you bastards going like this? she wondered. And why was there not a bunch of Council jet fighters hot in pursuit? It probably meant that the reinforcements from Earth had still not arrived yet. What the hell was taking them so long? And what about the jets that were already on the ground at base, all fuelled up and ready for take-off? *Things must be a real mess back there,* Williams decided. Ary had not given any details about the other casualties, apart from the ones in the sports hall. Perhaps the jets were not flying because they were all out of pilots... Well.

"Never mind," she muttered under her breath. "Keep your focus, L5, and get going."

She shook sand off of her armour, stood up, and shouldered her rucksack. She had no way to guess what was happening, and worrying about those things, imagining disaster scenarios, and wondering whether Ice was still in one piece would not help her with her current endeavour. Nor would fantasizing about what Ary's reaction when she discovered that she had gone AWOL on her once more would be. Williams kept her eyes on the prize, and she ran hard and fast toward the trees. She tried to keep a straight line, as hopefully Nic would have done. When she got there, she would be able to pick up her trail. Her lover was alive, and they would be reunited soon. It was the only thing that really mattered.

CHAPTER TWENTY-ONE

Unfortunately, it was not the long-awaited rescue team that Nic had hoped for, but a troop of Scythian soldiers. She almost screamed out loud in abject terror when she spotted their typical, loathsome features and armour markings. *Scythians!* A hybrid race from the Orion system, they were one of the Council's oldest and most feared enemy. *Jesus Christ!* she thought, as sudden tears welled up in her eyes. *What am I going to do now?* Even though it was still dark, Nic's vision had grown accustomed to it by now, and she could clearly see them walking through the trees. It was a long column of maybe twelve or fifteen soldiers, advancing two by two, and moving toward her location in almost complete silence. Were they looking for her? What would they do if they found her?

Well, what do you think, Nic? a little voice at the back of her mind sniggered. What do Scythians normally do to Council soldiers, uh? *Torture and kill,* Nic reflected, her heart pounding. That was what they did. The Scythians were the cruellest people in the known universe, and her blood turned to ice at the thought of what they might put her through. She knew what the Council military advised their soldiers to do in this type of situation. She had no laser weapon on her, nothing to defend herself with, but she had a small knife. She could slice her wrists, and avoid being captured.

With trembling hands, she reached for it. But before she could clasp her fingers around the handle, she felt both a strong arm wrap itself around her body, pinning her own arms down, and a heavy gloved hand land over her mouth, effectively silencing her. Her heart almost stopped beating. Too late. They had found her. *No! NO!* She was screaming inside her head now, and she started to struggle to free herself.

"Sshhh…"

She felt a warm breath flutter against the side of her face.

"Nic. It's me."

It was only a whisper, yet loud and clear in its meaning, laced with urgency.

"Don't make a sound."

She immediately went still. *Evan?* She blinked hard. Had she heard it right, or was fear making her hallucinate? The hand over her mouth slowly released its painful grip, and Nic caught a glimpse of red and black armour behind her.

"I've got you," the voice murmured. It was warm, and reassuringly calm. "We're just going to let them pass. Stay quiet, okay?"

Nic nodded, just once. *Evan!* Evan had come for her! She almost fainted with relief. At the exact same time, a Scythian soldier suddenly showed up close, way too close to them. She could have touched him. She clearly saw the laser rifle he carried, and the large hunting knife strapped to his shoulder. Perfect for skinning animals, and Nic knew very well that they used those things to skin people, too. Soldiers in particular. She had watched footage of it. It was shown to every new recruit when they joined up, whether they wanted to see it or not. It was drummed into everyone's head that it would not do to be captured by a Scythian. Better to kill yourself when you got the chance. *Oh, God…*

She tensed, almost panicked, and she felt her lover immediately press herself tighter into her body. It was a subtle message for her to keep calm. Williams remained silent, but she gently stroked the side of Nic's face with her gloved thumb. It was an almost imperceptible gesture, and one that was not likely to attract attention, but it helped. It was fair to imagine that killing herself to avoid capture would never be a part of Major Williams' combat strategy. Nic had immense trust in her. She closed her eyes, and she attempted to relax against her. She tried to forget where she was. She thought of the beach instead. She did her best to focus on Evan, and nothing else.

"Good," Williams whispered.

She could feel how badly Nic was shaking against her. From the freezing cold, fear, stress, probably a combination of the three. She tried to keep her as still as possible, as soldier after soldier passed through the trees, in front and to the sides of them. Nic had thought there were fifteen, but Williams had counted closer to forty. The two Council marines were stuck in the middle of their line, and it was an exceedingly good thing that Nic had managed to find those thick bushes to hide in. Now, they just had to keep doing it for a little while longer, and they would both be just fine.

I've got you… It's okay, Nic.

Williams had spent half the night looking for her. But the operator had made it kind of easy, really, with the clumsy way that she had left such an obvious trail of broken branches, and disturbed stones and dirt in her wake. It had probably never occurred to her that she needed to be really careful with those things, too. In fact, given what her day job actually was, it was nothing short of a miracle that she had managed to make it this far. Williams could not wait to be able to talk to her, and make sure that she was okay…

And it felt like ages to her, but eventually, the sound of boots and marching soldiers started to fade. Nic stirred.

"Stay still," Williams instructed in a whisper. "We need to wait a little more, to make sure they're really gone, and that it's not a trap. Okay?"

Nic nodded. Still silent, still careful. *Okay.*

Williams allowed her lips to brush over her temple.

"I'm really proud of you," she murmured. "You did great. Now, just a few more minutes."

She made the few more minutes a safe fifteen. She felt Nic fall asleep in her arms after about five. Williams went into a deep meditative state herself after a while. Body quiet and still, mind awake and spread out wide over the forest, receptive to and searching for any danger. But thankfully, there was none. After a while, the normal sounds of the woods returned. Birds started singing. A couple of squirrels chased each other up a nearby tree. A beam of warm sunlight pierced through the canopy, and Williams angled her face toward it. It was time to make a move.

"Nic," she murmured. "Wake up…"

The woman came to with a startled jump, and for just a second, she looked confused at the sight of her lover looking like she did. Evan was in full armour. Blond hair hidden under a black cap, and her face smeared with thick layers of camouflage cream. Almost unrecognisable. Until she smiled, of course, and her blue eyes sparkled.

"It's me, Nic, I promise," she quipped.

The operator burst into tears, and she flew into her arms.

"Evan."

She had been on the brink of cutting her wrists open, desperate to avoid unbelievable pain and relentless torture at the hands of the Scythians, and now the relief that she felt was indescribable. And it was not just anyone who had come for her. It was the woman she loved. Evan had come for her. This meant everything in the world to Holson.

"I thought I was dead when I spotted them approaching through the trees," she gasped. "Oh, God, I have never been so scared in my entire life... I am so glad you're here."

She was panting, trembling still. It was obvious that she was in shock, and she was shaking so hard that Williams was pretty sure she would collapse if she released her.

"I am glad as well," she whispered. "So glad to have found you, Nic."

She would have liked to spend more time reassuring and comforting her, but she was conscious that they needed to keep going.

"It's all right now," she said gently. "Those fighters are long gone. Nic, please, I need you to calm down, okay?"

"Yes. Yes, sorry..."

"Don't be sorry," Williams smiled. "Just breathe for me, all right?"

She rested both hands over her shoulders, and took a long look at her. Nic appeared exhausted, and she was filthy from head to toe after her arduous trek through the desert and the woods. Her face was covered in dried blood. Her eyes were red from crying, and too little sleep. Lips an unhealthy shade of blue, and she still felt so terribly cold. Williams immediately reached into her rucksack for the fleece jacket that she had brought, and she passed it over to her.

"Here, put this on," she advised.

Nic slipped into the thick warm top, which was too big for her, but felt wonderful because it smelled of Evan. She zipped it up, and immediately felt its warmth.

"Thanks," she murmured.

Williams nodded, and she took off the top part of her armour. She helped the injured woman to get into it, and then she turned up the heat. Nic flashed her a tired but delighted smile.

"Oh, yeah," she said. "I love that."

Tears were still rolling down her cheeks, and Williams was sure that she was not even aware of them. It was probably fine, she decided. Just the body processing too much adrenaline, and letting go.

"Sit down for a minute," she invited.

She passed her an energy bar.

"Here. Have some of this."

"I'm not hungry, Evan..." Nic protested.

"I know, but I want you to. And drink some juice as well. You'll feel better for it, I promise."

Williams flashed her an encouraging smile, and she took her gloves off. She dribbled some water onto a piece of cloth she used to clean Nic's face. She bent her head forward a little, and ran her fingers over her scalp until she found the rather deep cut that was the source of all the blood. It was covered in a thick, unhealthy looking crust by now. It looked painful, and she winced at the sight of it.

"I need to have a proper look at your head," she stated, "but first, I want to put a bit of distance between us and this particular spot."

Nic instantly looked up.

"Why?" she asked. The blood drained from her face once more. "You think they're going to come back?"

"They might do, once they realise they've lost your trail."

Nic started to panic all over again.

"But what are we going to do?" she whimpered. "Where can we go? I don't know what to do, Evan. I..."

"Hey. Sshhh. It's okay."

Williams cupped her lover's face in both her hands, and she brushed her lips over an errant tear on her cheek. Then she did the same on the other side. She kissed her nose, and when the woman closed her eyes, she kissed each eyelid in turn, softly, smiling all the while. She held her hands, and she waited until she had her full attention. Then she spoke to her in a gentle, quiet, reassuring voice.

"Remember this is what I do every day, Nic?"

The operator tightened her grip on her fingers.

"Yes. I do. I'm sorry…"

"There's nothing to be sorry for, my love. Just trust me, okay? I know exactly what to do, and where to go from here. We're not lost. We're not going to get caught. I promise."

Nic nodded, a little calmer now.

"Okay, Evan," she mumbled. "Okay…"

"Good. I'm here now, and you're safe. I won't let anything happen to you. Before you even know it, we will both be back on Mars, enjoying margaritas in the sunshine, and taking long walks on the beach."

This caused fresh tears to fall over Nic's cheeks, but this time Williams also caught a flash of joy sparkling in her eyes. There was hope in there too, although accompanied by a little glint of something darker. Some reticence was definitely showing. Again. Williams felt her heart tighten inside her chest. This was her own fault. She was responsible for putting that fear in there.

"You really mean that?" Nic murmured.

"I do. We are not going to die here."

"But I mean…"

Her lover nodded before she could finish.

"I know what you mean. You and me? Right?"

Nic smiled again, a little stronger this time.

"You and me," she said. "Yes."

Williams glanced down at the ground. A muscle in her jaw flicked. She sounded a little hesitant when she spoke again.

"I would love that, Nic," she confessed. "I'm sorry I acted like such an idiot with you. I didn't know what I was doing, and I hated myself for it. Even now, I do. It was wrong. *I* was wrong."

Nic leaned in for a gentle kiss.

"Don't worry about it," she whispered. "Don't worry about me. And don't you hate yourself either, ever."

She caressed Evan's cheek with her finger, and lifted her head so that she could meet her gaze. She loved to see the way the marine's eyes immediately lit up in pleasure, and she was touched to realise how much she tried not to let it show too much. And failed so miserably. She kissed her again, deeper and more intently this time.

"It's okay," she assured her. "You're an idiot sometimes, but you're *my* idiot. I forgive you."

Williams chuckled. She exhaled deeply. She had been holding her breath, in anticipation or dread, she was not really sure which. But now, she could not help but smile. It was that blazing, strong, confident smile of hers that Nic loved to see so much.

"All right," she grinned. "I'll improve, I promise."

"So, what do we do now?"

"Now, you can stay right here, finish your juice, and recover for a few more minutes while I go take care of your friend."

Eyes full of tears, Nic nodded.

"Her name's Janet."

"I'll make sure that Janet is safe, and protected."

Another nod. Nic was holding hard onto her wrist, and the sad look in her eyes almost triggered Williams' own reaction. She blinked to clear her head.

"When this is over, we will come back for her. I promise."

"Okay. Yes."

Williams picked up her hand, and she kissed the inside of her palm.

"I won't be long. You stay right here where I can see you, all right? Don't move. Any problem, just yell, and I'll come flying."

She was true to her word, and she made sure that Burton's body was properly hidden, and covered up. She worked quickly and precisely, and ensured that no animal would be able to get to her for at least a day or two. If the fight with the Scythians took longer than that, if they were prevented to return for a significant amount of time... Well. Better not to dwell on that too much. She pulled the woman's tags over her neck, and she shoved them inside a zipped pocket on her armour. Then, she took a few seconds. She did not say a prayer exactly, but she just squatted down for a moment, rested her hand on the makeshift grave, and was grateful for the woman's life. Not just for the work that she had done, but for the human being that she had been, too. And still was, of course, just in a different form. She closed her eyes, and she sent that thought out into the universe. *Rest now, Janet.* Then she got to her feet, turned around, and ran back to Nic.

CHAPTER TWENTY-TWO

It became hot again incredibly quickly. As they gained altitude, fewer trees meant never finding enough shade to cool off, and they were forced to stop often to rest. But it also meant more space, and better views. They would see any Scythian troop trying to creep up on them approach from a long way away, and Williams was pleased about that.

"Sorry, I know I am slowing you down," Nic apologised after a while.

"Actually, I like this kind of pace just fine," her partner insisted, eyes sparkling as she turned to flash her an encouraging smile. "And in actual fact…"

They had been climbing over naked boulders for a while now, and just ahead of them was the entrance to a small cave. It was perfect for what she needed to do, and she offered Nic her hand to climb the last few feet up toward it.

"Let's take a break," she proposed. "There is some shade inside there. You can sit down, and we can both rest for a little while."

"But is it safe?" Nic argued.

All the same, she sat down almost immediately. It was obvious that she was struggling. Williams knelt on the bare rock in front of her. She looked her in the eye, and raised an amused eyebrow.

"Do you think I would suggest stopping here if it was not safe, Sergeant Holson?" she enquired.

"Probably not."

"So. Don't worry about it. Trust your idiot to get it right."

Nic gave her an amused smile.

"Okay, then."

She rested her hand on the back of her neck, and pulled her in for a soft kiss.

"But it is Nic to you, Major Williams," she reminded her.

Williams flashed her a brilliant smile.

"I know, *Nic*. Only kidding."

She had not wanted to upset her by explaining that she had debated leaving Burton's body out into the open, on display more or less, in case some of the Scythian soldiers came back to investigate. It would have been nice to make them think that the person whose trail they were on had just died, that they could move on, and get the hell out of the area. Now, if they did find the body, they would know for sure that someone else had been with her. But Williams also had massive confidence in her own field skills. Nobody could ever track her down on L5 trainings, and if her talented Council colleagues could not do so, then a bunch of stupid Scythians would certainly not be able to do it either. All in all, she did not really need the diversion. Also, she doubted that Nic would have allowed her to use Burton's body in this manner anyway. It was true that she did not need her permission, and she could very well have lied to her, and done what she wanted. But if one thing was clear in Williams' mind right at this time, it was that she would be completely honest with her lover from now on. No more lies, ever. She would share everything. No matter what.

"Water?" she offered.

Nic looked elated.

"You still got some?" she exclaimed. "I thought we'd run out."

She accepted the full bottle gratefully, closed her eyes in relief as she felt the cool liquid on her lips, but forced herself to give it back after just one sip.

"Go on," Williams encouraged her. "It's okay, you need it more than me right now."

She searched in her bag for anything else she had to give, and came up with a single ration pack.

"Bread and butter pudding," she announced with an appropriately excited grin. "I think it's still in date. You want some?"

She managed to make Nic laugh, and she was proud of that.

"Yeah, I do. What else have you got in your bag of tricks?"

"Let's see. Explosives. Extra ammo. And a first-aid kit," Williams replied as she dragged it out. "You can eat while I take care of your head."

"What about you?"

"I'll eat straight after. But that thing looks bad, Nic. I need to clean it up. You'll probably need stitches, too. So, why don't you relax, and tell me what happened during and after the crash?"

As the operator related the story, and explained what she had done once she realised that help would probably not come, Williams cleaned up her injury thoroughly. She disinfected it by pouring alcohol straight into the wound, apologising often as she worked. Then, she got a stitch kit at the ready. The laceration was still bleeding, and she needed to close it up properly. She did pause when she heard Nic say that Janet Burton had been unconscious the whole time.

"You carried her with you this entire way?" she murmured, impressed, watching her lover intently.

Nic nodded. She gave a light shrug. She stared down at the ration pack in her fingers that she suddenly had no desire to open up.

"She was my friend, you know…"

Williams gave her a gentle hug.

"I'm sorry," she said. "I'll get you out of here soon, I promise. I'm going to make contact with my team in a minute, so we should get a useful update on the situation. Hopefully, it will be safe to call for a medivac for you."

It suddenly occurred to Nic that Evan was on her own. This was extremely unusual, and puzzling really.

"How did you…" she started, only to flinch when the first stitch pierced her skin. "Ouch," she winced, clenching her fists in sudden pain.

"Sorry," Williams apologised, again. "But I need to do this. I'm working as quick as I can, okay?"

"Yeah. Sorry."

Williams smiled.

"Stop saying that. You're doing great," she promised.

Nic was silent for the rest of the procedure, simply doing her best not to whimper out loud, as her lover secured three more stitches into her head, thankfully with minimum fuss, and in record time. Then, Williams took her own head cover off, dribbled antiseptic over it, and covered Nic's short hair with it.

"There. Now, you look like a real commando," she joked, hoping to make her feel a little better.

She caught the questioning look the woman threw her way, before she yawned, and rubbed her eyes. She looked about ready to fall asleep now. She really was beautiful, and Williams smiled again, feeling her heart melt a little at the sight of her.

"What?" she murmured. "You okay?"

"Yes. Thank you for taking care of me."

"Well. You know that's something I enjoy doing, right?"

"Yes, I do. But Evan, where is the rest of your team?"

Williams grabbed her medical equipment, and she shoved everything back into her bag. She found her comms piece abandoned at the bottom, and she put it on.

"My team are over there," she said, pointing toward some higher peaks. "They dropped me off at the wreckage, and then I made my way to you overnight."

"Were you sent in after us? Why are you alone?"

Williams shook her head, smiling.

"No, Nic, I was not sent," she confessed. "I wanted to go check for survivors, but Ary kind of told me not to do it. What the hell, my team all agreed we wanted to go anyway. And so, we did. When I realised that you were still alive, I told the guys to go on without me."

Nic raised a confused eyebrow.

"Ary *kind of told you not to do it?*" she repeated.

"Yeah."

"Doesn't sound like her."

Williams could not help but chuckle at that.

"Yeah, well," she shrugged. "The colonel said I was not to come and check, and to head straight for the mountains instead. I disobeyed a direct order. Probably more than one, now that I think about it."

"Oh, Evan!"

"It's no big deal, Nic."

"But you know Ary. She's probably got you listed down as AWOL by now."

Williams gave another light shrug.

"Yes, that is quite possible," she agreed. "Although my crew should have informed her of my whereabouts by now. And anyway, what else was I supposed to do, uh?"

Her blue eyes had darkened suddenly, and her features hardened. In her armour and cam cream, and with that tightly focused look on her face, she looked almost frightening.

"I lost a lover once," she murmured. "I was not going to lose you too."

"You did this for me?"

Williams shrugged, shook her head no. Nic loved her even more for the response that she gave.

"I would have done it for anyone else. You don't just abandon people like that. Some asshole above Ary relied on AI to tell them there were no survivors. She got handed down a set of orders, and she decided not to question them. Well, I couldn't do that."

Williams smiled, and her entire demeanour changed in that instant. Even through the heavy camouflage cream, which was rapidly melting off by now anyway, Nic could see that she was blushing.

"So, I didn't do it just for you," Williams admitted. "But I was so worried... I had to come for you, AWOL or not. I know it might not be obvious at first glance, Nic, but I really am extremely fond of you."

Using Holson's words from the first time she had told her, and the operator gave a soft laugh.

"You think it's not obvious?" she giggled.

"You mean it is?"

"Oh, just a little."

"Really?"

Williams looked surprised at first, and a little confused. But then she just sighed, and her shoulders slumped. She looked down, and that little muscle in her jaw twitched.

"Well. I assume that you are really okay with that," she murmured.

It sounded like a statement, but really it was more of a question. *How can she be so unsure?* Nic wondered in amazement. *How can she be so wonderful, brilliant, and yet so unsure of herself at the same time?* She decided to leave her in no doubt whatsoever about it.

"I love you, Evan," she declared. "I am in love with you. Big time. Get it?"

Williams looked relieved. She sat up a little straighter.

"Yeah. Come to think of it, that's pretty obvious too," she reflected, smiling faintly. "But after the way I treated you, I was a little worried…"

Nic reached out for her.

"Come here," she said warmly.

She pulled her against her, and she brought Evan's head to rest on her chest. She slowly ran her fingers through her hair. She felt her resist a little at first, but not for long. Williams had not stopped moving and pushing herself in going on over ten hours now, and when the opportunity presented itself to rest for a second, her body made her grab it.

"I love you so much," Nic repeated in a whisper. "Why did you faint that day? Is it okay to tell me now?"

Williams let out a heavy sigh.

"Yes," she murmured. "That morning when I looked at you, all I saw was Maxx. I saw her face just as she was dying. She saved my life during that mission. She sacrificed herself for me. Did you know that?"

"No, I didn't. I'm sorry."

"She slipped. She fell into a vat of acid. I took two laser hits through the shoulder trying to get to her in those last few moments. It cost me my arm. And I know that as soon as she started to fall, it was too late to save her. There was nothing I could do. But at least I was able to make eye contact with her."

Williams shivered.

"It was a horrible way to die. She kept her eyes on me until there was nothing left of her. And I've been having flashbacks. That morning when I looked at you... It was all I saw."

Holson tightened her grip on her.

"I am so sorry, Evan."

"After they brought me back, not a single day went by that I did not wish I were dead. And then, I started to enjoy being alive again. It was little things at first, like feeling good when I was training, or smelling lily of the valley. I felt guilty that I was enjoying being alive when my team were all dead. It felt terribly wrong to me. And then, I met you. I mean, properly met you for the first time."

"I know that you struggled with it."

"Yeah. It felt like..."

Williams went silent, and Nic caressed her cheek with the back of her fingers. She gave her a little time to think. She knew it was probably the first time that Evan even admitted this stuff to herself.

"What did it feel like?" she prompted her after a while.

The marine shivered again, and she pressed herself tighter into her lover's embrace.

"It felt to me like I was killing her all over again, Nic," she confessed. "Like I was killing Maxx. I mean, she had only been gone a few months, and there I was, already falling for someone else."

"I felt the same way," Nic reflected softly. "Although it was a little longer for me. But I will never forget Kate. I will never stop loving her."

Williams sighed again.

"So, what do we do now?"

Nic smiled. She kissed the top of her head.

"Well. We are both alive, you and me. Right here, right now," she said. "And loving each other, I don't think this sort of thing can ever be wrong. Maxx saved your life, Evan. I'm sure she would want you to enjoy every second of it now. And Kate would be the same with me. If they could see us now, I think they would be happy. Don't you think?"

"Yes…"

Williams nodded. *No histrionics, L5,* she reminded herself. Of course, Maxx would want her to be happy. If the roles had been reversed, she would want the same thing for her. She allowed herself to smile.

"Yes," she murmured. "I know you're right. This is good."

She wrapped her arms around Nic's waist, and she allowed herself to drift for just a few moments. Not to go to sleep, really, but just a few minutes of complete relaxation. And enjoying being in her arms. She was the one wearing armour, and yet, it was wonderful to feel so protected. Eventually, she raised her head, and she met her glance.

"I love you too, Nic."

"I know, baby," the woman replied with a coy wink at her.

Williams chuckled. Her eyes sparkled in undiluted joy. *Baby?* she thought. Yeah, well. She could get used to that one pretty easily.

"How is your head now?" she enquired.

"Throbbing. But I'll live."

"You better."

"I promise."

"Good. I am going to… OW!"

The sudden burst of static in Williams' ear really hurt, and it was followed by the even louder and incredibly pissed-off voice of her commanding officer.

"Ah. Colonel…" she started.

"Shut the fuck up, Williams, and listen good," Ary hissed. "I need you in the field, L5, otherwise I would land your ass in jail this very second, and throw away the key forever this time. You hear?"

"Yes, ma'am," Williams nodded, grinning at her lover.

Ary could frighten the shit out of a lot of people when she wanted to, but Williams was not one of them. The colonel was just blowing off steam, she knew, making empty threats, and she suspected that a lot more interesting conversation was about to be dished out soon. She was not disappointed with what came next.

"Your team are on their way to your location now, Major."

It was good news, although it also effectively wiped the grin off of Williams' lips.

"Oh," she remarked in a flat voice. "You got me tagged."

Ary snorted arrogantly.

"Chipped is the correct word to use, Major."

"Through the lace?"

"Indeed, it is. I decided to activate it right after your last little escapade when you were on Mars. Turns out I was right to do so."

Ary sounded pleased, and Williams simply nodded. She had wondered about that a few times. Suspected that it might be the case, and done her best to not think about it. Now, she knew the score. Well. Whatever. It still did not mean that Ary owned her, and she was pretty sure that she could find out how to disable that trace if she really put her mind to it.

"Anything else you want to tell me, Colonel?" she asked.

"Yes. Look to your right, Major."

Williams glanced in that direction at the very same time that the medivac craft appeared over the horizon. She gave a huge sigh of relief at the sight of it.

"Your team are on board. They'll jump out, and brief you on the mission. Meanwhile, Holson hops on, and she'll get flown straight back to the ship. There is a pillow with her name on it at the infirmary."

"Thank you, Colonel," Williams murmured.

"No, thank you," Ary snorted again. "Now, you ace that mission for me, Major Williams, and I might even buy you dinner again when you get home. Ary, out."

CHAPTER TWENTY-THREE

There was a surprise for her on-board the medivac too, one that Williams could have done without.

"What the hell is going on?" she exclaimed, as soon as she spotted the young recruit jumping out with the rest of her regular team. "Ice? What are you doing here?"

Not really sure whether to be angry or pleased at first, and leaning toward the former. She was glad to see the woman in one piece, of course, but dismayed to be seeing her at all. This was a combat situation. Ice was not trained yet. She should not in a million years have been allowed in, and anger flashed across Williams' features at the thought of what stupid idiot might have authorised such a thing without consulting with her first. Ice spotted her reaction, and she swallowed a little thickly. But she reacted well, and she did not allow the less than welcoming greeting to affect her too much.

"Hello, Major," she replied.

"Answer my question. What are you doing here?"

As was her habit, the young marine blushed furiously as she stood at attention in front of her superior officer, and explained that Colonel Ary thought more firepower was always welcome, and that since she was top of her class on her current training, she could go.

"Just like that?" Williams commented, incredulous.

"Yes…"

"Why just you, then?" the L5 insisted, knowing there had to be something more that the woman was not telling her. "Why not send you with your entire squad, if firepower is so important to her?"

"Well. It's also because I asked her if I could go," Ice finally admitted, turning even more crimson. "She wanted to know why, and I told her I want to be on your team. She looked pleased, and then she said yes."

"Gotta admit, Boss, that takes some balls," O'Neil chuckled appreciatively.

Williams shook her head, frowning. She was extremely tempted to just throw the blushing marine back onto the medivac, and send her away. She knew that Ary would have enjoyed the woman's request, and got a kick out of a young recruit approaching her with such a crazy, ballsy suggestion. The colonel would think nothing much of parachuting a mere kid right into the middle of a kill zone.

"Next time I ask you a question, recruit," she said to her instead, "don't try to lie to me."

"Roger that, Major," Ice replied.

Eyes front, and assertive with it this time. *Well,* Williams reflected as she watched her attentively, making her own private assessment. Even she had to admit that Ice looked the part. A simple few weeks on basic training had already chiselled her into a fit-looking marine. She had a new, confident glint in her eye as well that had not been there before. She still blushed like a schoolgirl, granted, but she also looked strong, and ready to prove herself. Williams suddenly remembered that it had once been the case for her too. And that she had also not been out of basic training yet at the time.

"All right, you can stay," she muttered.

Ice looked relieved. Ary had told her she could go, and the rest of the team had not seemed to mind her presence, one way or the other. But she knew that the woman she would really need to convince when she got there was Williams.

"Thank you, Major," she murmured. "I promise I won't let you down."

"Obey my orders, and don't get yourself killed is all I want you to do," the officer grunted in response. "Think you can handle that, marine?"

"Yes, ma'am," Ice said loudly.

Williams flashed her a quick smile, all the while wondering whether Colonel Ary was not simply trying to replace her disobedient L5 with a more pliant, less troublesome soldier. She snorted ironically at the thought.

"Get ready to go," she told her team. "I'll be back in five."

∞

Nic was already safely strapped onto a stretcher inside the medivac when her lover jumped in to go and check on her one last time. The medics had hooked the injured operator up to an IV line the instant she got on board, and hit her with a heavy dose of painkillers. Now she appeared a little dazed, Williams noticed, and extremely sleepy.

"One minute," she instructed the attending medic as she climbed in.

He did not look too pleased with her request, and she knew they were eager to take off again soon. Staying on the ground for too long in this type of situation was not advisable. But she needed at least sixty seconds to say goodbye, and she was not going to budge until he moved.

"Okay, you got your minute," he agreed reluctantly.

"Thanks."

He walked over to the front of the cockpit to give them some privacy.

"Evan?" Nic called, struggling to raise her head.

"Yes, I'm right here. Hey, what's the matter?" Williams asked when she spotted the tears in her eyes. "Nic, please... Don't cry now."

She knelt by the side of the stretcher, clasped her hand in hers, and leaned over for a gentle kiss. Nic looked awfully scared. She used both hands to hold tightly onto the marine's wrist, as if she never wanted to let her go. Williams could feel her trembling.

"This is safe, my love," she whispered. "Medivacs like this one are well-armoured, and the pilot is combat-rated. These guys don't get shot down. Trust me on that. You'll be fine."

Nic stared anxiously into her eyes.

"I know," she murmured. "But where you are going isn't safe. What you're going to do there isn't safe. I don't want you to go..."

"But it's what I do, Nic," Williams reminded her gently, smiling reassuringly all the while. "You've been on the net with me more than once, right? You know how I work. I am safe, and I always come back."

"But I need you to come back *alive!*" Nic exclaimed.

She tightened her grip over her wrist.

"Please, Evan. Promise me that you will be careful."

Williams nodded. She kissed her.

"I promise," she whispered against her ear. "I'll be careful, I'll stay alive, and I'll be back to see you soon. Now, your job is to rest and get better, okay? Do it for me."

"Okay," Nic replied in a small voice.

She was obviously fighting to stay awake, and Williams knew that her emotional outburst was more due to the effect of the drugs she had been given than anything else. Nic was a marine too, not a teary girlfriend. And she certainly did not act like one. Under pressure, she was one of the coolest and most level-headed operators that Williams had ever worked with. And so, even though this was really out of character for Nic, she understood that it was simply due to the shock and tension of the last couple of days, as the emotions of her ordeal started to get released. It was bound to happen at some point, and Williams was glad that the recovery process had already begun. *Thank God for those drugs,* she thought.

"Here, take this," she said.

She pulled off the thin steel chain that she wore around her neck, and passed it over her lover's head. Nic's smile was immediate, although she looked a little drunk.

"Your tags..." she whispered, instantly wrapping her fingers around them.

"Yeah. They open the door to my cabin. Will you go check on my flowers for me? Make sure they get watered, so they smell nice when I get home?"

It was a way to get Nic's mind off of the painful things, and help her to focus on something good in the future. It worked well.

"Yes, I will," she replied urgently. "And I will keep those close to my heart, too..."

She managed another smile, but her eyes were closing in spite of herself. Williams stayed with her until she fell asleep. It only took a few seconds. By then, the medic had returned, and he was swivelling his index finger in the air in a *'let's wrap this up now'* kind of motion. Williams nodded her understanding. She touched her fingers to the unconscious woman's cheek.

"I love you, Nic," she whispered. "Take care of yourself. I'll see you soon."

And then she jumped out of the craft, signalled to the pilot to get going, and she watched them gain altitude, and disappear quickly into the atmosphere. She exhaled softly. *Safe,* she thought. Nic was safe, and now she could concentrate on the mission. It was time to get to work.

"Velez?" she called.

"Boss?"

She clasped a hand over his shoulder.

"Thanks for covering for me."

"Anytime, Major."

"Now fill me in. What's the mission?"

"Assess and destroy," he replied.

"Sounds good to me. Tell me more."

"All right, Boss. Guys, gather round," Velez instructed.

They all knelt in a circle on the ground, sweating under the beating sun. Ice was sandwiched in between Binks, the team's specialist sniper, and Red, the seasoned officer who had more kills to her name than she could count. Looking every bit as professional and intent as the other two, Williams noticed. *Good for you, kid,* she thought.

"So, the situation at base is this," Velez explained. He was brief, and to the point. She liked his style. "Evac operations are underway. None of the jet fighters on the ground there are currently operational."

"Why not?" Williams asked.

"That's where the second bomb went off, Major," he replied. "The jets suffered major damage, and it'll be a while before they can fly again."

She shook her head. *Should have known,* she thought.

"Carry on," she instructed.

"Right. The fighters we got sent from Earth to assist are busy ensuring air space security over the area. There's not many of them. They're outnumbered, and finding it a struggle to stay on top of the situation."

"Things must be really hairy if they can't even divert to assist at this location," Williams remarked. "No air support for us at all, I assume? Even though we know the Scythians are putting boots on the ground?"

"Affirmative, Major," Velez nodded. "No support. And yes, we have reports of troops massing up on the western side of the mountains. It appears initial sightings of enemy activity on the island were incorrect."

"Numbers?"

"Couple hundred. Unconfirmed at present. Could be more, could be less. We just don't know. They've dug themselves in pretty well. This," he added, spreading a vague map on the ground to show them, "is how we think maybe their camp is organised."

Williams stared at it for only a couple of seconds. The map was pretty useless as far as she could see. They would need to make their own assessment when they got to it.

"Okay, what else?" she asked. "What do those Scythians want?"

"That is also unconfirmed at present," Velez replied with a little apologetic smile, as if it was his fault he could not offer her a better answer. "They're putting troops on the ground, so there must be a reason…"

"Maybe they want to storm the base at some point," O'Neil interrupted.

"But if they wanted to take us over completely, they would have done it by now, right?" Ice blurted out excitedly. "I mean, that's clear to me."

Everybody's eyes turned to her, and she went bright red, but carried on anyway.

"When the bombs went off, it would have been the ideal time for them to do it," she remarked. "It was complete panic over there, absolute chaos. But they didn't. They must be here for another reason."

"And that reason would be, rookie?" O'Neil countered, not unkindly.

Ice simply shrugged.

"I don't know," she admitted.

"Maybe that's because we need to look at it from the other side," Williams remarked. "Ice, good observation, and O'Neil, I think you're right, buddy. Why didn't they strike when they could do the most damage? What are they waiting for?"

O'Neil resumed his previous argument.

"Exactly," he stated with a light shrug. "My guess is they're waiting because they think they can inflict more damage. I'm pretty convinced this initial bombing must have been aimed at doing just enough to attract more people to the base, like troops from Earth, emergency personnel, people like us; all that stuff."

"But the Crimson Peak exercise was already going ahead," Velez pointed out. "Lots of people were going to be there anyway. All they had to do was strike then."

Williams took a deep breath.

"Maybe they got their timing slightly wrong. A little too early, maybe. We'll never know," she admitted, "and it doesn't really matter at the end of the day. Not our problem. But I agree they are probably just waiting to do much more, and run a secondary wave of attacks. I think that's why they're here, waiting in the woods until the right moment, and then they'll pounce."

Red stared thoughtfully at the map. She shook her head.

"Wish I knew when that right moment was going to be," she remarked.

"Doesn't matter," Williams assured her. "Because we are going to get there first, and make sure we spoil the show. I mean, the six of us against two hundred *'maybe more'* Scythians seems like pretty good odds, right?"

She received a bunch of amused chuckles in response.

"Yeah, standard job," Binks replied.

"Another day at the office," Red agreed.

"Boring, boring," O'Neil yawned.

Velez just grunted, grinning dangerously all the while. They all looked at each other, and laughed. Ice appeared fascinated as she watched them.

"All right, then," Williams concluded, satisfied. "This is how I want to run this op. Feel free to pitch in when you want to. But since we have been tasked to assess and destroy, I think we need to sneak in under cover of night, place explosive charges in as many hot spots as we can, and retreat back. Then we blow it all up, and all we need to do afterward is pick out the ones who are still standing. Makes sense?"

"So far, so good," Red agreed.

"Sweet. So, when we get there, we'll do an initial recce to get a better sense of where everything and everyone is positioned inside the camp. Then we go in pairs. Red and Velez, O'Neil and Binks."

"Yes, Major," they all replied in unison.

"You'll each be carrying charges. Your job is to distribute as many of them in a tight circle around the outer perimeter. As far inside of it as you can get, but don't take too many risks. Don't get spotted. If you do, we'll have one hell of a battle on our hands. Clear?"

"Clear."

"Ice, you'll be with me," Williams decided, meeting the woman's gaze. "You'll place the charges, and I'll watch your six. We'll go deeper inside the camp together, make sure that when it all blows up, those fuckers don't stand a chance."

She saw the shocked expression on the young soldier's face. It was surprise more than apprehension, or even nervousness. Ice had clearly expected to be given a lesser role in all this. But there were so few of them that Williams could not afford not to use everyone present. Plus, it would give her a chance to keep an eye on her.

"Happy with that, marine?" she asked.

"Yes, Boss," Ice replied immediately. "Happy."

The L5 suppressed a smile. *Carry on like that, buddy,* she reflected, *and you'll earn yourself a place on this team a lot sooner than you think...*

CHAPTER TWENTY-FOUR

They were at their target destination by 14:00 that day, after six exhausting hours of hard tabbing across the sweltering mountains. Even at altitude it was uncomfortably hot, and Williams was impressed and extremely pleased with Ice's general level of fitness. So far, she seemed equal to the rest of the team, which was a major improvement on what she remembered from their time training together on Mars. Her tactical skills still had some way to go, of course, but that was to be expected after all. Whenever they encountered thickly wooded areas for instance, everyone else could make quick progress in total silence through the trees, but every once in a while, Ice would let something slip, and create some involuntary, unwelcome noise. Slide on a loose piece of rock, stumble over a root, that kind of thing.

Before her boss could even offer any guidance to her on the matter, Red stepped in. She hung at the back with the youngster for a while, giving her advice, pointers, and showing her what to do to improve her performance. Red was a good teacher, Ice a quick learner, and pretty soon, she too was moving just as well as the others.

"The kid's good, uh?" the Cretian officer remarked to Williams after a while, sounding quite proud. "She's got real potential."

She seemed to get a kick out of having the younger woman with them. Williams had noticed how extremely patient she was with her, and how she shared excellent tips that yielded immediate results. Red definitely appeared to be instructor material. *Might even end up torturing L5 hopefuls at some remote Council training centre one day,* Williams reflected.

"Yeah," she agreed.

She rested her eyes on Ice, who was walking slightly ahead of them. The woman was doing well, despite the fact that she should not have been there.

"Just needs to stay alive long enough to pass out of basic school," she remarked. "Spending time with us on ops like this might not be the best way to achieve that. I am far from pleased with Ary for running all over me on this one."

Red flashed her an amused grin in response.

"Well," she pointed out, "you agreed to let her stay."

"Yeah," Williams muttered. "Must be crazy too."

"Anyway, I did raise the point with her, Major. I said that perhaps you would like to be consulted on the matter before we all jumped onboard that medivac."

"And?"

"And the colonel replied that what you think of her methods is the least of her concerns, and that you would do well to remember she is the one in charge. She looked a little incensed that I would even dare to bring the subject up. And her language was quite colourful, to say the least."

Williams smirked, imagining the scene. She had watched Ary grow 'incensed' with her on more than one challenging and 'colourful' occasion.

"I'll bet," she said.

She glanced at Red.

"Thanks for spending time with Ice, by the way."

"No problem," the officer smiled. "She's keen. I like that in a woman."

Williams pondered that confusing comment for a short while. She wondered if she should revise her opinion about Red being such good instructor material after all, or whether her motives were of a more dubious nature. She found it quite amusing. After a few more minutes, she called out a halt for everyone.

"We are only half a mile from camp," she declared. "Let's lay low until it is time to move on. Invisibility shields up, everyone."

Unfortunately, there was no such easy thing, not even for those equipped with neural lace. The marines dug into the ground instead. They used natural hollows in the terrain, and bits and pieces of surrounding vegetation to make themselves completely invisible to anyone who might come walking by, and whoever might happen to be flying high above.

Waiting for night time to come, and for their mission to start officially, Williams whiled the hours away by eating and sipping her water, making sure that she would have the right energy reserves to be effective when the time came. She sent a quick message to Ary, using her lace to access the ship's comms system. She confirmed that they were in place, and what their plan of action was. She only received a terse, 'Acknowledged - Proceed', back in reply, but it was all she needed. Then, she rested her head on a patch of dry moss, and she dozed for a while. She allowed herself to think of Nic. Her lover would be back on the ship by now. In clean clothes, and safely tucked into a bed at the infirmary. With a nice bandage over her head to protect her healing wound, and some happy drugs to keep the pain at bay, and lull her into a restorative sleep. *Hope you get well soon, my love...* Williams thought, smiling.

Then, her thoughts drifted to the next time they would be together. Dare she even ask Ary for a few days' R&R? She grinned at the thought, and almost laughed out loud. Now this, more than the way she disobeyed orders so easily and often, might cause Ary to have a heart attack. She resolved to ask her anyway, and see how the colonel handled her request.

She checked the time next, and sighed impatiently when she realised that they still had several hours to kill. She decided to check on Ice. She could just see her little shelter from where she was, and it was damn near perfect as far as she could tell.

"Ice," she murmured into her comms.

"Go ahead, Major," came the immediate reply.

"How you doing, buddy?"

"Perfect, boss."

Williams rolled her eyes. This was a bullshit rookie answer if ever she had heard one.

"Nervous?" she enquired.

Something in her tone must have conveyed the message that it was okay to speak freely. And it was.

"I feel a little bit nervous," came the quiet, honest reply. "But excited, too. And very focused. I just don't want to let you or anyone else on the team down."

"You won't," Williams assured confidently. "And focused is good. Excited, too. You won't feel nervous as soon as we get going, so don't worry about it. Make sure you eat, drink, and get some sleep. You got that?"

"Yes, Major. Thank you."

Williams could hear the smile in her voice, and something told her that when the time came to fight, Ice would react well. Next, she checked on everyone else, and then she decided to try a little remote viewing exercise. She was surprised that it had not occurred to her to do it earlier, but then, she was still getting used to the new skill, and it did not come naturally to her. Yet. She relaxed, allowed her mind to drift, and she concentrated on what she wanted to achieve. Pretty soon, she found herself floating high above their hiding place. It was eerie how easily she managed to do that these days, just get out of her physical body in this way...

Not allowing herself to be distracted by the thought, she flew into the forest, and over to the enemy camp. The reports had been accurate. Those Scythian guys were pretty well camouflaged. She managed to pick up on a few shapes, some bigger than others, and get a sense of the general area. From what she could feel, and perceive, she concluded that her plan had potential. And really, what else were they supposed to do when it was only the six of them?

They would do their utmost to achieve success with the limited resources they had available, and hope for the best. Williams was not prepared to push beyond all reasonable limits. She was going to bring everyone home this time, safe and sound. Satisfied with the results of her exploration, she allowed herself to settle back into her body. She closed her eyes, and drifted off.

∞

"Major Williams?"

It was a whisper from Velez in her comms piece that brought her out of a sound sleep. Immediately alert, she peered out of her shelter. It was dark.

"Roger that," she acknowledged. "Time to go."

They got ready quickly. Distributed extra ammo and explosive charges between themselves, checked that everyone's comms were working fine, and made sure they were all clear on the mission once more.

"Get in, plant your charges, and get out," Williams repeated. "Be quick with it, don't linger. Remember, the more time we spend in camp, the more chances we have of being spotted. We'll RV back in the forest a safe distance away, and ignite the charges. Everybody clear on that?"

"You got it, Boss."

"Any questions?"

"Just one," Red piped up. "Ice, you got your FUP with you?"

The young marine appeared puzzled. *Shit,* Williams berated herself. She had forgotten to check. It was not something she normally had to worry about with her guys, and she was grateful to the Cretian officer for reminding her.

"Nice catch, Red," she thanked her, and the woman just nodded politely. "Ice, what we call our FUP is this little pill right here."

She fished the small plastic cover out of her pocket to show her. O'Neil slapped the young marine on the shoulder, grinning wildly.

"FUP," he informed her. "Fuck You Pill."

"What?"

Williams shot him a warning look. He flashed her an apologetic smile.

"Ice, you've seen the training videos about the Scythians I assume?" she asked.

The soldier nodded.

"Well, when you join a team after training, and become active, they give you this. If you ever find yourself in a situation when you think it might be preferable to die, rather than be taken alive, you can just swallow it whole, plastic and all. You'll be dead in seconds, guaranteed no pain. If you use it, that's a nice final fuck you to your enemy."

Williams shrugged before she carried on. She always hated delivering this kind of talk.

"I won't give you Dos and Don'ts about it, or specific examples. If you're ever in that kind of predicament, the choice will be yours. You'll know what to do exactly when you need to know it, and not a second before."

Ice stared rigidly at the little white pill in the major's hand. It suddenly dawned on her exactly what she was about to do, who she was with, and how inexperienced she was compared to the rest of them. It made her feel a little light-headed, and she breathed slightly harder for just a second. Velez and Binks exchanged a concerned look. But Ice recovered quickly, Williams noticed. Her eyes were clear when she met her gaze, and her voice steady when she spoke.

"Understood, Major," she nodded. "And no, I haven't been issued with one of those yet."

Red smiled broadly at the way that the rookie said 'yet' with such aplomb, like it was only a matter of inane formality that kept her from being integrated fully into the elite commando team of her choice. The L5 grabbed her hand, and she dropped her FUP into her gloved palm.

"Carry this one with you. You won't need it tonight," she added, her tone intense, reassuring. "But we may as well do things by the book on this one."

"What about you, Major?" Ice murmured, looking worried.

"I won't need it either," Williams replied. "Trust me on that, marine. None of us will."

She flashed her a dazzling, insolent grin to accompany her remark, and it seemed to do the trick with Ice. She smiled in return, and shoved the pill into her front pocket. Her confidence was back, it seemed.

"Thanks," she said.

Williams nodded. She wanted to bring a good dose of that death-defying arrogance with her on the mission tonight. She needed to switch on that other side of her personality, and awaken the L5 within her. The tough officer who would laugh at anyone who ever dared to call her *'baby'*. The seasoned marine who had stared more than once into an enemy's eyes, as they died from a quick flash of her blade, or even her bare hands wrapped around their throat when that was all she had to fight with. She wanted to turn into the merciless assassin that she had trained so hard to become, and the woman who enjoyed being that killer.

"Let's go," she declared.

"Roger that, Boss."

They all fell into a silent line, following her lead. Williams thought about the scars on her body. Each one represented a specific moment in battle that had sculpted her into more of who she was. Some even held a particular memory of individual men and women she had fought alongside with. The new scars on her right shoulder were a reminder of her old team, Sanchez, Edwards, and Collinson. The one that ran across her face was dedicated to Maxx, because a Scythian soldier had tried to take her eye out with his blade, as Williams attempted to get to her in those final instants.

She thought about her fallen comrades as she ran furtively through the freezing night with her new squad, eager to accomplish the mission. She felt her blood heat up in anticipation, and she tightened her grip on her rifle. She was made of scars and duty. Nothing could ever change that. And as they reached the enemy camp, and she took up position amongst her crew, Major Evan K. Williams of the Interstellar Commando Unit knew there was nobody else in the entire universe that she would rather be.

CHAPTER TWENTY-FIVE

Everything went without a hitch. The pairs separated on the edge of camp, each headed toward their pre-agreed sector. Williams and Ice were able to push deep into the compound, placing their charges as silently and efficiently as a couple of ghosts.

As they made progress, the L5 was pleased to realise that she could recognise some of the larger-shaped canvas shelters that she had sensed during her remote viewing session. She risked a look inside one of them, and grinned at the sight of all the brand-new weapons piled up in there. *Idiots,* she thought. The Scythians were so stupidly confident that they thought they could leave this stash unguarded... *Well,* she reflected, *those will make nice fireworks indeed.* She beckoned Ice over, and the younger woman bravely slipped inside the tent to position one of her explosive gifts where it would do the most damage. She was serious as she worked, focused, calm, and Williams found it a little hard not to forget that she was still just a kid in training. *Good stuff, Ice,* she reflected.

They carried on working their way across camp, moving quickly yet safely through the darkness. Another tent was full of sleeping Scythians, and Ice left her charge on the outside doorframe this time. She was holding her breath, and her legs were shaking with the enormity of what she was doing. She was glad to be with the best marine in the entire ICU. On her own, or with someone else, she would have struggled to be so daring. And so, with all the explosives in place finally, they started to head toward the safety of the woods. That is when they came upon their first real hurdle of the night.

Right there in front of them, blocking the way forward, a Scythian soldier was standing guard. Looking intently toward the forest, he was armed with a laser rifle, and the obligatory long blade affixed to his chest. Williams stopped, and raised a hand up. Ice melted silently into the background, as she had been instructed to do. Williams considered her options quickly. There was not much of a choice to make there, she decided. Either they got rid of him, and disappeared into the woods, or they could retrace their steps, which would mean going back the same way twice. Too risky, as far as she was concerned, and this was no big deal to her. Scythians liked skinning people alive? Fine. She would give him a taste of her own blade, and see how he liked that.

Ice watched, eyes wide in excitement, admiration, and a whole lot of fear as well, as Williams reached for the commando dagger that she always kept strapped to her thigh. She held her breath as the L5 marine straightened up to her full height, and seemed to grow even bigger as she got ready to pounce. Even though he was taller, she still appeared to be looming larger over the enemy soldier. She stepped up right behind him. She was so close... Ice shivered in anticipation. If the Scythian had only turned his head slightly to the side, he could have spotted her. Heart pounding hard inside her chest, Ice observed the fascinating scene unfolding in front of her eyes. Williams took another step forward. *Now,* Ice thought desperately, clenching her fists to stop herself from shouting it out loud. *Do it now, Major!*

As if on cue, before he could see her, or even sense her presence behind him, Williams tackled the unsuspecting Scythian. The young recruit was amazed at how quickly and violently everything happened after that. Williams fell on top of him, grabbed the top of his helmet, and pulled his head back, hard enough to break his neck. She cut his throat with a single slice of her weapon, and Ice was certain that she even heard the cartilage crunch when Williams cut through his windpipe. Blood poured out of the wound. It made her feel a little sick, but also excited. *One day,* she resolved intently. *One day, I'll be as good as this.*

She saw the soldier give a few spasms, but he was dead in less than two seconds. Complete silence followed the swift and brutal attack. For just a moment, Williams remained completely still on top of her enemy's body, checking that she had not been seen by anyone else, and that it was safe to move. Then, she signalled to Ice to catch up with her. They crouched down together, just on the edge of the forest. Williams immediately got on to the team comms.

"Sit-rep," she murmured.

She was speaking as quietly as possible, her voice barely a whisper, and using the minimum amount of words required to convey her request accurately.

"Job done," Red immediately replied for her and Velez.

"Same here," O'Neil stated for him and Binks.

They had all had to deal with their own version of the same guard at some point during their mission, and they had all adopted the exact same approach. It was effective, silent, and not worth discussing over the net. Now, it was time to move.

"All teams, regroup to the RV," Williams ordered.

She instantly received several radio clicks back in acknowledgement, and almost heaved a sigh of quiet relief.

Great, she thought. Her plan had been a simple one, and in theory at least, extremely easy to execute. Minimum risk for maximum results. But she also knew from tragic experience that theory did not often survive contact with a bunch of ruthless Scythian soldiers. She allowed herself to grow excited at the realisation that they were probably only ten minutes away from successfully completing the mission.

"Let's go, buddy," she whispered to Ice.

Ice stood up. She shouldered her rifle, and she took one step to the left. There was no warning, no tell-tale click like they used to have in those funny Hollywood movies, in the ancient and mysterious times before humanity had started venturing out into the universe. Although it was true that some types of weapons endured throughout the epochs, because they were so efficient, and such perfect killers.

And so it was that the Scythians had developed a modified version of the fragmentation mines of old, designed to explode over two stages. One charge, when triggered, sent the mine shooting upward to approximately chest level. When that happened, it was lightning-fast, and almost impossible to see. During the second stage, it emitted a high-intensity, circular laser blast that would surely kill anybody unlucky enough to be standing within ten to twenty feet of it.

The only reason the two marines were not killed on the spot that night was thanks to the L5's neural-lace-enhanced reflexes, and her ESP abilities. When the mine blew, some as yet unknown, untapped part of Williams' brain reacted even faster than the charge. Quicker than the laser blast. It felt to her as if time had slowed down so much all of a sudden that everything appeared to have come to a standstill. It lasted long enough for her to step forward, grab a hold of Ice around the waist, tuck her into her body, and turn her away from the mine. Her shield activated. Then, and almost instantly, everything accelerated back to normal speed. The laser blast when it was triggered was so shockingly painful that it knocked her unconscious. She suffered a ruptured eardrum in the process, and a significant nosebleed. But the hit was blessedly very quick, and her shield held strong.

"Major Williams? Major Williams!"

When she started to come to, Ice was shaking her. Williams found herself lying on her back, staring up into the frightened face of her young colleague. The rest of the team were on the radio, yelling for her to respond. She was feeling light-headed, and nauseous. All the injured marine caught from her crew's heated conversation was that they were getting ready to turn around, and come back for them.

"Let's go! Fuck the RV point!" O'Neil yelled over the net.

It was enough to scare Williams back to full consciousness.

"No!" she ordered. "Stay where you are, and call for an extraction craft."

"Major, you can't be serio…"

"Shut up, O'Neil, just fucking do it," Williams snapped.

She looked up in time to spot what appeared to be an entire squadron of Scythians headed toward them. *So much for being so quiet earlier*, she winced. Ice had already recovered from her initial fright, and she was courageously returning fire. But it was only the two of them. They would not last for very long like this. Williams suspected that allowing the rest of the team to come back and help would only put them at risk unnecessarily. But maybe there was something else that she could do to complete the mission, and protect the Saran base. There was also no way in the entire universe that she was going to allow Ice to die. She was going to save her people today, even if it killed her. She landed a firm hand over the woman's shoulder.

"Move away," she ordered, stepping in front of her as she stood. "Get out of here, Ice, go join the rest of the team at the RV."

"What?"

Puzzled, Ice simply stood there, unsure that she had heard her right.

"I'll hold them back," Williams said, as she fired her shield once more.

And right in the nick of time too, because a line of Scythian fighters started aiming their rifles at them. Williams spared her a single glance.

"Go, Ice!" she yelled to make herself heard over the sound of laser fire. "I'll catch up with you guys. Go ahead, don't wait for me."

In true rookie style, the young soldier dared to question the order. Immediately, she found herself flung several feet away on the wings of a powerful energy blast.

"Don't argue with me, marine," Williams shouted furiously. "Don't waste my fucking time, or my energy either! You've done enough already, don't you think? Get back to the team. Go, NOW!"

She did not have a lot of experience with the shield, and she was not entirely sure how long she could keep it going like this. Maybe only a few seconds more. She could feel the energy draining out of her already, and she needed Ice to be long gone by the time she executed her final plan. And so, she made herself as loud, clear, and hurtful as she possibly could to make sure that the youngster would leave, and not attempt to come back. She achieved her goal. Williams spotted the wounded look in her eyes before Ice turned away, and disappeared into the forest. *Sorry, buddy,* she thought. *But you can't be here when I finish this thing.*

Alone once more, she faced the Scythian soldiers. *How many did Velez say there were supposed to be again?* she wondered. She was not sure, and it would not help to worry about it now anyway, because they kept on coming. More and more of them were pouring into the clearing from every direction, and firing at her shield with everything they had. She could see the blades they were carrying. She could feel their frenzy at the sight of a lone marine commando standing so close, and she knew they were already looking forward to carving her up.

But Williams was happy now, too. She had them right where she wanted them, straight in the middle of her own well-designed kill zone. It was perfect. Of course, it would have been better to wait until she too could get away to safety before she triggered all of their charges. Five per team, strategically distributed across the entire camp... That was fifteen in total, and probably enough to vaporise the entire Scythian contingent she was facing now. Would it kill her? Would the shield save her life? Williams thought about Nic, and her heart beat a little faster.

Shit, she thought. *I really don't want to die here today.*

What she wanted was to be able to return to her lover, safe and sound, and go away with her on R&R someplace nice. Somewhere that Nic would love. She wanted to enjoy this second chance at life that she had been given. She wanted to smell lily of the valley, and feel the sun on her face again. Swim in the ocean. Make love to Nic, and fall asleep in her arms afterward. Cook breakfast together, and stop pretending that she did not love it like crazy when the woman called her *'baby'*.

"I am not going to die here today," Williams resolved, muttering under her breath. "Not gonna lose my team either. And I am going to kill every single one of you freaks, in revenge for my crew."

She slipped the detonator out of her pocket. Ice would be far enough away by now. It was safe to do this. Annihilate the whole fucking lot, and trust that her shield would protect her. She stared right ahead at the crowd of enemy soldiers, and she raised her hand so that they could see the device.

"You want me?" she yelled. "And to skin me alive, do you? Well, fuck you!"

She hit the switch. There was a flash of white light, a whooshing sound coming toward her, and the whole world exploded into nothingness.

CHAPTER TWENTY-SIX

Everything was utterly silent at first. Eyelids that felt like heavy lead shutters. She was unable to move her limbs. The pain was intense, and it was all around her. Every muscle, sinew, and bone in her body felt like someone had taken a sledgehammer to it. It even hurt to breathe. Something inside her chest felt different, too, and not in a good way. Then her eyes fluttered open, but everything was blurred. There was just this thick, whitish colour everywhere she looked. White fog all around her, grabbing at her body, and pulling her down. She started to get a little scared. *Where the hell am I?* Eventually, faint sounds started to return to her experience. Voices. A bunch of words she did not understand. Shapes she could not make out, swirling in and out of her field of vision. She closed her eyes again. Or at least it felt like she did. Was she awake, or simply dreaming all this stuff?

Evan…

She heard her name being called out, and her heart leaped inside her chest. She knew that voice. She tried to respond to her. *Nic? Nic, what's happening?* In her head, she heard herself yell out her lover's name, but in reality, no sound came out of her mouth. She struggled against the stuff that kept her down. What was it? It felt like she had something packed inside her mouth. She felt pressure in her lungs, and her head was being held down in place. She hated that. Again, she wondered where she was. It did not feel like death, unless in death you ended up strapped down to something hard, unable to move, or communicate. Maybe this was hell… Maybe she was dead after all. And what were they doing to her this time around? Changing her? Messing with her body? *No. Not again!* As panic rose inside her chest, she fought to regain consciousness.

"Evan," Nic called again.

The numbers rose sharply on the heartrate monitor that Williams was hooked up to, causing a worried doctor to come immediately rushing into the room. Nic leaned over her quickly, and she spoke into her ear.

"Evan, calm down," she murmured. "I'm here. You're safe now, I promise."

Even though the wounded marine was thrashing and resisting like crazy in the dream, even though she was screaming inside her head, on the outside she appeared completely still, even peaceful. She was only a few hours out of surgery, and the sedatives that they had pumped into her system were way too strong to allow her to even move a finger. But Nic was convinced that her lover could hear her voice. Especially since the more she talked to her, the more she reassured her that everything was okay, the faster Evan's heartbeat seemed to be dropping back to normal. This had happened a few times already, and even the doctor was getting used to it.

"Good job, Sergeant Holson," he commented. "Call me if you need me, okay? But it looks like she's calming down already."

"Yeah," Nic replied. "She's okay, now. Doing well."

When he was gone, she rested a reassuring hand over Evan's forehead. She brushed a gentle kiss over her cheek, and caressed her hair.

"You're doing fine," she repeated. "I know you can hear me, baby. I want you to relax, all right? The more you do so, the quicker you will heal. And the faster we can get out of this place. Okay?"

There was no reaction from the unconscious officer, apart from the green digits on the monitor, but that was good enough for Nic for the time being.

"I love you..." she murmured.

When she had first caught sight of the marine, just as the commando team disembarked from the armoured craft, her heart had almost stopped beating in shock. Evan was covered in soot and grit. She was bleeding from her nose, mouth, and ears. She lay unconscious on the shuttle floor, surrounded by the rest of her crew. And they were all silent, looking sombre. Velez, the one who was medically trained, had been the first to jump out. Immediately, he started yelling instructions at the assembled team of onboard medics.

"Right, guys, we've got an intra-pulmonary haemorrhage due to severe blast-lung injury," he recited intently, as they transferred her over onto a stretcher. "Oxygen saturation into the low 80s. BP's hovering between 225 to 250 systolic. Airway is blocked. I had to intubate on board."

Evan was alive, Nic realised, elated. But once again, only barely. She ran with everyone else toward the infirmary, her heart pounding, praying that her lover would be okay. Hours later on that same day, she sat with Ice and Red at her bedside, as the young woman recounted the events that had led up to the blast.

"I had absolutely no idea that she was going to do this," Ice murmured. "Absolutely no idea..."

Her eyes were a little vacant, as she stared at the array of tubes and IV lines that surrounded the injured soldier.

"She said she was just going to hold them back. If only I could have guessed…"

Red gave a small chuckle.

"Major Williams would have done what she did regardless of your opinion about it, kid," she remarked. "Don't take it the wrong way. It's nothing personal."

There was obvious admiration in the Cretian woman's voice as she spoke.

"She did the right thing, you know. She used her shield. She wiped out all those Scythian motherfuckers, and she got her team back home in one piece. That's an L5 for you. And she's tough, this one. She will be back on her feet in no time, you'll see."

Nic had simply nodded in agreement. Yes, she thought. Her lover was tough, she was strong. And she would survive this, just the same way that she had survived everything else. Thank God for the neural lace though, and that protective energy field she could generate. Evan's injuries had been listed as severe. But without her shield, they would have been lethal.

∞

The battered marine came to a little over two days later, in the middle of the night. Everything was quiet in the infirmary. She could hear the noise of the ship's engines down below, that droning sound that she always found so reassuring. Maybe because she had been born on a vessel. Who knew? Her doctors had extubated her several hours earlier, and discontinued the sedatives that kept her unconscious. Still, no one had expected her to wake up quite so quickly, and so, she was on her own when she did. *Seem to be making a bloody habit of waking up alone in hospital these days,* she reflected. After spending so long helpless in the middle of that horrible white fog, her mind felt surprisingly clear when she opened her eyes. It was a relief. She could see, and hear. She tested her limbs. Arms, legs, everything sore, but in working order. Williams started to fiddle with the IV line attached to her forearm. She tried to pull it out, eventually only managing to rip it off in frustration. It stung a little.

"Ow," she muttered under her breath.

Her throat was dry, painful, and she turned to the table next to her bed, looking for some water. She reached over to grab it. But her grip was still weak, her coordination pretty appalling, and the bottle slipped from her fingers, and rolled under the bed.

"Damn it," she exclaimed.

Voice a little stronger, and temper rising accordingly. She was about to grab the covers, and attempt to swing her tired legs over the side, when a strong hand landed in the middle of her chest, and pushed her back down. The simple touch was enough to knock the breath out of her. Williams looked up, gasping in sudden pain. She found Ary standing there, smirking, condemnation plastered all over her face.

"Col... Colonel," she gasped.

"What the hell are you doing, L5?" Ary barked.

She released her, and spotted the fresh trickle of blood on her forearm where the IV needle had previously been attached. She rolled her eyes at her in exasperation.

"Here you go, Major," she snapped, handing her a roll of surgical gauze. "Why don't you clean yourself up."

Then she glanced under the unit, nodded, and retrieved the bottle.

"That what you were headed for, before I stopped you falling out of bed?"

Williams said yes, and she was relieved when the colonel unscrewed the cap for her, poured some liquid into a plastic glass, and handed it to her.

"Thanks…" she murmured.

When she struggled with it, fingers trembling a little more than she would have liked to show Ary, the colonel slipped a supportive hand behind her neck to help her drink. All of a sudden, her movements had turned unusually gentle, and kind. It was not a side of her that Williams got to witness very often. It made her feel a little suspicious, but she was too exhausted to hold on to that thought for very long.

"Sergeant Holson did not leave your bedside for over 48 hours," Ary informed her. "I ordered her back to her quarters to get some sleep just over an hour ago. She will be sorry that she missed you waking up."

Williams nodded, her heart beating much faster all of a sudden at the mention of Nic.

"Is she okay?" she asked.

"Yes, fine. And I owe you an apology, Major. Yes, again."

Ary spotted the insolent little glint in the officer's eyes, and she matched it with an arrogant snort of her own.

"As a Cretian, I may not experience the same range of debilitating emotions that you humans do, you know," she added. "And I am glad of the fact. But I can recognise when I was wrong. You were right to go check for survivors. You also accomplished the mission I assigned to you, and in quite spectacular fashion I might add. No Scythians have been spotted on Saran since you blew up their advance location. Our Council base there is thriving once more, thanks to your heroic efforts. So, I will not throw you in jail for yet again acting like such a lone ranger. Next time though, just make sure that you avoid almost killing yourself in the process."

"And my team?" Williams murmured. "They're all okay too, yes?"

"Yes. All okay. And basking in that successful post-mission glow."

Williams allowed her head to drop back against her pillow. She closed her eyes. Yes, she had done good. She had brought her team back. Stood her ground against the Scythians. And pressed the switch on that detonator at just the right time, as soon as she was sure that Ice was out of harm's way... Her eyes flew open at the thought of her.

"What about Ice?" she asked, agitated all of a sudden. "Is she all right? Is she onboard the ship? Can I see her before she goes back? I wanted to tell her that I..."

"Shut up and take a breath, will you," Ary interrupted, alarmed at the way the woman's face had suddenly flushed such a deep shade of red. "Our little rookie is fine. She is onboard with us. And yes, of course you can see her, before I send her back to her basic training where she belongs."

Williams nodded with relief, the sudden lump in her throat at the mention of her young friend making it a little difficult for her to speak. She blinked away unwelcome tears she did not want Ary to see, but the Cretian did spot them, and she rolled her eyes again in reaction.

"Humans," she muttered in displeasure. "Now, Major Williams. Is there anything else you need before I go? Water? Painkillers? Another blanket?"

"R&R," the marine whispered.

Now it was Ary's turn to look astonished, as predicted.

"What?" she frowned.

"I really would like a few days' R&R, Colonel. If that's okay."

"How many?"

Williams hesitated. She could not remember the last time she had requested time off. Come to think of it, perhaps she never had. In the past, she always used to get assigned it, and she had always viewed R&R as a boring chore to be endured, rather than a pleasure to be enjoyed.

"Uh… 5 days?"

Ary grunted.

"Take two weeks. That's an order."

She turned to go.

"Colonel?" Williams called after her.

"What, Major? You want me to tuck you in or something?"

"No. I just have one more request, if I may."

"Fire away."

"About the R&R, can Sergeant Holson be assigned the same?"

Ary arched an interested eyebrow.

"So, it's like that, uh?" she mused.

"Yes, Colonel. It's like that."

Ary appeared decidedly nonplussed.

"As you wish, Major. Soon as your lungs have healed, you and your new squeeze can have your two weeks off. While we're at it, is there anywhere in particular you'd like to go?"

A small smile finally crept over Williams' lips. She felt just like a kid on Christmas morning.

"Earth," she said. "Key West."

Ary unloaded another smirk onto her. But she looked rather amused this time.

"Granted, Major," she agreed. "Now get some fucking rest."

CHAPTER TWENTY-SEVEN

True to form, Williams only waited a couple of minutes after Ary had left to get on the move. Gingerly at first, but the initial wave of dizziness over and done with, she took a few steps forward, and was pleased with the result. She was in no fit state to run a marathon, but she felt good enough to get herself back to her quarters, shower, get dressed, and go find Nic. After that, the next thing on her list was to spend some time with all her team, and talk to Ice.

She hunted around quietly for some clothes to wear, and settled on a pair of scrubs that were only slightly too big for her. Then she crept out of her room, slipped unnoticed past the nurse on duty, and headed back to her cabin. It took her a little longer to get there than it normally would, and she had to stop to rest a couple of times. But she made it eventually, and when she stepped inside, she immediately froze. It was a good kind of frozen on this occasion, discovering that her lover was fast asleep in her bed. Williams crept up to it, smiling all the while, and she leaned over her to land a gentle kiss on her cheek.

"Hello, Nic," she whispered.

The woman stirred. She raised a pair of sweet, sleepy eyes up to her face, and immediately blinked in surprise.

"Evan?" she mumbled. "Is that you?"

"Yeah. How is your head? Feeling better?"

"Oh, God, you're awake! Are you okay?"

"Hey, I asked you first," Williams chuckled.

Nic's response was to sit up on the bed, and to hug her tightly to her chest, until she felt her flinch rather sharply. Concerned, she pulled back.

"I'm sorry. Are you hurting?"

Williams shook her head no, but she looked a little pale.

"My chest just feels a bit sore," she admitted.

"Then you should be in bed. Come here."

Nic attempted to pull her under the covers with her, but Williams resisted.

"Wait," she said. "I stink."

She smelled of anaesthetic and disinfectant, blood and sweat. There were still bits of skin underneath her nails that she suspected might not be hers, but belong to the Scythian spotter that she had killed.

"I'm disgusting," she declared. "Let me take a quick shower first."

"Let me help you," Nic volunteered instantly.

She insisted on taking the scrubs off her, and very gently, tenderly washing the dirt and grime away. The L5 was a little uncomfortable with that at first.

"What's the matter?" Nic enquired, feeling the tension in her body. "Does this hurt?"

"No, I'm… I'm just not used to it, that's all."

"To what?"

"Somebody taking care of me, I guess," Williams admitted with a light shrug, instantly regretting it when a flash of pain shot through her chest. "And being naked with you for the first time."

"Really?" Nic questioned as she ran the soap-infused sponge all over the hard, exhausted body.

"Yeah..." Williams murmured.

She glanced down as Nic came to stand in front of her, and slathered scented body-wash all over her breasts. It was hard not to react to this, especially when her lover caught her glance, and dropped the sponge to use just her hands.

"Better get used to it quickly then, Major Williams," she grinned.

Williams flashed her a hazy smile. She leaned back against the wall, under the warm jet of water, and she exhaled heavily. This was all incredibly nice, and under different circumstances, she would have responded with a lot more enthusiasm. But everything was starting to catch up with her, and she felt dizzy all of a sudden. The only thing she could do was nod.

"I will," she murmured. "Can't think of anything better."

She allowed Nic to lead her out of the shower and support her back to the bed. Truth be told, she was glad for the help now, because she could barely stand.

"Lie down, darling," Nic instructed.

Williams stretched out under the covers, feeling exhaustion grab her by the throat, and squeeze. She shivered at the feel of her lover straddling her back.

"Are you cold?"

"No. Just happy. You feel amazing."

She was rewarded with a series of kisses along the back of her neck.

"Am I right in thinking that your doctor has no idea you've left the infirmary?" Nic wondered.

"Spot on," came the sleepy answer.

"Is that really wise, Evan?"

"Yep."

"Does Ary know?"

Williams grunted at that.

"She knows I never linger very long over there if I can help it. But not to worry. She's got me chipped, believe it or not. If she needs me, she will find me."

Nic dropped some massage oil into her hands, and she slowly rubbed her palms together to warm it up. She started to work her fingers over the tight muscles in Evan's shoulders. She felt her surrender to the touch, eyes still closed, and a faint smile dancing all over her lips.

"Ah… that's incredible," Williams mumbled.

"Good. Can you lift your head a little bit for me?"

Nic rested both hands against the sides of her neck when she did, and she rubbed her thumbs over the back in a series of long, relaxing strokes. Williams' head dipped forward, and she sighed into her pillow.

"Awesome…" she murmured.

"Great. Just let go, okay?"

"Hmm…"

Nic carried on with her expert massage, running her hands all over her back and shoulders until her lover was almost unconscious.

"Is it okay if I just ask you one thing?" she murmured.

"'Course…"

She sounded really drowsy now, and Nic hated to ruin the moment, but she had to find out. She needed to know the truth of what had happened.

"Evan," she whispered. "Baby, how certain really were you that this shield would save your life when you activated the bombs?"

The seriousness of the question brought Williams right back from the edge of sleep. Nic's voice sounded so tiny, so hesitant. She turned over onto her back, and met her gaze. She spotted the tears glinting there, and the way that her lower lip trembled.

"Nic," she murmured. "I did not try to kill myself."

"Are you sure?"

Wanting to believe her, desperate even, but still uncertain. Williams took a deep breath. She had promised herself, no more lies from now on. No more running from her feelings, or her emotions. She reached for Nic, and drew her under the covers with her. Naked bodies entwined, eyes wide open, looking at each other in the dim lights of the quiet bedroom. Nothing but total honesty could come from that. Williams took the opportunity to come clean.

"I thought there was a 70% chance that I would make it," she said.

Nic's mouth dropped open. She appeared utterly shocked by the admission.

"30% is a hell of a lot to gamble with," she gasped. "My God! What were you thinking, Evan?"

"Well. I know it probably sounds a little crazy now. But it didn't at the time. I thought it was acceptable odds, and worth the risk. I did not want to die, you know. I don't have a death wish. That's the truth, Nic."

"But what was so important, then?" the operator exclaimed.

Her voice was shaking in anger, disappointment, and more than a little fear, too.

"How could it be worth it to risk your life like that?"

Williams was silent for a few moments. She did not really want to discuss odds, probabilities, and the worthiness of the choice that she had made. It had been the right one, and she knew that in her heart.

"It was just something I had to do," she murmured. "For my people, and for myself, too. So that I could move on once and for all. Stop the flashbacks, and all the nightmares. And so that maybe I could let someone like you take care of me…"

"Maybe?" Nic challenged, and she sounded furious still.

Williams flashed her a timid smile, looking extremely unsure of herself all of a sudden. Tears sparkled in her eyes at the thought of what was at stake here.

"I hope so," she murmured. "If you want to. I love you, Nic. I really do, you know, and…"

Nic wrapped her arms around her neck, interrupting her. She held her tightly for a while, and in complete silence. She could feel her lover's heart, beating powerfully against her own chest. She felt frightened, although immensely grateful to have her back. Alive, and in one piece. But it was twice now that Evan had shown her a side of her that she would simply not be able to tolerate. She played with death way too easily, and casually. That had to change, and Nic had to ask. If the answer was no… Well. If the answer was no, it would feel to her like dying.

"I do want to be with you," she said in a raw, trembling voice. "But if I do, will you promise me that you will be careful from now on? Evan? Will you promise me that you will value your own life, at least as much as you value mine, and the lives of the soldiers on your team? And stop taking all those crazy risks?"

"Yes," Williams nodded immediately. "I promise."

She did not take crazy risks, but she understood what her lover meant, and her reply was genuine. She pulled back to kiss her on the lips, and she caressed her cheek with her thumb.

"I do value my life, Nic," she whispered.

Her fingers drifted down the side of her neck, and over her collarbone. She kissed her there, and she slid a little lower down against her body. Nic started to respond to her. She melted into her arms.

"Evan?" she asked.

"Hmm…"

Williams carried on with her gentle exploration of her body. She wrapped her lips around her nipple, and she felt Nic's hand caress the back of her neck.

"Evan," Nic repeated, a little more firmly this time.

Williams finally looked up, concern shining in her eyes.

"What? Are you okay? Is it me, am I doing something wrong?"

"No, you are doing everything right. But you do look a little pale, darling. Very pale, actually."

"Don't worry, I'm…"

"So," Nic continued, smiling warmly and paying absolutely no attention to her protest. "Why don't you lie back down, and relax."

Williams opened her mouth to speak, but Nic swallowed her answer with a kiss that dismantled any objection she may have had. Her right hand moved to settle over her breast, gently kneading the full and tender flesh there. And then her mouth quickly replaced her hand, and those gifted fingers drifted down between Evan's legs. It was the softest caress, the purest sensation.

"Is this okay?" she murmured. "Doesn't hurt?"

Williams struggled to open her eyes.

"Not where I got…"

She twitched and trembled all over at the feel of Nic's teeth teasing her nipple.

"…injured," she gasped.

"Well, that's good to know," Nic replied with a soft chuckle. "Maybe I won't be so careful with you then. How about this?"

She kissed her again, and this time she made it a whole lot deeper, and way more intense.

"Y… Yes," Williams mumbled.

At the same time, Nic rubbed her hand harder between her legs. She was pleased when she got a strangled cry out of her in response. She swatted her fingers away when Williams tried to regain the upper hand, again, and she paused for a second to glare at her.

"Now, will you let me do this, and stop trying to interfere?" she snapped in pretend annoyance.

Williams chuckled.

"Maybe..." she said.

Nic kissed her again.

"Let me take care of you," she murmured, serious now. "I want to. Please?"

She had never moved her hand, and now she started to rub small, slow circles all over the most sensitive part of her lover's body. Williams almost stopped breathing. Her vision blurred. There she was again, unable to move, except that this time it felt so good that she fiercely did not want Nic to stop.

"'Kay," she whispered.

She gave up trying to control what was going to happen. Gave up believing that she did not deserve any of it. She focused all of her attention on the sensations instead, and she simply gave herself entirely over to Nic's touch. She had never felt more alive... It was the best feeling in the world.

∞

Ary could be confusing sometimes, and she proved it once again the very next day. When Williams checked her messages, she found that confirmation for a two-week stay at an exclusive Key West resort had landed in her inbox. Nic squealed in delight when she showed it to her.

"But are you sure that we won't be bored over there, just you and me, stuck in that place for two long weeks?" her partner joked.

"Don't worry, baby," Nic replied, wrapping her arms around her shoulders to land a teasing kiss over her lips. "I have a lot of ideas for fun. And I am planning on keeping you plenty busy."

Their R&R was due to start the very next day, and so, that night, they shared a meal together with the rest of the crew. Ice was there too, and Williams was pleased to discover that the team had taken exceedingly good care of her in her absence. Not that she would have expected anything else, really. These were good people. Hers. And the very best. Everyone cheered when she entered the mess hall, hand in hand with Holson. Williams turned crimson.

"Come on, guys," she protested. "Keep it down."

"It's great to see you on your feet again, Major," Binks declared, smiling broadly.

"Yeah, Boss. I have to say you made me sweat a little on that shuttle flight back," Velez admitted. "Been a while since I'd done that medic stuff on a live body."

"Sorry about that, Velez. And I want to thank you for shoving that tube down my throat so expertly. You were a real gentleman."

Velez flushed a deep shade of red, and O'Neil howled with laughter.

"Sharp and funny, as always," Red noticed with a warm grin. "Welcome back, Major."

"Thank you," Williams replied, returning the smile. "It feels good to be back."

She stood up to raise her glass.

"To us," she said.

"TO US!" they all cheered in response.

Ice sat at the other end of the table during the meal, looking a little shy, but she was deeply pleased to be with the group, and it showed. Williams caught up with her at the end, and she drew her aside for a quiet moment.

"How're you doing?" she asked. "Enjoying this?"

"Yes," Ice responded politely. "Very much so, Major."

"So, are you still keen to ace basic training, and come back to work with us full time?"

"Yes. I can't wait."

Williams nodded, smiling, watching her. The enthusiasm was still there, but there was a definite reserve, and a hesitant look in the woman's eyes when she looked at her that she had never spotted there before. It looked like this was personal.

"Hey, Ice?"

"Yes, Major?"

"You know I didn't mean what I said to you that night, right?"

Ice glanced at her. She attempted a smile, but it was clearly forced.

"Right," she murmured.

"Are you sure?"

Ice eventually turned to look her straight in the eye. She had that pinched look in the face that left the L5 in no doubt whatsoever that she was fighting not to cry.

"Red talked to me about it. She said you didn't mean it. But I..."

Ice swallowed hard.

"Part of me wondered if maybe you really did," she admitted. "After all, if I hadn't triggered that thing, and alerted the entire camp of our presence, you wouldn't have had to almost die..."

"Ice," Williams replied, her voice gentle. "I said what I said because I needed you gone. Not because it was your fault. It could have been me who stepped on that charge. It could have been Red, Velez, any of us. It was just bad luck that it was you, that's all. I did not mean a single word of what I said."

Ice swallowed back her tears.

"Okay," she murmured. "Thank you."

"In fact, I sent a comms report over to your boss this morning to tell him how well you performed during that op. And I have already put in an official request to have you transferred over to my team, as soon as you've passed out of training."

The young woman remained speechless, eyes open wide in shock. Williams raised an amused eyebrow.

"Well. Is that okay, marine, or would you rather I didn't do it?"

Ice shook her head.

"No, I… This is great, I… I love it!"

Finally, at a loss for words, she threw her arms around Williams' shoulders.

"I am so fucking happy!" she exclaimed, beaming. "Thank you, Evan!"

"Wow," Williams laughed. "Calling me by my first name, and swearing too? Never thought I'd see the day. Now, rookie, remember what I said to you when I told you that you could stay?"

Ice nodded, eyes bright.

"Obey your orders, and don't get myself killed, Major?"

Williams nodded.

"That exactly. So, look after yourself, and I will see you soon, my friend."

∞

EPILOGUE

∞

Williams walked over to where her lover was standing, looking out the window, waiting for her. She wrapped her arms around her waist from behind, and rested her chin over her shoulder.

"How're you doing?" she whispered.

"Great. Excited about tomorrow. You?"

"Excited about being with you, period."

Nic turned around, smiling broadly. She locked her arms around Williams' neck, and leaned into her for a gentle kiss.

"You are so gorgeous," she murmured. "And you say the sweetest things."

"Not trying to be sweet. It's the truth."

Later on that night, Nic lay nestled against Williams' body, with her head resting in the crook of her shoulder, and the fingers of her right hand splayed out over her breast. Evan was asleep, breathing deep and slow. Nic could feel her heart beating. It felt so delicate, and yet so strong at the same time. So fragile, and so immense. Nic knew that she had found the woman she wanted to spend the rest of her life with. But she was also filled with a deep measure of sadness and worry at the thought of it. Because she realised that falling for Evan was the ultimate risk, the craziest gamble. No matter what the woman said, regardless of how strongly she may believe her own words, Nic knew full well that if faced with that particular choice again, Evan would always put others first, and perhaps make the ultimate sacrifice. Even though the thought terrified Nic on a regular basis, it was also the reason she had fallen so hard for her. Forget the L5 designation, the ranks, the medals, and all the recruitment posters. When it all came down to it, Major Williams was a marine to the core. She fought for justice, duty, peace, and hardest of all for the people she loved.

The possibility that Nic might lose her one day precisely because of this, just like she had lost her Kate, was very real, and excruciating to even contemplate. Yet, for Evan, it was a risk that Nic was willing to take. To love again, and to live, knowing that in the very next second everything could be taken away from her. She unconsciously clung a little harder to her lover. Evan was there now, so real, and warm. *I could never bear to lose her...* Nic shivered at the thought, and her heart suddenly felt to her like it might break. *Don't cry, stupid,* she thought to herself, even as big, painful tears welled up inside her eyes.

"Nic?" Williams murmured.

"Sorry. Did I wake you?"

"Are you okay?"

"I'm fine. Why?"

"You're trembling."

"I was... I was just thinking."

There was a long pause, and for a moment Nic thought that she might have drifted off again. But then the marine rolled over to gaze into her eyes.

"It's frightening, uh?" she said.

Nic simply nodded. Of course, Evan would know exactly what was going through her head.

"Yes," she murmured. "Very."

Her partner brushed a gentle kiss over her lips.

"But you know, Nic," she remarked, "sometimes stories can have a happy ending. Ours will be like that. Trust me."

Nic could not help but shiver a little.

"You're an L5 marine, Evan," she murmured. "You know? That stuff scares the hell out of me. It's dangerous. It's brutal. And you... You just go about it as if..."

She let her voice trail off, and Williams nodded. Eyes sparkling, she flashed her a gentle smile.

"I understand," she said. "And it's okay. So, I will make you a promise, Nic. Right here and now, I promise that I will always find you. No matter what happens, no matter where you are. I will always come for you. And I will always come back to you."

Nic was crying now, but it was crazy because at the same time, she was feeling better. Evan did not, she could not know that any of the things she was saying were true. But there was also something insanely seductive about losing herself in the belief that she did. Maybe that was what made all of her marines want to follow her into hell the second she clicked her fingers. They loved her. They believed her. And they had faith in her.

"I'm sorry," Nic murmured. "It's just that..."

She chuckled through her tears.

"Well, it's just that I love you, I guess," she concluded.

She knew she did not need to explain anymore.

"I love you too," Williams whispered. "We'll be okay."

Something about the way she said that was like a switch being flicked off. All of Nic's fears suddenly evaporated into thin air. *This is my choice,* she reflected. *And I choose the happy ending. Together, we will make it happen, I know.* Embarrassed about her outburst, she tried to turn it into a joke.

"Are you using your neural lace spooky powers on me, L5, or what?" she mumbled.

Williams burst out laughing. Eyes glinting in the dark, she settled back behind her lover, and punched a bunch of pillows into place under her head.

"Tell you what. I've read plenty of military books about neural lace. But never one about sex." She giggled. "Maybe we should write one when we are in Key West. What do you say, uh? And take pictures. Give Ary a little something new to worry about."

"Evan," Nic protested, but she was chuckling now.

"No, I'm serious. Think about it. Levitating orgasms. Hey, we should at least try it!"

Nic was shaking, but it was with laughter this time. Smiling, feeling happy, Williams tightened her arms around her shoulders. She held her safely against her chest.

"Feeling better now?" she murmured.

"A lot better."

"Okay. Good night, Nic."

"Good night, baby."

That night, and every single one after.

THE END...

ALSO

BY NATALIE

DEBRABANDERE...

UNBROKEN

"I couldn't stop reading. Heart-warming love story, full of intrigue, suspense, and a touch of terror. Loved it."

STRONG

"Raw and heart stopping action in Afghanistan. As a Marine, the main character deals with the stress of battles and loss. Great story, highly recommended."

ASHAKAAN

"What a fantastic book! I love a good Sci-Fi adventure with a strong female lead who can kick butt, outsmart the bad guys but not totally, and fall in love."

FELUCCA DREAMS

"Excellent writing! Awesome love story! The sensuality between the characters is palpable. Natalie Debrabandere keeps hitting hit out of the park!"

LOOKING FOR ALWAYS

"One of the purest love stories I have read. Original and captivating story line, amazing characters. This book keeps you hooked until the very last word. Great job!"

BEYOND THE QUEST

"Fast-paced, addictive, full of twists and turns! A riveting, exciting tale of love and adventure!"

Keep up to date with Natalie's work on Facebook @ndebrabandereauthor & Twitter @1ndebrabandere

ET
6/19

40846527R00155